SAFETY IN BEAR COUNTRY

SAFETY IN BEAR COUNTRY

A Novel

HEATHER PAUL

N_1 O_2 N_1

CANADA

*Publisher's note: This book is a work of fiction. Names, characters, places and
incidents are either the product of the author's imagination or are used
fictitiously, and any resemblance to actual persons living or dead
is entirely coincidental.*

Library and Archives Canada Cataloguing in Publication

Title: Safety in Bear Country : a novel / Heather Paul.

Names: Paul, Heather (Novelist), author.

Identifiers: Canadiana 20220265771 | ISBN 9781989689394 (softcover)

Classification: LCC PS8631.A84969 S24 2022 | DDC C813/.6—dc23

Printed and bound in Canada on 100% recycled paper.

Now Or Never Publishing
901, 163 Street
Surrey, British Columbia
Canada V4A 9T8

nonpublishing.com
Fighting Words.

We gratefully acknowledge the support of the Canada Council for the Arts
and the British Columbia Arts Council for our publishing program.

For Aurora, Blaise and Jasper

THE NATURE OF BEARS

The doctor raises his silver Muppet brows and gestures to the beach ball on two legs in a yellow nurse's uniform clattering away at the sink. So, I say, or I think I say, "Everything's okay. I'm like totally conscious." But he doesn't seem to hear or understand. "There's nothing wrong with me." I try again, summoning a primal authority from within, willing my lips to form words and pushing them through, only this time louder. My garbled words are the nonsensical sounds of the brain addled; they echo around the brick walled room, the protestations of a caged beast. Something's not right. They talk over me as though I'm not here. I hear them, but I don't know what they're saying. I cannot understand.

The nurse tightens her frosted ponytail with both hands and wheels towards me a urine-coloured bag dangling from a metal tree. "No!" I scream, kicking my legs and flailing my arms in the direction of her nefarious fruit. Nothing happens. They're leaden, fluid filled sacks of inertia, and my *No!* an animal's shriek. The doctor leans on my shins, grips my right wrist hard. The nurse straightens my left arm and swabs my veins with something cool. "No!" I scream again.

She pierces my skin, my veins, and tapes a needled tube to my inner elbow. "Settle down. The doctor is a very nice man who's trying to help you. And let me tell you, Missy, you had some sort of guardian angel up there. Still alive after all those shenanigans." She scolds her head from side to side clucking her tongue.

Lucky girl. Silly girl.

"This special medicine will fix you right up."

"I don't need fixing…" My nostrils tingle with the smell of something familiar; it reaches through my nose so that I can practically taste it on the back of my tongue. Not antiseptic, not disinfectant, it's chemical, it's citrus, and then it comes to me: ADA. A hush of warmth ripples up through me, and all I hear is canned laughter from the TV in the adjoining room. Sunlight creeps through tilted blind slats. And on the speckled concrete, the shards of last year lie scattered, the broken kaleidoscope of my life upon the ground.

BARBARIANS ALL

Lillian shoves four guys at me, their innate slowness and lack of gross muscle control causing them to trip over their own feet, wide and large like clown shoes. She divvies up the remaining twelve, pushing them into motley line-ups behind Stuart, Tom, herself and me. I try to keep ahead of things, so she won't get pissed, put four identical plastic baskets filled with toothbrushes, paste, deodorant, talcum powder, combs, shaving cream and razors on the stainless-steel countertop beside the sinks and underneath the mirrors. The ease and completion of the task please me almost as much as the symmetry. Four clients, four staff, four prepping stations, four states of matter, four types of human blood, four chambers of the human heart, four Noble Truths of the Buddha, four seasons cycling back on themselves year after year after year.

"What a fucking waste," says Lillian, pointing to the masking essentials of modern hygiene. "Think these idiots know the goddamn difference?"

It's been weeks since I've been working here, and Lillian's unabashed verbal cruelty still shocks and frightens me. How can she work here and not know better? And if she is that far gone, how can anything a lowly know nothing summer student like me say to this adult, this seasoned institutional worker on the brink of retirement, to change her ways? So, on we carry with this charade, this parody of living that is the MNC. I nod and smile at myself in the mirror without showing my teeth, disgusted by myself: my powerlessness, or maybe my cowardice, just a soppy sea sponge human blob, both ineffectual and integral to the entire operating ecosystem by keeping my mouth shut up and letting all the bullshit filter through and squeezing green Crest mint onto a Blue Oral B.

"Open up, Barney." I wave the pasted brush in front of his face. He's done this every day for forty-odd years, but I still have to prod him toward the sink. Lillian stands beside me on her step stool scrubbing the inside of Harold's mouth as though it's a toilet bowl. No soft tissue is spared. I want her to be gentler though in a way I suppose I can't blame her—if there were a seismograph to measure stink factor, these guys' morning breath would bust the scale. It's probably the meds. Who knows what they are on. They only see a doctor every six months or so, yet every day, three times a day for some of them, it's a Dixie cup full of pills.

Barney is the tallest, over six feet. Unlike tiny Lillian, I can reach his face no problem. He stares over my head with an unflinching, unwavering blankness. Is he looking into the mirror, or through it? Is he staring into some alternate universe only he can access, gleaning information from the great beyond? Doubt it. I stare at our reflections wondering what it'd be like to climb foot first through some reflective membrane portal into somewhere better, or at least different.

Lillian whips a plastic razor up and down Harold's face with the confidence of a seasoned barber, which she probably is, if her fuzzy upper lip is any indication. I don't even shave my legs. I'm so pale I hardly have any body hair. Kids at school used to tease me by calling me albino. That use to make me so mad. Made me think of those little white rats with their pink eyes, whiskered snouts, gnashing teeth.

Barney squeaks, shifts his weight and rocks on the balls of his feet. Even he knows I have no business shaving a man. I steady my hungover hands and frost his face with foam, dragging the dual action blade down his cheek, around the bend of his chin, cringing at the sound of scrape.

"Atta girl, Serena." Tom flicks my bicep with a hand towel. "Go with the hair."

All our fucked-up faces in the mirror remind me of this painting I started in May after my first show closed at the Galaxy Gallery in Toronto. That makes it sound like I'm some fancy *artiste* always having shows and selling my work. It was actually just my graduation project from OCAD. A bunch of us showed. I got two red dots. One was from my parents. This painting, the one I started in spring and haven't worked on for the past three months, is enormous. Dark and drippy, a half feathered, half furred human face scumbled across textured canvas. Rough. Chaotic. Disjointed. Raw. Unfinished. At least that's what my prof said when he saw it before I brought it home. I kept it beside my bed until last week hoping it would trigger some unconscious inspiration and I'd know what to do, but its unfinished ugliness was just a tongue sticking out at me whenever I looked at it, which, being across from my bed, was pretty much every time I woke up. Finally moved it to the laundry room. Now mom's bugging me to get it out of there so she can get at the dryer.

I hold the end of Barney's bulbous nose contorting it I realize, but how else are you supposed to get at all those spiky little hairs that surround the nostrils at odd angles?

When I first moved in with Jinglenuts a couple of years ago, I would perch on the tub's edge agog with love and expectation and watch him shave. How quickly it can all go to hell.

The big mole in the centre of Barney's cheek always trips me up. My first few swipes around it are the effortless strokes of a painter, delicate and calculated. Then I fuck it up and slice the mole. Barney steps up the rocking, taps his fingertips together feverishly as I wipe away pink mousse to survey the damage.

"Sorry, sorry, Barney. Just a wee little nick." I dab at the mole with a tissue and pat his back. What's sorry to him? He looks right through and past me. Kind of reminds me of the glassy eyes of the taxidermied bears I saw with Jinglenuts at the ROM. We went there last fall to see this exhibit on bears. He only agreed because I begged him and because he still loved me then. We were kicking along Bloor Street, wet leaves sticking to the toes of our Doc Martens, tossing the ashes of our joint wherever we pleased and climbing the stairs between lion heads, elbows linked, not a responsibility to rub between us. We were Adam and maiden, young and easy under the apple boughs.

And when Jinglenuts was around the corner reading a wall plaque, I swear that something called to me from inside one of those hollowed-out bodies. I imagined tearing the stuffing out onto the museum floor and climbing into that bear shell so I could peer out at the world through the skin of another. A hide like that could be the perfect armor.

Lillian, Stuart, and Tom are on their third round of guys, my line is getting antsy, rife with murmurs, belches, farts. Henry Marshall is next. He's the only one on ward who actually speaks, though he only says one phrase over and over and over again while jerking his head and thrusting his chin up to the left and then to the right as though he has Tourette's. I swear to God Lillian took all the passive guys for herself. She's on Maurice right now who's so still and sturdy it's like shaving a potato.

A kid's pail in one hand, shovel in the other, Henry sallies up to my sink. "Where's that Henry Marshall? Where's that Henry Marshall? Where's that Henry Marshall?" he says, thrusting his chin every which way.

"All right, Henry. That's enough. Hold still so I can shave your face." He repeats his phrase another three times, louder, and with more vigorous head jerking.

Lillian sees Henry giving me trouble and intervenes. Grabs him under his right armpit and puts her ugly little pock-marked face in his. "Listen here, Henry Marshall. You shut up and keep still or I'm gonna take that goddamn pail and shovel."

"Nooo," Henry wails, clutching the sand toys to his chest, turning his body rigid. Looking up at me with cloudy blue eyes and grey cheek stubble, he obediently opens his gap-toothed mouth. With pasty suds dripping from the corners of his lips he says softly, in not quite a whisper, "Where's that Henry Marshall?" It isn't much, but we'll take it, Henry and me.

Wes Chapman's next. When it comes to allergies, few are worse off than him, his condition compounded by a crick in the neck disorder and his inability to blow his own nose. Gluey snot icicles drip from nose to vinyl bib, clearing his chin and creating harp strings of mucus that put a song in my heart whenever I see Lillian using a fistful of brown paper towels to puck them.

She glowers at him. Then launches into a profanity laced story of revenge and comeuppance. Yesterday, while she was wiping his ass, he shat in her hand. Think I see the snot icicles crack, the corners of Wes's mouth hinting grin, but maybe I'm just projecting.

Mornings are cooler now, but it's still August so even though we'll need the air conditioner in a few hours, it makes no sense to have it blasting now. I mean, I could pull a snowsuit over my shorts and T-shirt and be A-Okay. Of course the air conditioning dials are under a locked cage on the wall of a locked utility room and can't be altered until someone fills out a requisition form and takes it over to maintenance and by the time someone from the ministry reads it, approves it and assigns the work, it'll be September. I'm gonna be as far away from here as possible by then.

Is anywhere far enough?

Maybe I can convince Marty to join me at the beach for lunch.

We corral the guys into the TV room and Tom puts on Much Music. Stuart stands, tucks his extra-large golf shirt into his pants underneath his ample belly, reads the info sheet from the night staff and announces the morning schedule. Charlie has a doctor's appointment to fix the toenail he ripped off during the night. Gordie has a dentist appointment to have a crown placed on a front tooth he broke two weeks ago. Recreation staff is coming today at nine-thirty to take whoever's left on an outing. Stuart claims the appointments, and Tom, the recreation. I hate to even look at Lillian, but there it is: the two of us on jizz patrol.

Grab a bucket of warm and soapy with a generous squirt of disinfectant from the big, mysteriously unlabelled pink jug in the storage closet and pull on the rubber gloves, industrial strength tan. Not Lillian. She goes bare handed into the fray, cleanliness and order on her side, vicious in her attempts to restore a semblance of righteous normalcy to this place. As if all anybody really needs to be right-minded is a good smack and a scrub.

"Stupid disgusting idiot," she mutters, elbows pumping as she scours semen from one of the more prolific masturbator's plastic sheeted bed. She takes it as a personal affront, says, "I can't stand that Lenny bastard."

I deliberately start my scrubbing in the dorm room across the hall, so I don't have to listen to her. Suppose things could happen to a person that could turn her nasty inside out. Still, you'd think after twenty years here Lillian would've made peace with the place. Everybody knows you have to kill a little part of yourself to work here. Sew up just one chamber of your heart so tight you can't feel certain things. Fine line, I guess. In shutting off one emotional valve, you run the risk of drying out the whole heart. It sure ain't Lenny's fault. Why fight the rain is all I'm saying.

Wring out my jizzy cloth and moisten the dry smear of cum on the next bed. Think about semen as spilled seeds, about squandered potential, about the randomness of being. If an omnipresent energy field shrouds our lives, if from the moment of conception our beings are infused with the energy of infinite potential, what the fuck happened with these guys? How much influence and control do we really have in our own destinies?

The first time I almost died, I had not yet been conceived. That probably sounds all paradoxical and cryptic but it's not that complicated. After Stanley was born, my parents tried unsuccessfully for a sibling. Four years later, doctors pronounced Dave and Margaret an 'infertile couple'. They were urged to be grateful for their one *normal, natural* child. Stanley, all model dinosaurs and flaxen hair, was a blessing. My folks wept then for the dreams in themselves not realized and spoiled Stanley rotten. Two years later the Angel of the Lord descended upon Margaret and said, "Lo, unto you a child is born." And you'd think just having got my self born would have been good enough.

At lunch, I set the four round oak tables in the dining room for *family style* eating. What a joke. How do you take the institution out of the institution? You can't just change what it is and how it operates by calling it something different especially when you have the old guard running the place. You can't pretend that they're the kids and we're the parents and we all sit down together to polite conversation over roast chicken for Sunday lunch. I mean, I appreciate the sentiment, the notion of trying to give a more normal, nuclear family experience to the guys but that's not what it looks like, or feels like, that's not what's happening. These are adults with serious physical and mental conditions who require constant care and monitoring for their safety and have been institutionalized since childhood, some since infancy. I'm sickened pretending that any of this is ok and even more so that I am a part of it yet unable to tear it down. Round oak tables and new politically correct labels do not a family make. Surely, we can do better than this; I mean it's 1994!

Two of the tables are designated for the guys with teeth who can chew and swallow normally, safely; they're called The Regulars. Two are for those who need their food through a blender: The Grounds. Nobody seems to know why half these guys need their food pureed. Could be their teeth rotted down to blackened stumps through years of neglect or they might have had the chompers punched right out of their mouths and don't have sense enough to keep a bridge in place. Could be they've got some throat contraction disorder that prevents their esophagus from squeezing down lumps of food. Could be all the meds screwing with their chew reflexes and hunger impulses. Could be they're gorgers, one of those guys who compulsively shoves as much food as possible into his mouth stuffing himself beyond all sense of pleasure. Like every time they eat it's a carnival hot dog contest except, they wind up choking and subsequently vomiting.

I know from my museum trip that bears binge eat, hyperphagia, to store up fuel for the winter. Then they grow these hairy, gristly butt plugs to block in the whole works until spring. But humans have no such needs. And bears don't go choking themselves in the middle of said binge.

I asked Lillian once why they don't feed the *grounds* soup, oatmeal, things that lend themselves to the form. Is putting pizza and iceberg lettuce with Thousand Islands dressing through the blender really a solution? *It's 'gainst their human rights*, she said. Bowls on plates, forks to the left, spoons to the right. It's the mental health of the staff such rituals serve to protect, a reminder of our common humanity. Otherwise, it'd be like a zookeeper throwing fish to the seals.

—

Toward the end of it all, Jinglenuts asked me if I was ready to climb out from under my dark cloud and accompany him to his Religious Studies wine and cheese. I pulled the afghan up over my shoulders and told him I was working on my butt plug. I can see him now: a sunny late August morning, brunching on the patio of some trendy Queen Street bistro. Light bearing down from the heavens highlighting his blond hair, no, his beret, creating a halo of intellectual, no of spiritual supremacy, that overwhelms his busty, undergraduate companion. *"Oh Jinglenuts,"* she'd gush, *"you're like so spiritual."*

"Well, you know I've always believed that two souls are brought together by something grander than the material, that divine sources guide us toward those individuals from whom we need to learn the most." And taking her hand across vegan burritos, he'd encourage her gaze to connect with his and say, *"I'm looking forward to learning from you, and all about you."* And it wouldn't be long before he'd show her the way of the Buddha all night long.

I swirl the mop around the toilets diluting the piss into soapy water figure eights that evaporate into the institution air with an ammonia bite. The freight elevator bings open, and a grey-faced laundry lady emerges from the depths with a white cap and a wheeled tub full of pressed clothes and linens. She is speechless or should I say she doesn't speak. I can't tell if this is defect or decision. Lillian intercepts the bin says she's making beds and that I'm putting clothes away. As if I give a shit. I've been around here long enough to know whose pants are whose, and that Edgar doesn't wear shorts.

Candice, the floating staff, spells us off after lunch so we can take our breaks. Hop on my bike and follow the paved path through the pine trees to the admin building to find Marty. He's engrossed in something on the computer with his back to me, so I peer over his shoulder in time to see the green screen from his solitaire game exploding into shuffling zigzags across the monitor.

"Is this what you've been doing since seven this morning?"

He smiles and shrugs. "I made a trip down to archives. Dropped off a few files, made some coffee for the *Ladies*, played a little Tetris, maybe some Solitaire. Government institutions rock."

Of course Marty gets posted in admin while I get stuck on a male behaviour Ward. "What's in the archives?"

"Files. Incriminating photos. Ancient restraining devices. Total shop of horrors."

"I wanna see."

"In time, curious one. In time."

I extend my middle finger. "Lunch? Beach?"

"Elaine," Marty calls to a plump woman in a pink crocheted cardigan and black nylon slacks, "mind if I go for lunch now?"

Of course Elaine doesn't mind. He smiles an Eddie Haskell grin, grabs a bag and a couple of drinks from the little fridge under the coffee maker. Marty's too short for me, and we've known each other since kindergarten. But with those brown sugar curls and permanently rosy cheeks, I can see how some girls might be attracted to him. He balances himself on my bike seat, lunch in one hand, cans in the other. I stand, balancing myself on the handlebars, and head toward the waterfront pedaling like mad.

"Not so fast, Serena! My balls!"

I'm laughing so hard that by the time we hit the train tracks I've lost control and we almost topple over from Marty's squirming, so I veer off the dirt path to the grass and jump. He rolls around clutching the baggy crotch of his brown corduroy shorts. The pair of us a laughing heap of tangled limbs.

He rights himself, hands me a root beer. Walk down to the beach from there, flopping on the hot, damp sand at the edge of the field.

He offers me half a sandwich, says, "What've you been up to? Still painting?"

"A bit," I lie. "Hanging out with Trace and the guys from the Royal Frenzy mostly."

"What for?"

I shrug. Bite my sandwich.

"We should hang out more."

Nod and chew. "How do you keep sane living here?"

"Mariposa's all right. My brothers and I loved it when we were growing up."

"Yeah, yeah, I know—parks and trees and lakes, Stephen fucking Leacock. Easy for you to say, you're off to Osgoode in a year. It's not like you're a lifer."

"You never know. Dad's trying to get me to take over his practice."

"So, you'd actually move here for real?"

"Gotta make a living somehow. I'll write my 'gripping' legal dramas on the side. Worked for Grisham."

"What happened to you? You sound like my parents. You used to be Mr. Joseph Campbell, hero's journey, follow your bliss and all that. Don't you want to have any exotic adventures all Kerouac-style before you sign on the dotted line?"

"Sure. I just don't feel the need to plant trees or smoke pot in Amsterdam right now."

"Hello? Your midlife crisis is calling. Remember what Janis said: *You can destroy your now by worrying about tomorrow.*"

"It's not like you're a lifer, Serena. You got a degree, lived in Toronto. Didn't you just have some big deal art show in the city? Aren't you going travelling in the fall?"

"Yeah. Yeah. But look at you. You're all organized with a life plan and everything. My life, my supposed trip seems so way out there, slipping out through the cracks between my fingers."

He puts me in a gentle headlock, rubs his knuckles along my scalp in an ape-like display of affection. "Call a travel agent, map it out. Anyway," he says, "can you believe what's happening with all this incinerator bullshit?"

"I know. How did those jerks ever get elected? My parents are totally involved with the whole anti-incineration campaign. Have you seen those SIN pamphlets? My dad did the research, design and printing."

"Stop Incineration Now. I like it. I should get involved since I'm here and everything. Good karma."

"They need help with green ribbon distribution, want as many people as possible wearing those things. C'mon over some night, lend a hand." I light a smoke and raise it. "To dioxins!"

Marty grabs it from me and takes a drag. "To all indiscriminate carcinogenic particulate matter!"

I bury the butt in the soft dirt with my finger then pick at the grass, plucking out two extraordinarily long pieces and knotting them. We lie together, the tops of our heads touching, looking at the sky, then out at the water. Marty swallows. The nearness is comforting at first then feels too intimate what with our hair entwined and all. I sit up, breaking the trance. Roll the grass knot between my thumb and forefinger, then flick it over there into nowhere, into the moment between us that like the summer, and my aspirations, seems also to have evaporated.

September: Nine Months Before

QUANTAS OF SOLACE

Three Aboriginal men in batik loincloths are captured in a mid-whirl tableau, their eye-light frozen by a voyeuristic photographer. Bodies brown-black like soil, dotted white with lime, dance into consciousness, dance into being through communion with the ancients. The image rests on my palms, a stolen spiritual centerfold. Flung far from YYZ aboard this giant boomerang, I'm not sure I'll ever return but am grateful the option exists. Can people do that? Just up and leave forever? My in-flight Qantas magazine article promises to *Unlock the Secrets of the Aborigine.* A flip of the page reveals a second photograph of a cave-drawn kangaroo with mysteriously large genitals that hold the key, apparently, to creation, to the dreamtime when the gods sang the world into being. A time when all spirits for eternity were born. So says the caption anyway.

I fiddle with the armrest dials and with the window cover and my mind circles the idea of dreamtime. In that frozen moment where those men dance, I'm sure I glimpse the divine. Not just in their eyes, but in the air that surrounds them. Within me there is a knowing; I, too, must return to dreamtime. When I rub my hands on my seat in an effort to still myself, the woven texture of the grey synthetic fabric grates against my palms turning them red and itchy. My mind is spinney, can't concentrate for long. Got to get ahold of myself. Press my temples, inhale, deep breaths, deep breaths. Keep it together, Serena.

The gleaming ashtray flip top catches my fidgeting digits and I blurt to the woman next to me, "This must be an old plane, there are ashtrays here from when you could still smoke."

She barely raises her eyes from her page where she too is hoping to unlock the secrets of the Aborigine. Back straight as a pianist's, ashen hair clipped severely at her nape, she reminds me of a friend of my mom's who'd always correct my sloppy *yeah's* with crisp *yeses*.

"Way back then." She turns the page.

I look at the magazine. Everyone is always looking for conclusions, solutions, explanations. No one ever says that life is an Escher staircase. That the most you can hope for is to find some way to simultaneously *be* and to temporarily transcend *being* like those dancer guys in the photo.

In the magazine there are tear-out postcards of the dancers and of the kangaroo. I rip them discreetly, one perforation at a time, hoping that Lady Di beside me won't notice, and stick them in my sketchbook. Leaving is not the same as disappearing.

Of course you wouldn't know that from Dave and Margaret's reaction when I told them I'd booked a flight. Dad removed his glasses and pinched the bridge of his nose like he was trying to stop a nosebleed or something. Mom shot watery rays of concern from her blue eyes to my father's who, catching the distress, reflected it anxiously out. One cannot cellar-dwell forever, folks. Back and forth they looked at each other, choosing words carefully, understanding perhaps for the first time what it really means to let go. Why are they so afraid? It's like they see deficiencies in me even I don't know are there.

Lady Di closes her eyes and tilts her head away in what I suspect is an attempt to ignore my agitation. She can't. I'm effervescent, a bottle of Lime Rickey my brother Stanley has shaken.

I attempt to read *Frankenstein*, but am incapable of the concentration required to make sense of the first paragraph, plus it's boring as hell. I thought it would be a fun read, a monster terrorizing people, not some long drawn-out letter writing sequence in antiquated prose. I'm about to read the instructions on the vomit bag when food arrives.

"Do you have Pinot Gris? I think it would be lovely with the snapper."

The flight attendant apologizes to my neighbour and smiles through red lipstick while suggesting an alternate.

"Sauvignon Blanc? Yes? Fine. I'll have Sauvignon Blanc, preferably from New Zealand."

I order the same. We're all equals in economy *milady*. Eating my puddings out of little plastic compartments and sipping wine is diversion enough. Then a baggie, a night kit, drops in my lap. Blue socks, lip chap, an eye mask with an optional sticker proclaiming *wake me for meals*. A giggle fizzes up inside of me. Wake me for life, wake me from life, wake up to your life. I peel and stick the motto cockeyed to my mask, offering my seatmate a grin. Lady Di slips hers into her purse. I want to shake her, laugh in her face. Not nasty-like, just saying none of your pretensions matter, we're all connected to the same stream of light. Swig the last of my vino giddy with the promise of new and drink away the doubts of others that have plagued me since the day I was born.

No one believed I would do it. Even I had my doubts. Here I am, though, Thursday, September twentieth, bound for Cairns, Australia with an open-ended ticket to stay or leave as I please. One stop in Honolulu, one stop in Sydney. Even after airfare, I still have a few thousand socked away and I can always get a job serving drinks, wiping asses, painting t-shirts—sky's the limit. And I owe it all to Jimmy Birchbark and his ill-gotten egg.

Tracy foisted upon me the St. Christopher, Patron Saint of Travelers medallion that her grandmother gave her for a reading week trip to Daytona Beach the year before. I tried not to accept but she insisted, hanging the necklace right over my head. A loving gesture for a normal person. For a subnormal such as myself, the silver disc embossed with an old man and praying hands creeped me the hell out. So, while sitting under the white pine in the MNC graveyard one night and saying my metaphysical good-byes to Jimmy and Mariposa, to my friends and family and to my former self, I decided that in spite of the intention with which it had been given, it was cold and oppressive and had no business bouncing against my heart. Cross-legged in the dirt under the cover of pine watching the grave tops for my squirrel friend and digging in the soil with a stick, I unearthed a flat, circular piece of tree that fit my thumbprint perfectly. It must have been a knot in a branch once. I carved a J and a B with my handy dandy jackknife on the thickest side and poked a tiny hole in the top end. Later at home after tucking Tracy's medallion in the jewelry box on my dresser for safekeeping, I took out from the same box a piece of leather lanyard from some never finished summer camp necklace and looped it around the wood piece etched with Jimmy Birchbark's initials. The way I figure, whoever you pray to keep you safe ought to be as close to God as possible. Jimmy Birchbark, JB, to be known forever after as the Patron Saint of Winkies.

At 2:46 AM, Ontario time, I sit on the floor of the Honolulu airport. The lack of sleep, fresh air, and the four-hour stop-over has stilled and sobered me enough to attempt *Frankenstein* again. Was supposed to have read it last year for a Women's Studies course but managed to scrape by without having done so. While I was packing, I heard the guilty whispers of the uncracked spine from across the room. So far this geographer guy is spilling his guts to his sister. Makes me think of absolving my own conscience. Pull out my free postcards: let the verbal purging begin. *Dearest Marty*, I write. Pause. Tap teeth with the wrong end of my pen. Speech balloons pop and fizzle in my head each encapsulating apologetic clichés. I really do like him. At least, I don't want him to hate me. Traditional Hawaiian ukulele Aloha hey music wafts down from ceiling speakers infiltrating my thoughts and laying down a soundtrack for the fat men shuffling along in palm treed shirts, socks and sandals, carrying tins of macadamia nuts. Looking around, I'm struck by my complete anonymity. It's as though people can see through my worn jeans and dancing bears shirt. Not that I'm entirely invisible, more that I'm translucent, a sliver of shell held up to a light.

I'm sorry Marty made assumptions about us. I'm sorry he's hurt. I guess I'm sorry I used his affections to feed my ego. And I'm tired of feeling sorry, apologizing for the actions of this person I've turned out to be. And there's a limit to how bad I can feel about his poor little feelings before I just say fuck it. Wasn't it enough for him that we were friends? I write him a jokey postcard, printing microscopically small, just to make him work for it.

My ass is getting sore from crouching on the cold cement, suppose I should move around before the flight to Sydney. Touch the wooden talisman at my chest, rub it with my thumb in silent commune, imploring Jimmy Birchbark to keep me safe. Stand, stretch and lean against a pebble-covered planter brimming with tropical leaves. A man's voice from over my shoulder.

"You waiting for a flight to Sydney?" He's tall, fit, older than me but not *that* old.

"Yep." I would lie, but with my luck, he'll be in the seat next to me.

He extends his hand. Black hairs on white knuckles. Touching his palm, dry and smooth, I want to retract my hand as soon as I've given it to him. He pumps a couple of times and I allow it, inwardly resenting the intimacy thrust upon me as a result of my ingrained good manners.

"I am Sergio. I am from Argentina." The strap from his black shoulder bag slips down his arm; he crosses his other hand over the shaking one to fix it. His black hair is cut short, sideburns flourish into points.

He wears a black Kappa tracksuit with white stripes up the sleeves and down the legs, sets assorted black bags on the floor. Bounces on the balls of his feet as he talks about his thirty-seven years, about his divorce, about his spirituality and his extensive Tai Chi practice. He tells me all the *must do things* in Australia and the Margaret in me appears to listen intently though I'm really wondering why he's bothering with me, what he wants, and do evil people do Tai Chi?

Pulls pictures out of his bag of Uluru or Ayres Rock, in the heart of the country, right in the centre of the outback. Amazing, this giant monolith jutting out from the otherwise flat earth like a smooth red iceberg.

"It is a sacred place to connect with the dreamtime. Ever been somewhere you could feel was special? Spiritual? The holiness coming up through the ground into your body through the soles of your feet?"

I shrug. He's not really looking for a response. If you count the in-flight magazine, this is the second recommendation I've been given to journey inward. Gotta pay attention to these things. Maybe this Sergio is not some lech, maybe he's a Joseph Campbell supernatural forest helper.

"The Aborigines knew Uluru was such a place more than two thousand years ago and there are artifacts and drawings to prove it. You must see the red kangaroo. Magnificent." Sergio fills the conversational lull with a primer on Taoism. Why do I always attract pseudo gurus and guitar players?

"Tao, once you embrace the feel-os-ofee, you become like a fish in the water who does not have to think to breathe. You move about your day in the flow of life, with ease, without questioning. Do you see? It is so simple, so beautiful. We humans complicate. The Tao is the way and the way to do is to be." He looks straight into my eyes. I squirm. His hazel eyes shift quickly to the ground as though looking for something lost.

The first thing Jinglenuts said to me when I met him was, *Ah, Serena. Serene. Calm to be, to be calm. Being calm is one with God and on course to the eightfold path.* Was I really so gullible?

Sergio looks at his watch. "I've heard Qantas is strict with their carry-on limits. I have so much camera equipment, electronics, cords for my computer. I worry they might not let me bring it all on the plane. Maybe if you do not have much to carry you could take one of my bags?"

And there it is. Do I look like I just fell off the turnip truck? "Sorry." I shake my head and back away. He bends down, opens his black nylon bags, looks up pleadingly, protesting that he doesn't have any drugs or guns or bombs or anything. That he's already been through airport security so he's clean. He drags out cords, cameras, beckons for me to observe the cavernous insides of his case. Tendrils of cords spill out encircling us. It's a test. It's like Dave and Margaret teamed up with *Candid Camera* and arranged the whole thing. Maybe I'm just being paranoid. He's probably perfectly normal, but you don't just walk up to some strange girl and ask her to do you a big, creepy favour. So I say, No. I won't do it. And the effort of saying no belies all my girlhood training and makes me sweat and stutter. I touch my JB amulet. What would Jimmy do? Ha! Jimmy wouldn't *do* anything. Jimmy would just *be*. Imagine that! Jimmy Birchbark the original Taoist.

"Sorry. Can't help you." I blither a little, say oh you'll be fine, hoping to ease the sting of rejection. Why is it that I even care? Step over the circle, Sergio's lengthy exasperated sigh burning in my ears as I scuttle away leaving him to gather his belongings. See him a little while later when I come out from the bathroom. He's in front of a restaurant, his junk spread out like a dragnet around an old lady in a navy pantsuit, pink bow frothing at her neck shaking her grey head.

In Sydney, on the way to boarding the next plane to Cairns, I pass a kiosk of kitschy Australian postcards. One shaped like a boomerang makes me think of Stanley. I ought to make more of an effort to keep in touch with the prick. I purchase it along with some others. Make small talk on the plane with two Canadian girls also flying up to Cairns. They seem oddly impressed by my lack of planning. They've prearranged a shuttle service with their hostel booked by their travel agent in Toronto and invite me along. One of them asks me what it is that I do that allows me to have so much free time to travel.

I tell her I'm between lives.

The only free beds in the hostel's dorm are top bunks. My new pals seem concerned, but this doesn't faze me. I've been sleeping on top bunks at camp since I was seven. Throw my pack up, slip into my silver bikini, eager to submerge myself in the pool. The screen door snaps behind me, slams hollow, transporting my memory to August cottage days. A moist, tropical heat seizes my first deep breath. Insects buzz electric in amongst the poolside ferns and palms. It smells different than home. Less earthy, more vegetative and greener and there are creatures hidden in the plants burbling with throat songs and noises peculiar to my Northern ears. An errant blob of sunscreen on the lens of my sunglasses attracts a small, dark fly. I watch it lift its legs and trudge through the stickiness. A triangle of sailcloth strung up with rope hangs over the pool guarding from sun. Though the pool is empty, the deck seems filled with bodies basking in, or shirking from, the light.

My first conscious act as new Serena in Australia will be purifying, baptismal. With toes gripping the edge of the deep end, I stare down the length of pool. Imagine my body like a newly gessoed canvas anticipating being drenched in shades of blue. Warm water rushes over me and I open my eyes underwater, swimming to the shallow end without once coming up for air. Faces dance, parade through my mind, Sergio, Marty, Tim, Jinglenuts, Tracy, Lillian, Jimmy, Stanley, Dave, Margaret all dissolving into the water. Am I far enough away now? Is it safe now to become myself? As I thrust up through the pool's surface, I can't stop smiling and my face muscles ache as though out of shape, as though I haven't smiled since before I was born in a million and one fucking years.

ENLIGHTENMENT,
BUT FIRST LET ME POUR YOU A DRINK

Saturday night, there are a few tables with pitchers of beer but nothing we can't handle so I refill my draught and offer Lisa one.

"Don't drink," she says. "Dad was a drunk before he passed, my brother is too. I seen what it done."

"You're going to work at the casino when it opens?" I say.

"I'm going to be a *host-ess*." She smooths her hands along her front. "Wear a pretty uniform and vest." She wipes the counter with the bar cloth. "You think Reg came up with *surfing in Costa Rica escape* all by himself?"

"You don't?"

"Him and Willy Simcoe were talking after sweat lodge. I heard Simcoe suggest it to him."

"What, he got stocks in Costa Rica or something?" She laughs, no sound comes out. "He's the one who made the whole casino thing happen right?"

"Yeah. He could sell ice to Eskimos, that one."

Tracy walks in waving. "I keep calling your house, obviously this is the best place to find you."

Concoct her a chocolate martini: vodka, crème de cacao, a dash of Frangelico. "Getting excited about the big move?"

"Can't wait." She pulls out a smoke, taps it on the bar a couple of times before lighting and looking up at me like she's about to get serious. "Tim says you told him to get lost?"

I nod. "I tried to do the friends thing. Told him I met someone, that there wasn't going to be any messing around. You know what he's like. He was pushing and pushing, calling me all the time, showing up here and shit."

"You've been friends—and then some—for like, ever."

Busy myself with bar work. "Had to, Trace."

"It's sad."

It is sad. Being in Mariposa this close to Tim but without him feels a bit like a slow to heal puncture wound I keep lifting the bandage off to inspect only to find it's the same gaping hole as the last time I checked. "Heard anything about Marty?"

"Saw his brother couple weeks ago. Far as I know he's still working at the Ward trying to make money for school. He's leaving April, like me, I guess. Get a head start on the year." She rounds the heater of her cigarette on the edge of the ashtray.

Tracy's going to Ottawa. Marty's getting ready for law school. And here I am back at the Queen. I mop up the accumulated slush around the tiled front door. Unmelted snow in the shape of Tracy's footprints trails along the playing card rug leading to the bar stools. In flurries Byron Williams, who tips his olive green fedora to me and jumps my mop.

"Ladies, I have seen it all," he says, face aglow. "Joshua Smith riding his lawn tractor on the sidewalk, a foot deep in snow."

"Is the LCBO even open at this time of night?" Lisa asks. "Shoulda give Crapwalker a lift while he was at it."

Joshua permanently lost his license for repeated DUIs a couple of years ago. Cars honk and wave as they pass him on his lawn tractor driving to and from the liquor store. Byron interrupts, "Serena, my budding artiste. There have been new developments. You are aware of the giant mural of Leacock, flanking Keaton's Flower Shop at the base of Missinaba Street?" I nod. "You are aware also, perhaps, that the opposing side you see when driving up from Lake Wissanotti is currently a real estate sign for my ex-wife's brokerage? We had a kind of deal when we divorced that we would share ownership of the sign, of the wall. We purchased the rights to the ad space years ago thinking we might create something meaningful, artistic and culturally significant for the town as a kind of legacy. But like everything else in our marriage the idea fizzled much like the Alka Seltzer tablet in my morning tonic. Millicent's sold her soul to real estate and her five years are up as of July and my five years begin. I would like to offer you the space, uninhibited, to create whatever 'artscape' you feel is meaningful to Mariposa. I will have the surface prepared and whitewashed. As a patron of the arts, I offer you this huge blank canvas."

"You trying to get back at your ex-wife or something?" asks Lisa.

"Absolutely and isn't Serena lucky to benefit from my childishness."

"You should do something about that incinerator BS," Lisa suggests.

Guess I could do something with the incinerator. Paint faces with ashes raining down, blurring all expression into versions of Evard Munsch's *Scream*. But that's so public servicey. Might be irrelevant in a couple years. I don't want something pretty either. I want something to fill people with wonder. Not something that would look nice in a living room over a brown corduroy sectional. Something as real and raw as baked bean night at MNC.

The Queen is filling up now. Each time the door swings open a breath of cold air gusts in from the street and straight up to the bar where I'm stationed. Lisa waits tables. Byron has found someone to play chess with him. The ebb and flow of drinkers continues and keeps me popping beer caps, mixing drinks and pouring wine. Tracy slowly gets pissed and entertains me.

When I get home, I take a look at all my Australia sketches. Use an Exacto knife from Dave's downstairs workshop and slice each page free from the book so I can spread the pictures out, rearrange them and have a good look at them as a whole. All told, I've got an MNC foot, a spilled ashtray, Jimmy Birchbark, client's humping the beach, the politically corrected bronze monument, wildflowers on the concession side road, Santa in a cigarette boat, Crapwalker, the band shelter, the incinerator, The Royal Frenzy, the Opera House, the guy from the army surplus store, the Queen of Spades, the highway filled with cottagers and Joshua Smith on his lawn tractor. I move things around, consider and rearrange and suddenly, I'm exalted: blessed with a genius idea. Sketch a plan on the back of a piece of white Bristol board I find in the laundry room that once served as a poster for the digestive system in my high school biology class. Mr. Richelieu gave me an A.　　Minus.

Early May: Almost Two Months Before

DRIVE

Wednesday, around nine AM, we load my Grandma's old Tempo with mismatched gear. As well as the car, Dave and Margaret have passed along their Coleman stove, a four-person Crappy Tire tent, some blackened cookware and the oldest surviving potholder in the history of humankind with crusty food still cooked into the thumb. Parents have a lot to offer; sometimes it's hard to know which the wheat and which the chaff. Aubrey packs the trunk humming happily to himself while I hang my grandma's brass dowsing pendulum over the rearview mirror. I'm still wearing my Jimmy Birchbark amulet and the opal necklace because I have this weird feeling that if ever I need assistance with astral projection, it'll be now. In black Sharpie, I write on the pale grey perforated vinyl ceiling in 3D letters like the beginning of *Star Wars*, Serena and Aubrey: Voyage into the Unknown.

Driving toward city hall on the way out of town, we try to eyeball my parents and the rest of SIN at the *community information session* offered by McLaughlin and Banbury. Aubrey stops the car for a look in front of the main foyer window. Could probably park there for hours. It's not like there's a security guard around. Sitting on a trolley in the centre of the room is a model of an incinerator about the size of a small desk, complete with green Astroturf and surrounding painted blue water. The architecturally accurate model incinerator is encircled by rows of seated people with large yellow and black signs that either accuse SIN, SIN, SIN, or show circles with lines slicing through silhouetted incinerators. An expansive banner above the door reads, *Stop Incineration Now*. Dear old dad certainly has outdone himself.

"Look at those nincompoops," says Aubrey, meaning the mayor and his deputy. "Good for the economy, my ass. Bunch of selfish boomers trying to make a quick buck on the backs of the next generation. Your parents are great and everything, but singing songs and waving signs? The evil ones laugh with fists full of cash when backs are turned."

He loosens his grip on the steering wheel, wipes sweaty palms on jeans. "I wanna do something. Something to let those guys know we're on to their game and they aren't gonna win."

"I did that granny shit for the Queen's Park protest already."

"Yeah. Something more aggressive. In your face."

"Like literally? Maybe we should throw balloons filled with red paint at their heads. A drive by splotching like Greenpeace."

"Yeah," he nods enthusiastically. "I'm not afraid."

"Joking."

"I know, but there are things we can do besides march around in a group and pump signs in the air like a bunch of coffee house hippies no one takes seriously. It's the nineties. Think. What's the best way to undermine someone in power?"

"Sex. Drugs. Scandal."

"Humiliation. You wicked deviant. Where's the nearest grocery store?"

We load up on supplies at the IGA three blocks up on Missinaba Street then head back to city hall. I drop Aubrey off to the left of the main doors, leaving the car up the street for an easy and inconspicuous exit before sprinting back to meet him in the bushes. We work quickly, using my knife to separate the two legs of a pair of pantyhose so we each have a mask to pull over our heads. Aubrey fills four aluminum pie plates with Reddi-Whip. On three, we rush the front doors, push our way through the gathering until we're between our intended targets and the model incinerator. With perfect athletic aim, Aubrey fires. McLaughlin reaches up to wipe whip cream from his face with fingers as cameras flash. The second one hits his chest and splatters. Banbury slowly rises from his orange plastic chair, head turned. I nail him first on his ear, milky sweetness dribbles down his cheek, the second creams his suit. It's no Texas book depository but if you played the cream-pieing in slow motion, it might bear a slight resemblance.

Cameras flash, people heckle and applaud. Aubrey clutches my hand dragging me along with him out the door and into the car. Tearing the stockings from our heads, our laughter trickles out open windows as we peel away. Aubrey hoots, fist waving through the window and one hand on the wheel, eyes wild and exhilarated like a nicotine addicted MNC client who's broken free and is about to gobble up a dumped parking lot ashtray. Sometimes all it takes to make yourself known is a tin plate and can of Reddi-whip. I write *Cream Pie Assassins* in fancy script with Sharpie on the ceiling and roll my window up. The faster we drive, the chillier it gets. May first already. Spinning, spinning, spinning. Almost a full revolution round the sun.

Three hours later, we're in Sudbury smoking a pipe of Reg's weed in front of the Big Nickel. I hug and kiss Aubrey, grateful we're together and on our way to somewhere. I want to smear him all over my skin, let him ooze into my every pore. How long will this loving smother last before I'm scraping disappointment off with a razor blade? Insecurity thunders through, rumbles deep. Aubrey's foolish and confident, well-intentioned and doesn't give a shit. He says he loves me, and I almost believe him though I'm sure, in the end, the disappointment will be his. Sooner or later, I'm going to have to let the bitch out of the bag.

He laughs at the colossal beaver on the big, stupid nickel. Makes comments about hosers. "Wait till we get to Wawa," I say. We continue driving, forced North by lake shape, before we can head west.

Aubrey's taller than me, not that much taller. Tall enough that when he pushes the seat back until it almost touches the rear bench, his legs flop open into forty-degree angles like some kind of humanoid frog. Flips his hair side to side as he drives, eventually attempting to solve the problem by tucking the amber-brown strands behind his ears. I put us both out of our misery and hand him an elastic band.

He fusses with the radio, digging around in the bag of tapes between the front seats so I pull the bag onto my lap and read out titles for his rejection. Nothing seems to hit the right note. Then *I Can See Clearly* comes on the radio, ringing out through tinny Tempo speakers. "Yes!" he shouts, slapping palms on the dashboard. Sings along, voice loud and true. I anoint the ceiling with the song title, which seems apt, and give the dowsing pendulum that dangles from the rearview mirror a little twist, watching it spin and circle round.

Eventually I say, "I feel trapped in here."

"In the Tempo?"

"Yeah." But that's not exactly what I mean. I mean I feel like a zombie or something. Wonder if that's how Crapwalker felt. Wonder if his body just chased around after his mind that was too broad to be contained inside his tiny skull. Lucky for him his heart took mercy, deciding he'd had enough and letting the rest of him be free. Used to think Mariposa had strength enough to snare me. Now I'm wondering if it's me. That all along I've been bigger than Mariposa could ever possibly contain, and that I'm more like Crapwalker than I care to admit.

Then I figure what the hell, we're gonna be in the car for hours, days even, and tell Aubrey about the third time I almost died. How I floated above watching myself go through the motions of life.

"Cool," he says. "You remember having an out of body experience from when you were like three."

So I tell him about the other times I almost died as well. That I've been spared because, well, I think I might have some kind of purpose to fulfill on earth before I can transmigrate. I'm not sure what, but I believe the answer lies in my ability to transcend my current Bardo. "Bardo is a state of limbo," I tell him. "After you die, your physical body goes back to the earth and your being or whatever, flies off, hoping to improve its karmic position for the next life by trying to rise above the temptation of earthly pleasures and the repulsion of earthly ills in order to reach the heavenly realms and avoid rebirth. Makes me think maybe all those times my parents prayed for a baby, maybe they prayed a little too hard and a desperate soul rushed into a womb-cave, and they wound up with a defective, imperfect child who wasn't ready to be born. So here I am, one foot in this world and one in the next."

He doesn't run screaming, not that he has anywhere to go. He takes a drink from his paper coffee cup, looks at me best he can while driving and says, "I'd say you hit the fucking karmic jackpot."

We listen to the radio awhile, then Aubrey says, "Once a week my dad used to hold what he called *meetings of the mind.* Our living room would fill with philosophy students from the college, a few older professors. My dad held court, crossed-legged on the floor with prayer beads on his meditation pillow, my mom in a frock serving sweet tea from a tray. I'd watch them from the top of the stairs. They seemed so glamorous. Not happy but pulled together. Retrospectively, of course, my dad was probably getting off on all the young men gathered around his feet like he was some kind of guru. And my mom probably want-ed to kick him in the balls and tell him to take out the garbage."

"Was he meditating?"

"Probably. Transcendental meditation was the big thing at the time, that and psychedelics. I only mention it because of your Bardo thing. These guys were toying with ideas of transcendence too. My dad totally admits to using acid and other drugs through-out his 'research'. He had his sixties hangover well into the seventies."

"Tune in, turn on, drop out."

"I love that you know that!" Aubrey twists the volume knob left, repositions himself in his seat. "I remember seeing some real-ly weird shit but didn't understand it, just thought, hey that's what philosophers do. They reach way back into their brains and pull it all out like one of those never-ending magician's scarves, and that's what you get when someone's turned inside out. They wail, laugh uncontrollably, writhe, scream, run around, dance their subconscious minds outside the house. My mom and I would go to my grandparents' in Miami sometimes to avoid the wildness. I missed a lot of school when dad and his groupies would take over the house, I was just a little kid. Weirdly, it felt normal."

"You guys ever talk about it?"

"Oh sure. We've had some good chats. He said they were testing out Leary's philosophy, the one about the eight levels of consciousness."

"What's that?"

"Leary and a couple of other philosophers created this hierarchy, eight levels of consciousness each activated by different drugs, and if you work through to the final level, you can achieve a transcendence that is not just an outside of the body only when you die thing, but an actual reality."

"Like you can live on earth in your body but still roam around in a state of transcendence?"

"I guess. With the help of brain-altering chemicals."

"A post-body society. Interesting." Wonder how Crapwalker and Jimmy Birchbark would fit into that. Would there be no mental illness? No intellectual impairment? Would all be recognized as equals? "Kind of weird they'd think putting all these chemicals though your brain was a way to open channels. I've never really thought of drugs in any positive kind of way, like, as a portal."

"Lots of cultures have been doing it with natural plants for centuries."

"Toad licking."

"Yeah, sure, peyote, mushrooms. Vision quests, shit like that. Let's face it, humans are always coming up with new ways to get high. There's some weird drive in us to alter our physical, mental reality."

"Escape."

"Or, to tap into our subconscious. Or ancient consciousness."

"Yeah, but you can totally drop acid and not be moved by the experience. Like knives, it all depends on intention. Cut an apple, cut a throat." I open a sleeve of saltines setting a small stack on the dash in front of Aubrey for easy access. "Does your dad believe all this?"

"He's not as free as you might think. Or as free as he'd like people to believe. Not now anyway. He says all the drug junk

was experimental, mostly left him fucked-up instead of enlight-
ened. Says transcendental meditation is as close as he ever got. He
doesn't discount everything, though he does have a bit of trouble
thinking big enough to include contact with extraterrestrials as an
evolutionary inevitability."

"Extraterrestrials?"

"Okay, so the last level's when the space time continuum is
obliterated, speed of light barrier is broken, total transcendence
via LSD or similarly psychotropic effect is achieved. They
thought angels or guides or any extraterrestrial beings are simply
ourselves in the future coming to warn and help us which is kind
of cool."

"What do you think?"

"I think it'd be great to reach that level. Anyway, sounds like
a person could have a lot of fun trying."

He finishes the rest of his coffee, wipes his lips on the sleeve
of his T-shirt and repositions his hands on the wheel.

I sneak looks at Aubrey as he drives. Admire the way he
sings, the freckles along the slope of his nose, the shell pink of his
lips. Reach out to him. Stroke his earlobe.

"It's all in there for us to access," he says, "sometimes we
need help getting to it."

On the side of the highway, we see our first *Don't Drink and
Hunt* public service billboard and he nearly wets himself. Then
there's Wawa. And, in the shadow of giant Canadian goose
wings, we sit on the green wood bench blessing Reg and his
offerings by refreshing the pipe. Aubrey's foot taps out the
rhythm of an imaginary song. Fingers, hands, feet, always a part
of him is tapping out the song playing in his brain. In this way,
he has managed resilience, perhaps. Me, I draw and write things
in my sketchbook and on the ceiling of my dead grandma's car.
The sun thinks about punching out, the sky at the horizon just a
lick of mauve.

The early evening light casts a twisted shadow on the road as
it winds toward the interior of Lake Superior Provincial Park, still
technically off-season. We drive around the keep-out arm and
over campground gravel that crunches like broken dishes under

the slow roll of our wheels. If you were going to murder some-one and didn't want anyone to hear the screams, a provincial park off-season would be a great place to do it.

Now that the light has disappeared, it's so cold there's no time for conversation or concern for others, just the desperate taking care of number one, layering up in fleece pants, mitts and knitted toques. You can tell a lot about a person by the way he sets up a tent. Jason loved instructions. If he were here, he'd bumble around in the dark with a flashlight and a rumpled piece of paper laying out each pole in its proper pile and assessing the situation before proceeding as per the written directions. I shake the contents of the nylon bag out in the dirt and start put-ting poles together by the glow of headlights. Aubrey cracks us both a beer, leans up against the car watching. "You know what you're doing?" He's relieved when I nod. Helps unfurl the brown mesh and nylon square. Points the door towards the fire pit. What I mean is that I know what I want it to look like in the end.

Wordlessly we assume gender role stereotypes. He gathers wood for the fire. I cook macaroni over the camp stove. I guess I don't care. Collecting wood sucks. I like making fires, though. Typical, my dad would say. While the pot boils, I crouch on the ground building a little stick teepee inside a log cabin of larger sticks. Light a small crumple of paper with a match. It burns and fizzles leaving only a red edge to work with. Breath comes out of me and into the sticks igniting them with flames from I don't know where, Prometheus, I guess. Aubrey drops a mélange of branches, long, skinny, young and green, thick and spongy from his arms beside the fire. Fortunately, previous campers left a cou-ple of stocky, dry logs to save the day. He squeezes me with gloved hands. I stoke the fire until it crackles. Drain the pasta and empty the neon orange powder packet onto the noodles. It's cold by the time it hits the black and white enamel plates satisfying even though it tastes like crud. Aubrey drags the picnic table clos-er to the fire pit. We sit and eat and warm ourselves.

"Think there are bears around here?" he asks, mouth full of noodles.

"They're just waking up from hibernation." Quietly rustling around in the forest fresh from shitting out their butt plugs. I can feel them watching us, sniffing us with noses raised, imprinting our scents into memory. "Lisa told me an old saying: A pine needle fell. The eagle saw it, the deer heard it, the bear smelled it."

Aubrey sits for a minute, fork raised. "Fuck, Serena, you're freakin' me out."

"Relax. I've been camping my whole life and only ever seen bears once and that was at a garbage dump."

Aubrey says he's never really been camping before. Plays Pink Floyd on his guitar. "You're right. We're gonna be fine. There is nothing to fear. Fear is all in your head. There is nothing to fear but fear itself," he adds with a Winston Churchill lilt.

"There is nothing to fear," I add quietly as he resumes playing, "but yourself."

"Oooo, heavy, man. I like that. Where's the Sharpie? I'm gonna write that on the ceiling."

He returns from the car without his guitar. He has one of Grandma's wool blankets over one shoulder and something shiny in his hands. "Are these the infamous dowsing rods?"

I laugh. "What should we divine?"

"You think they work?"

He sets them on the ground and sits beside me. Looking up into the black star speckled night I'm silently lost in thoughts that span time immemorial to infinite possibility. Galileo sat staring at these same stars, more or less. Of all the things he could have dreamt, I'll bet he never would have thought to think of the tiny, plastic glow-in-the-dark stars people stick on their ceilings.

"There's a recreated Indigenous village near Mariposa where the Hurons and Jesuits lived in relative harmony like three hundred years ago before all the European diseases and the Iroquois wiped them out. The village is one of those historical sites where people dress in clothes of the day, run blacksmith shops and First Nations women make bannock over open fires. Anyway, I was there one day petting a fox pelt in the longhouse when this old woman with black and gold sunglasses pushed up on her head told me that my country is very young and that she is from

Europe where there are castles and churches from the time before this country was civilized. I told her things were a lot more civilized here before Europeans came."

"Yeah. Nomadic people don't need castles and churches."

"These trees were the castles and the churches."

Aubrey pokes a stick in the fire. Smokes billows up in our faces. "White rabbits. White rabbits," he coughs.

I stand, turning my back to the smoke. "The most civilized thing about it was they lived for thousands of years here without wrecking anything. Look at Toronto with their garbage. Mariposa with their dumb ass incinerator plan. It won't solve anything, just creates a new problem. Then they'll have to come up with a new solution to solve that problem and so on." I pull out a baggie of magic mushrooms, a gift from Reg, and wave it at Aubrey. "Want to see if we can navigate the sixth level?" Take a few and pass him the bag as though sharing a sack of sunflower seeds.

"Why not? Can't play guitar with gloves on."

I grimace and nearly retch while chewing the putrid blue fungi. Funny the way your body knows you shouldn't eat this shit, tries to warn you, but your mind fights through the animal instincts and forces it down. Aubrey grabs us a couple of fresh beers. Rinse the mushroom funk from my mouth by spitting a cheek full of beer on the fire. It sizzles and spurts as though in pain, like an evil spirit or something being doused in holy water.

Aubrey dances across the fire from me, his arms rove through the air undulating like a belly dancer or a die-hard Grateful Deader. He waltzes his way around the fire pit, gathering my hands and pulling me into him so that I catch the rhythm and join. Beneath us are layers of million-year-old bone that belonged to animals who grew and changed and became and followed their desires and the parrot lizard became the parrot bird, and the saber-toothed tiger became the pussycat. In the cold, white moon the dowsing rods are shiny, crossed and inert in the dry leaves and soil next to the fire.

I fetch the flashlight from the tent and the photocopied park map from the dashboard and squeeze Aubrey's elbow, interrupting his own little space voyage. "Let's go for a walk," I say, leading him to a narthex of cathedral pines. We wait for the mushroom's poison to take further hold, for our entry into another reality. At first we follow the road toward the water but veer off shortly onto the trail system where every tree becomes a threat. We are Dorothy and Toto, lost in the forest, branches reaching down with gnarled fingers hooking the hoods of our jackets. The twigs and leaves crackle underfoot and the woods, save for our noise, owns the silence.

We continue walking, destination unknown, as a game show hallucination metastasizes in my mind. A glittering wheel of choices. A smarmy man in a burgundy suit barking into his microphone as he spins the giant wheel. *Serena!* he shouts, *You can ride a horse, take a boat, jump off a bridge, go to jail, go to school,* his voice speeding ever faster, *ride a camel, kill a baby, jump out a castle window, give birth to a yak.* The visions whirl and swirl like the celestial currents in a *Starry Night,* becoming increasingly random until they spin throughout my mind, and I lose track of them visually as they blend into white light and flashing circles, a vortex of choices in the centre of the wheel. And then I'm jumping on a lit walkway, a real live board game that lights up like *The Mad Dash* when I step on a square. I breathe in the cold air deep, drink water from my Nalgene. The burgundy-suited host follows me. I follow Aubrey. The game show dissolves, nothing resolves. Eventually, there is a merging of trails and a sign indicating directions. I am both exhausted and refreshed. "Should we look at the map, Aubrey?" At first he's frantic, afraid, then looks up seeing muffled light edging through the trees and breaks into a smile.

Fear and Self-Loathing in Mariposa

Last night I sprawled across the blue tweed couch in the basement and stared at the walls. Propped my head up on one of mom's cross-stitched duck pillows and listened to the automatic ice machine in the kitchen pinch off frozen crescents that echoed through the house as they dropped into the plastic bin one by one by one. Drunk, unable to sleep, I flipped through the channels hoping for something that wasn't fuzzy or shilling Dick Gregory's Bahamian diet or wasn't showcasing some pony-tailed guy flogging his revolutionary exercise machine the motion of which promised bodily transformation via creepily imitating the act of Neanderthal copulation. Then I heard that ubiquitous, disembodied voice of the male documentary narrator and stopped flipping channels. Sand swirled on the screen across the cursed valley of Tucume, somewhere in Peru. Archeologists discovered a whole bunch of pyramids built by ancient tribes. Problem was, as soon as the people would get close to finishing the last pyramid, natural disaster would strike and wreck everything. This happened a bunch of times over hundreds of years. Of course, nobody ever said, *Hey, maybe we shouldn't build here because of all the droughts, windstorms, and torrential rains.* Nope. It was all *someone must have angered the gods. Off with their heads!* Whoever didn't get decapitated would move on down the valley and start building pyramids again. Then the Incas popped in and warned of an impending visit from the Spanish. Well, instead of making pyramid bricks, the valley folk started shitting them. Something must be done to stop the Spanish invasion, someone must be responsible, someone must be sacrificed to appease the gods. When decapitations didn't end the rumors of the Spanish, the tribe took drastic action and all were suspect. They ripped the still beating hearts from each other's chests and offered this life force to the gods. Guess what? The tribe extinguished itself and the Spanish never came.

Lillian barricades herself in the central Plexiglassed office to record the morning routine in the logbook. And while Tom and Stuart toilet the guys, I sneak to the staff room to choke down a cup of coffee and rummage around the cupboards for a cracker to settle my lurching stomach. After a few bitter sips, sourness churns within so I dump the remaining coffee down the drain, take a few deep breaths and catch up with the others for a session of yard time before lunch. Take solace in knowing that if I have to puke at least I'll be outside.

"Won't be many days like this left before winter," says Tom as he unfolds us each an aluminum chair webbed with orange and yellow nylon strips. He lights a cigarette and offers me his yellow lighter. Tom's in his forties and has nearly twenty years institution time under his ample belt. He reminisces fondly about the good old days when staff could smoke wherever they pleased, as three guys crowd in on us, surrounding the chairs, hoping we'll drop our butts.

Tom's voice drops an octave. He becomes the alpha dog. "Yous guys get the hell outa here. Go play on them swings." He leans into me speaking softly as though in confidence. "Some of them dickheads that used to work here didn't give a rat's ass about these guys and would just throw their butts any old place. They'd laugh, think it's funny that these guys'll put anything in their mouths, gobble up butts from the ground like a gaggle of geese with breadcrumbs. That's why half a the picas are addicted to nicotine."

"Gross," I say, shaking my head sympathetically and taking a big drag of my smoke.

Rupert, about thirty-five, crawls in front of us on the ground. He wears diapers and has not developed past the infant stage. He has Cro-Magnon features, a huge forehead and dark, bushy brows. His diapered bottom rises higher than his head as he scoots along on his shins. Rolls on the ground with his feet in the air like a baby except he's less agile and otherwise resembles an adult man, hairy legs and all. He giggles randomly, swings his head side-to-side, flashes a pristine, white-toothed smile then puts his face into the grass happily munching. There is beauty somehow, in the simple pleasure he takes. We let him chew his cud and joke about who's next to change his diaper; it looks and smells like horseshit. Natalie, our supervisor, would probably tell us it's our job to stop him from eating grass. But it's the only thing he does all day that he alone can choose. That's got to count for something.

Mucker, in his one-piece blue jumpsuit with white mitts Velcroed onto his wrists, walks up to us, stops and grins.

Stuart clears his throat, hoarks a loogie over his shoulder. "Shit eaters always have the best teeth."

"You wouldn't believe what I seen go down 'round here." Tom stubs his cigarette out on the bottom of his shoe and jiggles the butt around in his palm as we all do until we can flush them. Arms straddling knees, belly in his lap, he brushes a shock of thinning, sandy blond hair from his eyes, lights up another smoke and says between breathy puffs, "Couple of weeks ago, Leon busted up his finger. Tore the nail clean off. Bleeding like a son of a bitch. Had him over to Emerg. You wouldn't believe this fuckin' doctor. Said Leon needed stitches and dove right in 'n tried to start stichin' 'im up. I'm the one holding Leon, who's strong as an ox and trying his damndest to be good, but there's only so much he's capable of, you know? So I tell that doctor he ain't touching Leon until he gets some anesthetic. I'm the first one to stand up for these guys, ain't that right, Stu?"

"You betcha."

"Why, that doctor give me the dirtiest look! I was *this close* to punching his fuckin' lights out. So he gives a big huff and gets a needle ready—I'm sure it was fake—jabs it right in Leon's nail bed. Did he howl. So I'm basically trying to reassure the poor guy and he's trying not to lose his shit. It's like the doctor thought *fuckin' Winkie he'll never know the difference.* I been to vets with more class."

"Oughta report him," says Stuart.

"What do you say? What can you do?"

"That's pretty fucked up," I say.

Stuart sucks in air and it sounds like "yep." His hands smooth the denim on either side of his gut.

"It's fuckin' ignorant that's what it is." Tom's teary. He sighs, blows the air up through his bangs. He might have been cute once. If I was ugly and desperate. The silence sits between us, a deaf mute on a swing.

Meds distributed and downed, grey food trolleys arrive with post-it notes delineating which dishes are for the *grounds* and which for the *regulars*. We herd the guys into the dining room. Stuart stands on guard in front of the food to prevent attack. Jimmy Birchbark outmaneuvers him and snatches a chicken leg. Stuart saves him from choking himself by grabbing his wrist and shaking it until the leg drops, leaving a greasy smear across the concrete.

"Why don't we just feed him before or after everybody else instead of going through this everyday?" I say to no one in particular.

Lillian answers without looking up as she clears dishes from the tables. "It's against his human rights."

Tom chips in, "Natalie told us he's got to learn proper meal-time behaviour if he's ever to function *in the community*. All these guys gonna be living in group homes one day after this place shuts down."

"Aren't you worried he's gonna choke?"

"Not my job to make those kinds of decisions. That's why Natalie gets paid the big bucks." Tom flips the hair off his forehead and resumes clearing the plates. Locks Jimmy outside of the dining room anyway where he watches through Plexiglas as the others tuck in. His anxiety is frothy-mouthed and frantic. Puts us all on high alert. I fix a plate for Jimmy to eat when the others are through. He knows he's not supposed to do it. Gotta admire his relentless spirit, every meal it's the same.

After lunch the guys usually have rest time, meaning they can pretty much do what they want and staff are supposed to walk around making sure no one's getting into mischief like climbing on top of a dresser and catapulting himself, while holding his ankles, knees first to the concrete floor like one guy did. On my rounds I pass through two sets of locked doors and straight into Andrew Tildon banging on the Plexiglas with his fist. Sorrowful, groans effuse from somewhere deep within the hollow of his being. He lunges at me while screeching, his face red with what I can only interpret as anger. Yell for back-up. No one comes. He's my height, nearly six feet, has begun to bald and currently sports a Fu-Manchu. Stuart must be shaving him in his own image. Andrew grabs my wrist with one of his massive man hands and latches on so tight I remember squirming under one of my brother Stanley's sunburn 'games'.

"Don't you touch me, Andrew Tildon!"

All the pressure points from self-defense training workshops loop de loop in my mind. He puts the squeeze on. Fuck! I hate walking these halls alone. Every open door, every corner I turn, someone ready to pounce and attack. These guys may not have their wits about them, but they also don't know their own strength and sometimes the only way to save yourself is to go full beast, let 'em know they can't mess with you. A length of slobber dribbles out the corner of his mouth and dangles precariously close to my forearm. Why do the ones with Hep.B always drool? It's like a fucking prerequisite. Just as I'm about to give him the Vulcan death grip, he releases his hold. I turn on him, bend his arm behind his back, not hurting him, just disorienting him so I can direct him into his room where I order him to sit down and behave himself. He screams and laughs from his puddle of limbs on the floor like he's just had the best time of his life. My T-shirt palpitates. Hands sweat. Adrenalin pumps a rapid rhythm through my heart, and I feel like a horrible person for doing the job I've been taught to do. I'd be happy to give him whatever he wanted if only I knew what that was.

Tom and Lillian are nowhere to be seen, probably in the common room on the other wing watching soaps in spite of Natalie's mandate to only ever play the music channel. She believes that since the clients cannot follow storylines, the only

TV they should watch is the music channel. She's such a Nurse Ratched sometimes. No one wants to see the guys zoned out on TV all day but soap operas are emotional and have plots and can usually be followed by people with little or no intelligence. Bombarding mentally challenged men prone to violence with cleavage-jiggling, ass-gyrating, gun-toting images with no story-line is kind of messed-up. Should be watching kiddy shows where they learn to make friends and share and not stick their fingers in electrical sockets.

Stanley and I used to love watching this show with kid reporters. A guy from our street's aunt was one of the producers so he got to be on it once interviewing a teenaged, blind Jeff Healy who was playing guitar on his lap, and a doctor who was talking about heart transplants. They spoke about experimenting with mechanical pig and baboon hearts, a big thing in the eighties. Stanley convinced me, because of the scar on my chest, that I'd had a heart transplant when I was a baby and that the doctors replaced my heart with a baboon's. He teased me mercilessly, dragging his knuckles along the carpet hooting like a monkey. Mom eventually had to sit me down on the white chenille bedspread in my room and open up my baby book to an article from the Mariposa News Packet tucked in beside a lock of white hair titled, *Local Baby Survives Heart Surgery*. I'd had minor surgery to repair an atrial septal defect, a hole between the two chambers of the heart, a common and uncomplicated surgery that I refer to as *the second time I almost died*. Miracle baby once again. No wonder Stanley never tired of telling me that if I'd been born into certain South American tribes, I'd have been covered up with leaves and left for dead because my heart was so weak it could not go the distance.

Pig, baboon, no way. If I had any animal heart it'd be a bear's. Like a manticore with a lion's body and a human's face, I'd have the body of a human and the heart of a bear thumping inside my chest pulsating and driving me ruthlessly forward at times, then at others barely beating at all, never fearing a thing.

September: Eleven Months Before

UP TOP DOWN UNDER

The Canadian girls, and a couple of others I've met from around the hostel, invite me out for drinks. But so far, night three, I've been in hiding. After days full of exploration, I've been keeping safe and out of boozy trouble by tucking into my purple plus-zero sleeping bag and reading *Frankenstein* like I'm ten years old all curled up with the *Sweet Valley High* series. Walton, the geographer guy, is trying to make a name for himself charting the Artic waters when he meets this half-dead scientist trudging along the ice. The setting is cold, bleak, desolate, the mood hopelessly disappointed and lonely. Though I'm more alone than ever right now, I'm not lonely. And I understand lonely like I understand trying to fall asleep in the dark next to a man I live with but no longer love.

The scientist turns out to be Victor Frankenstein, who confesses that he tried to create life and that the creature he made didn't exactly turn out as planned. Do they ever? Anyhow, rejected by his "father," the monster exacts revenge on Victor and his loved ones. Victor, realizing at last his responsibility as scientist parent, follows his creation to the Arctic to finish it off.

I fold the page corner of my novel, stick it under my pillow and prepare to do a little sketching. Use my knife to sharpen some pencil crayons into a paper cup. My head almost touches the ceiling as I'm sitting on the bunk, but I'm comfortable enough. I draw an MNC client's foot in a blue Velcro shoe. Add a slouching white and red striped sock and a bit of scab-addled hairy shin to fill the page. Since I left home, I'm only inspired to draw images from memory, mostly of Mariposa. Last night I drew apples with bites out of them floating down a culvert into the flow. It's weird. Here I am, seeing all this exotic flora and fauna, all these fresh new sights and smells and all I can do is write little verbal sketches of what I might draw in the future. Like today, I went on a rainforest excursion and saw these curtain fig trees that look like dreadlocks hanging down from the sky. Fruit bats eat fig seeds and shit them on the trees. The seeds land in crevices in the treetops then grow roots from the top down. They're not parasitic because they take their nutrition from the air, rain and sun. They're epiphytes. Some of the roots reach down the length of the existing tree trunk all the way to the ground and surround it but don't necessarily harm the host tree. So I write in my sketchbook, *Rastafarian trees let loose twisted tendrils to the earth. Original tree supports them, and though usually survives, occasionally becomes a casualty of living.* Kind of a weird relationship. It's all fine and dandy until one of you gets smothered.

The next day, I tag along whitewater kayaking with the Canadian girls. The kayaks aren't what I expect. They're open-faced, blue, inflatable rubber. Everyone in the group is partnered but me and this goateed guy named Steve who says he's originally from Liverpool but lives in Australia now. I restrain myself from saying anything about the Beatles or using the word Liverpudlian though I long desperately to do both. His thick brown hair is pulled into a low ponytail and he walks with what appears to be a contrived swagger. Smiling, he exposes two white Chiclet teeth with a space between them, and thrusts his hand out toward me. Steve, he says, and suggests we paddle together. The guide distributes yellow plastic helmets and gives a demonstration of paddling techniques. I only half listen, letting the rest of my brain wander to where I am in the world, almost in New Guinea. Cairns is the place where the rainforest meets the reef. Picturing myself here, I see an aerial view of a map, and I'm standing on the edge of the continent falling into the blue part that stretches between land mass and Great Barrier Reef.

Once the Japanese couple figures out how to paddle together so that they don't keep going in circles, each boat descends the first drop. We wait our turn under the umbrella of rainforest leaves draping out from the shore shielding the sun. Water explodes onto smooth boulders, fear replaces adrenalin, then whoosh! My stomach plummets as I plunge down into the froth, and, like Paddle to the Sea, my boat submerges, springing back up in a wake of bubbles. Steve and I laugh and scream in unison. For a moment there is only cool water over sweaty skin and the mineral scent of wet stones. If I could smile wider, my eyes would disappear into themselves.

After the next set of rapids Steve says, You can paddle as well as most blokes. He thinks it's a compliment to hold me up to a male benchmark. He's underestimated me from the start. Sometimes I wonder if this is my greatest asset.

The hostel is plastered with yellow photocopied party invitations promising free wine and kangaroo steaks for guests in the courtyard. Guess I can't spend every night holed up in Serena land. I step through the screen door threshold onto flagstone and wave at the hostel owner who is expressing oil from a squeeze bottle onto a sheet of metal that covers a wood-fired stone oven. The barbie of *Crocodile Dundee* legend, I presume. Meat sizzles on the metal sheet. He nods toward a box of wine on the picnic table, tells me to help myself. I'm awkward and conspicuous. Steve from kayaking waves to me from across the courtyard. I should leave. I probably shouldn't drink. I depress the plastic spout of the wine box dispensing a tumbler's worth.

A sparrow of a girl looking nervously around leans against the edge of a picnic table. "Cheers," I say, holding my glass up to her. "Been here long?"

"A week. I'm Gemma." She scopes the patio, strokes her thin neck and short-cropped hair. "From Denmark." She removes a white and gold package of Marlboro Lights from her pocket, taps the bottom toward me until one pops up. I accept.

Clad in long plaid shorts and a peach tank top, Kara from Amsterdam, whose walk emulates the gait of a rhino, sallies up to our picnic table holding a green can of Victoria Bitter. Her head is almost shaved except for little orange wisps feathering down crowning her face.

"What brings you to Australia?" I ask.

Gemma waves her hands, rolls her eyes at Kara. "Don't get started."

I look from one to the other trying to make sense.

Kara says, "Just let's say I need holiday."

"Your job?" I ask.

She shakes her head. Gemma lights another cigarette, throws the pink lighter with the Sailor Moon sticker on the table. "It was not my job, my job, I work for the government is no problem. My girlfriend and I have some problem and I had to leave my apartment. Some legal problem. Not good. I decide to myself, I need holiday." And in the same breath she calls to a tall brush cut blonde guy with a big gut and high cheekbones. "Hey Mats," she says. "Come join us."

Mats nods at Gemma, Kara and me, and plops two VBs on the table. Condensation from the cans beads and drips leaving instant rings of wet on the wood. The sun has dipped, the heat given up leaving a less intense warmth, though it's still sticky and without breeze. The owner tugs a string that clangs the dinner bell. A line of hostellers juggling mismatched china plates and cutlery from the hostel kitchen snakes through the flagstone courtyard and picnic tables toward the BBQ. The kangaroo, Mats says over the din of increasingly drunken chatter and letting everyone know he needs raw meat to enhance his virility, is a little overcooked. But that doesn't stop him from eating two steaks the size of his head. Kara's a vegetarian and is scandalized by the whole eating of kangaroo thing. Tastes a little tough, bit like a cross between venison and beef.

After dinner I excuse myself from the group, refilling my tumbler and heading to the row of phones across from the showers to call Dave and Margaret. Mom answers the phone and wheezes. I picture her clutching her chest, as though she can't believe I'm alive, that I actually managed to not get myself killed over the last few days. Tell her about the hostel, about the rainforest and to make her feel better, about how the Canadian girls and I are such good friends. Tell her something funny too, so she won't worry. Change the subject from me to my grandma, who is status quo, and then to the incinerator.

That's when she really gets going revealing that my dad has been putting up SIN billboards and knocking on doors to encourage people to put signs on their lawns. She sounds exhausted and inspired. Explains all about how dad is trying to get the two Missinaba Reserve bigwigs, Willy Simcoe and Tommy Snake, the guys who were responsible for bringing the casino to Mariposa, to get on board with SIN or at least use his company for the casino signage. Then she asks if I remember Mary Weider from high school and, of course, I do. She was always getting awards for public speaking and perfect attendance.

Mom says, "Mary's been very helpful distributing our green ribbons and SIN pamphlets. It's nice to have a young person involved."

"She a cellar dweller?" Silence on the other end. "Does Mary live in her parents' basement?"

"I don't know whether she's in the basement or not, but she's living with her parents. She's had an awful time trying to find work. There doesn't seem to be much out there for young people, not in Mariposa anyway." Big sigh.

I wind things up. Who gives a flying fuck about Mary Wieder?

Back at the table, Steve and the Canadian girls have joined Gemma, Kara, Mats and a few others.

Wagging a chubby finger at me, Mats says, "We'll beat you next year, almost this year too."

I must look puzzled. Kara whispers, "Junior hockey. Sweden."

One of the girls says, "We just signed up for scuba diving at Cape Tribulation, the Great Barrier Reef! You should come." She passes a sheet of paper that I promptly sign.

I bum another smoke from Gemma. Mats leans over, puts his hand on my shoulder and flicks his lighter, smoothly resuming his conversation with Steve and forgetting to remove his claw. Mats' skin is rough, there's a little scar in the shape of a fishhook on his cheek. I shift. His hand retracts. Steve winks at me.

Empty boxes of white wine litter the tables, a few of the tea lights fizzle. Ours is a disheveled picnic of knocked over beer cans and foil ashtrays. Mats retrieves the last box of wine from the hostel fridge, raises it triumphantly and fills our glasses. His arm keeps finding a way to slither around me until Steve inserts himself between us. Then, an English nurse slurs way too loudly for the quiet of night, "Any of you lot ever had a threesome?"

Gemma and I laugh, and it isn't long before most of us turn in, though Mats seems newly intrigued by the nurse's tales of ménage à trois. Before I fall asleep, I draw a picture of an incinerator that looks like a giant souped-up garbage receptacle with a red bow around it and a caption that reads: *Happy Bicentennial Mariposa, love Mayor Muffinpump and Deputy Mayor Bumblefuck.*

Early morning, the hostel shuttle deposits us on a white sand beach with turquoise water. To me, more shocking than its beauty, is its desolation. Then I see the giant red and white warning sign. *Danger! May through October. Box jellyfish. Take precautions. Bring vinegar to the beach.* Just when you thought it safe to swim, killer stinging jellyfish with invisible two-metre-long tentacles lie in wait. I'd almost rather have winter. Almost.

A dinghy makes two trips from beach to diving boat and soon we're out at sea. Scuba diving is all about going against your natural instincts. You've got this heavy tank on your back that makes you feel like you're sinking but you have to relax as you slip down into the water so that you can be calm, breathing through this mask thing and trusting it will sustain you. The second you panic, you're sunk. I love swimming, feeling weightless in the water. I imagine I'm falling deep into a never-ending well of darkness looking up into the glassy light of the surface. For the rest of the afternoon, we are human submarines in the briny deep weaving in among fish and waving coral both as diverse in colour and form as any flower garden.

The fifth time I almost died, I was fourteen, a junior counselor at camp. I was on the other side of the camp making bracelets with some kids at the craft hut when the emergency waterfront bell rang. Frantic, thinking about a drowning child, I ran all the way to the beach, and dove in wearing cut-off jean shorts and a cotton shirt with a tie at the back. I followed proto-col using a grid pattern to search the swimming area of the lake, even searching under the steel girders of the dock, which some-how caught my shirt. I panicked and struggled under the water to free myself from the shirt, from the dock, anything for air when a senior counsellor swam up like Neptune, seized me around the waist and ripped the shirt free. He was tall and strong, and I remember thinking at the time, remarkably hairy. He squeezed me tight absorbing my tears into his furry chest. Turns out it was only a drill.

The following day, we bungee jump from a tall suspension bridge, hike into the Atherton Table Lands, swim in waterfalls and stay overnight at a rustic hostel deep in the rainforest. On the way back to Cairns, the van is subdued, a residual effect of over-consumption of Bundaberg sugarcane rum the previous evening. We had a little circuit going: passing the bottle around in the wood-fired hot tub, jumping in the cold rainforest river, then heating back up in the wood-fired sauna. The owner told us in the morning that the river was lousy with freshwater alligators but since we were having so much fun she didn't want to inter-fere. Mats and the English nurse totally got it on. Gemma hooked up with an actuary from Auckland. And, stupid me, I made out with Steve. At least I stopped myself from going any further even though I kind of wanted to. The last thing I need right now is to get involved with someone for the sake of convenience. Despite my protestations last night, Steve still made sure to sit beside me on the ride home today and, in between catnaps, keeps pawing me and asking me where I'm going next. I keep it all non-com-mittal, saying, I'm not sure, and, Just down the coast toward Canberra, never letting on that I'm escaping on a southbound Greyhound first thing tomorrow.

I glance out the window at cane crops and banana trees and think about the family of platypuses we saw earlier this morning in a freshwater stream. Weird little creatures like oily, furred, duck-billed wiener dogs paddling along with their webby feet. I think of Darwin too. Platypuses have spurs above their webbed back feet that are attached to poison glands, a genius adaptation.

In Australia's early days they were hunted for fur. Dogs would try to retrieve them, bite the spur and be poisoned.

I sketch to pass the time, resulting in an excellent likeness of Crapwalker in full highway stride. Wonder if booze and drugs, maybe even certain mental illnesses, are human adaptations. Genius ways to cover up and protect all those infinite ways in which we are excruciatingly vulnerable. I colour his parka shades of grey, his cheeks in tones of pink and red to burnished orange. Could a guy like Crapwalker's adaptation be his ability to not be present in the world his body inhabits?

The cane toad postcard I bought for Tim falls out from the pages of my sketchbook, so I figure it's a sign. I write "scratch and lick" over the frog's posterior. Then I stare and stare at the blank side. Where to begin? I use the scissors from my knife to cut out all of the eyes from an Australian beauty magazine I pinched from the coffee table in the hostel. One after another, I glue them to the back of the postcard in undulating ribbons of blue, brown and green. It will be enough for Tim to know I'm thinking of him.

Fugima, an older Japanese man who joined our crew and doesn't speak English particularly well, stands up in the van and does his best to ask if anyone has a knife he can borrow. The question is directed at me since I am holding mine. Reluctantly, I hand it over. He plops down near the nurse who's beginning to look a little green. She rolls her eyes at him and readjusts the balled-up sweatshirt under her head. Fugima pulls off his blue nylon sock, flips open my knife and starts carving yellowed skin from his feet.

"What the fuck are you doing!" screams the nurse. "You can't do that here! Put your sock back on, man. That is absolutely disgusting."

I hold my hand out for my knife. Gross. Now every time I go to slice a bit of cheese or spread a little peanut butter, I'm going to think about Fugima, that hot blue sock and his yellow corns. I must have some first aid antiseptic somewhere in my pack.

Holding my soiled knife makes me think of this crazy drunken high school bush party. One guy, Eddie, lost his shit and pulled a knife. Eddie, iconic in his head banger uniform of stringy brown hair, red and blue flannel jacket, Player's Lights in the breast pocket, white high-tops and Scorpions T-shirt, was stumble down drunk and nearly fell in the fire. Nobody knows how or why, but he brought out a giant machete and chased his girlfriend, Sharon, around. Some older guys tackled him and wrestled the machete away, then Chris Lahey cranked up the Zepplin on the stereo of his Z28 and we rocked it until the sun came up. But it was Machete Eddie in the end that everyone remembers. I heard that Sharon soon after begat them both a child to be known ever after as Baby Butter Knife. I draw them in my sketchbook as Joseph, Mary and child in a state of grace, except for the glint of a butter knife poking out from folds of blue blanket.

Confined to this van and surrounded by snores, I figure it's as good a time as any to write the boomerang card I got for Stanley. I remember being trapped in the backseat on some endless family drive, him drawing hideous pictures of me in the style of *Mad Magazine* caricatures. A tiny zit would become a pus-filled volcano erupting from my chin. Then he was off to university, and I haven't seen much of him since. I only know about his life from what my mom tells me. He lives in Lethbridge and is finishing his PHD in Paleontology, the same thing he's wanted to do since he was six. My parents are glad he's been able to use his art skills to illustrate dinosaurs and that he has an *Asian* girlfriend. *Asian* is what my mom always says as though it matters, as though attention must be paid.

I saw Stanley two Christmases ago and he was still the same old jackass, mocking my artistic aspirations, pulling me aside to let me know he thought Jinglenuts Jason was a pompous fairy. Granted. But still. People are always talking about how their big brothers take care of and look out for them. Suppose I just have to accept that Stanley's the kind of guy who would stand there pointing and laughing if you slipped and fell and ripped the arse of your pants while you were crossing a busy street. I wouldn't go so far as to say he'd kick a cat. He's not into acts of violence. More like he gets his kicks from acts of violent humiliation.

Tuck the postcard in between the sketches of Crapwalker and Machete Eddie and read *Frankenstein* the rest of the way back to Cairns. So, the creature Dr. Frankenstein built was too ugly, too different, too far from the perfect human image for him to stick around and love and nurture his progeny. When the so-called monster, not even worthy of a name, learns the truth of his abandonment and the extent of his father's cowardice, he aims to kill anything the scientist ever loved. Except for the revenge part, I'm reminded of all those kids dumped off at the gates of the Mariposa North Centre and the hubris of the *normals*. As though those kids had no value when really, if you think about it, the most vulnerable among us often have the most to offer, they teach us compassion, acceptance, that all humans are human. Yet, we refuse to revere them believing we learned these life lessons independent of our teachers. Sometimes, through willful or ignorant acts, we create the monsters. Sometimes *we are* the monsters. And sometimes, the monsters we create teach us how to be human.

March: Three Months Before

BAG OF BONES AROUND YOUR NECK

Dave and Margaret arrive Sunday night fresh from a SIN meeting at the Public Library. Both are seething. Hell hath no fury like middle-aged do-gooders scorned.

"It's time for David to take on Goliath," says dad as he hangs his heavy leather coat and scarf in the hall closet with Margaret at his heels. "No longer will rural communities be trodden on by big business and corrupt small-town politicians." He's shut the door to the closet before realizing that Margaret is standing there with her coat and scarf in hand. He apologizes, kisses my mom saying sorry dear, takes her garments and hangs them up too.

I remove the heated-up shepherd's pie from the oven and place it on the marble topped island next to the salad bowl and some low-fat dressings. Peel back the foil of the pie cautiously, allowing the steam to escape without burning my wrist. Dad walks straight to the kitchen to wash his hands; he hasn't stopped talking since he came through the door.

"Dave, try and relax," my mom says. "You don't want to get yourself all worked up." She has a hand at her heart.

"McLaughlin's going ahead with the incinerator building, he's bought land out by Nichols' corners. We're not going to give up that easily. SIN has booked a bus to Queen's Park for an official protest, the Raging Grannies in tow."

"Raging Grannies?"

"Those old ladies, well they're not really *that old* necessarily. They dress the part and sing protest songs under the guise of sweet, little old, non-threatening grandmothers," mom says. "You're welcome to come." And then as an afterthought, "Mary

Wieder's coming over tonight to start the postcard writing campaign on behalf of SIN. Why don't you help us?"

"Oh, well, if Mary Wieder's coming over."

"I think she's lovely. And, she's been invaluable to our collective."

We dig into dinner, the three of us chewing quietly for a few minutes then mom says, "You know, you did such a good job with those difficult clients at the MNC maybe you might consider following in my footsteps and getting into social work. There's an excellent program in North Bay and of course at either of the Toronto universities."

"I'm gonna try and make some art." And get back to Aubrey.

"I understand that, and art is a wonderful hobby."

"I'm hoping that with a little time I can get some paintings together, build on the last show I had at school, and with a little luck maybe…"

Dad interrupts. "I am a great believer in luck, and I find the harder I work the more I have of it."

"Spare me the Leacock quotations. I've heard that one so many times that, if he weren't dead, I'd rip his fishing hat off and slap him with it across his bulbous, mustachioed nose."

Dad laughs. "If you're going to be hanging around Mariposa anyway, I could certainly train you in the printing business. Pay you the same, or more, as what you're making at that dive downtown. Who knows? Maybe you could wind up taking over Twin Lakes Printing one day."

Mariposa is a bunch of weeds fixing fast around my ankles as I try to swim up and through to the light.

"That's a nice offer. Thank you."

Neither one of them believes I am good enough to make it as an artist. Do I?

Mary rings the doorbell. Carrying with her a grocery bag full of paper, and a heart full of helpful ideas, she wraps her arms around me before I even have a chance to shut the door. I feel autistic in her embrace.

Suppose I should at least look like I have some social, some environmental conscience. I do have, I'm just not *that* concerned, not concerned enough to hang out with my parents discussing it all night long. Comfortably concerned at a distance, with a smoke and a drink preferably. Mary empties the plastic bag on the kitchen table and the three of us sort the contents into piles until Uncle George calls and my mom takes the phone to the living room.

"So, you're back from Australia? And before that you were at MNC?" Mary fluffs her straight brown bangs, sweeps the rest of her hair into a clip and says, "Crazy out there, eh? My mom used to work there before they bought the Marina out at Wissanotti Point."

We fill envelopes with ten SIN postcards, each pre-addressed with both federal and provincial members of parliament address-es. Label each envelope with one SIN member's name. Each member finds nine other people to send cards out. Given that there are at least five hundred SIN members, there will be approximately five thousand Stop Incineration Now postcards landing on office doorsteps in Ottawa and Toronto.

Mary proposes that dad reprint a new batch of cards for a random mail out to everyone in town. He leaves for his shop to get started on the printing. She easily organizes her mail outs into alphabetized piles looking woefully at my scattered group-ings of envelopes. She peers out at me from behind red, rectangle glasses that keep slipping down her sharp nose. "You still with Tim?"

Shake my head. "I'm pretty serious with another guy I met in Australia."

"Going back?"

"Soon as I can. What about you?"

"Finishing up at Queen's. Environmental Geography. Still have two courses. Been trying to commute but it's hard."

"How d'ya like living back in Mariposa?"

"I didn't exactly have a choice."

"What do you mean?"

"I mean you're really lucky to have what you have, Serena. Tell me, what's it like to have a charmed life?"

What the fuck?

"What's it like to have the perfect family, perfect face, perfect body, travel around wherever and whenever you want?"

"You're the one who was always Miss Perfect Attendance."

"As if you or your friends even noticed me."

"High school was like a million years ago."

"More like four."

Heads down, we stuff envelopes. "What's wrong with your life anyhow?"

"Oh, nothing, just that my father is a raging alcoholic and my mother's all bi-polar depressed scarfing down mood stabilizers like Tic-Tacs and I have to delay my plans so I can take care of all the books for the marina, so they don't flush their whole lives down the toilet. When's my life start, eh? How about that!"

"That's shitty."

She sniffles a bit. Licks the trace of a crusty purple cold sore on her lip. Dampens a sponge to seal an envelope and looks directly at me. "You're just really lucky to have the life you do."

Wonder if her mom is like my grandma, if that's why Mary and my mom get along so well, perfect daughters of cuckoo bananas moms.

Later, I call Tracy telling her all about Mary. Since her mom died, she's dismissive of people who gripe about mothers, and I wouldn't dare. When I ask if she'll come with me to the Queen's Park protest, she says she doesn't understand what the big frickin' deal is. She says the incinerator seems like a good idea, doesn't take up as much room as a landfill, lasts for a long time, brings money into the community, gets rid of garbage.

"First of all, trucking garbage north equals more emissions. Lots of the garbage is toxic and shouldn't be burned but will be burned then all that burning will produce more toxic emissions in the air we breathe and cause ash to flutter down covering everything in grey powder like the devil's snowflakes. Can you imagine going waterskiing and having to wear goggles to keep the carcinogenic ashes out of your eyes? Good-bye fishing, good-bye tourism and clean air, hello cancer. Second, third or fourth or whatever number point I'm on now, no one knows how these

chemicals that we'll be breathing will affect us or future genera-
tions, i.e., your unborn babies."

"You don't have to be pyscho about it. When did you go all
environmental? Last time you were at my place, Miss Nellie *Mc
Lung*, you threw a cigarette butt in the lake."

"Please come, Tracy. We should get involved with this.
What McLaughlin's doing is fucking outrageous. And we actually have an opportunity to do something about it, something
important. This is our time."

"Didn't you talk me into students' council using this same
kinda bullshit? *Come on, Tracy, we don't want to graduate high school
without having done something important.*"

"*Please.* If you don't come with, I'll have to hang out with
Mary Wieder all by myself. I kinda promised my mom and dad.
They think it's going to be such a *super experience.*"

"That sounds more like the Serena I know. All right. I'll
do it."

I think about Mary. Think a little bit about truth, too, about
the stories we tell ourselves. In one of Jinglenut's Buddha books
I read about a businessman whose house burns down while he's
out of town. The guy rushes home all worried about his young
son, sees his charred home and assumes the worst. He crawls
around weeping and kicking through the ashes until he finds a
small pile of bones. Decides these must be the bones of his child.
Leaves the village never to return to a place of such grief and loss,
puts the bones in a silk bag and wears it around his neck for years.
Meanwhile, the kid was rescued by neighbours the night of the
fire and taken to a safe place one village over where he was loved
and cared for. The foster parents eventually tell the boy that his
father is a rich businessman. Like any son he sets out in search of
his roots. The boy locates his father, knocks on his door and says,
"I'm your son." The man, who *knows* his son is dead, refuses to
open the door in spite of the boy's pleading and knocking. Father
and son never meet 'cause even when it is knocking at the door,
we don't answer because we already know the truth.

—

Lisa happily agrees to cover my shifts so I can attend the Queen's Park rally. She's tickled at the idea of me all suited up as a Raging Granny. Mom and dad said we needn't dress up, but I'd rather be incognito lest someone from my Toronto days sees me.

"How is lovely Serena tonight?" Byron asks.

"Let's just say I'm the living embodiment of the first noble truth." I place his order for steak and kidney pie with the kitchen guys round back.

"It pains me to know that you suffer so." He sips his beer, his shallow upper lip collecting foam. "The I Ching says times of growth are beset by difficulty."

"I must be having a growth spurt," I say before reassuring him that I'm just fine. Pour myself a glass of red wine and sit with Reg's accounts book and the intent to complete an order form for the liquor store. Feeling that lost lonely thing, that makes me want to find Tim after work and throw myself at him. Not that I would, but I might as well. Haven't talked to Aubrey in a couple weeks, probably forgotten all about me. Light a smoke, leave it smoldering in the ashtray as I file through papers and add sums as I've seen Reg do so many times. Hardly smoked at all while I was traveling, didn't even think about it.

During my table waiting rounds, I run into Candice, Stuart and Tom, my old colleagues from MNC. They're eating chicken wings at a tall café table in the back.

"Well, what do you know?" says Tom. "Serena Palmer. It's been some time. Suppose you've heard?"

"About?" I collect the empty guacamole and salsa dishes on the eaten-up nachos plate and hold it in my right hand.

"The Wink Ward."

"Oh, yeah, my dad read something in the paper about that. They're looking to close MNC?"

"That's right," says Stuart. "In five years, all the current residents will be shipped out into the community."

"Not just dropped off on the street corner, Stuart," says Candice, bouncing large hot-rolled locks over each shoulder. "They'll all be placed in group homes."

Tom wipes grease from his mouth with a white paper napkin, leaving rusty smears of sauce. "I feel sorry for some of them guys. They've lived their whole lives out there, never known another home. Guess that's what happens when you got people like Natalie in charge, more credentials than brains. Just don't want to be driving around seeing guys on every street corner stumbling around like Crapwalker."

"They're talking about puttin' a police training headquarters in the old MNC building," says Stuart.

Tom interjects. "Last thing we need in this town is more pigs."

"Was thinking it would be the perfect place for 'em," Stuart cackles.

"Will you be assigned to different group homes?" I ask.

"If we're lucky," says Tom.

"It's five years away," Candice says. "Plenty of time to figure things out. Transitional training for staff and clients starts in a few weeks."

"What does that mean?"

"Clients will spend an afternoon a week with a staff member at a model group home. Take the bus, go to the grocery store. None of the guys out there will ever be able to get jobs or anything. It's like they are trying to get the community used to having clients around as much as they're trying to get them used to being out in the community. Anyways, I thought you were off to explore the world, Serena. Please tell me you got somewhere."

"Yeah, I wound up in Australia for a few months."

"And…"

"And it was incredible. Beautiful country, met some great people, did some cool stuff."

"But here you are? The way you talked about getting out of here, I thought I'd never see you again."

Tell her about Aubrey, about my grandma. She nods knowingly. I'm ashamed. It's as though I'm some kind of big talker whose ideas never come to fruition.

"Just don't be like me. Next thing you know, you're thirty-five years old eating wings with a couple of old farts at the Queen."

Stuart swipes a fiery wing through blue cheese sauce, leaving a trail of red in white gloop. Tom pats his belly, "Whole lot a lovin' right here." Candice throws a crumpled paper napkin at him. Gross. I bet Candice and Tom are doing it. Offer to bring them a new pitcher of Canadian.

May: One and a Bit Months Before

MOTION PICTURE

The Trans Canada Highway cuts a winding river of asphalt through blasted rock as though an ancient glacier ruthlessly carved the route through northern Ontario to Manitoba, and on melting, left nothing but two yellow lines. Gravel on the shoulders gives way to rubble, then stones, then rock cliffs marred by blast holes and metal stakes. The granite never stood a chance against a frozen will to destroy, to create. Wonder if the broken scrubs and roadkill lumps shoulder-side were people once who climbed out from fast moving lives and stood on the edge hoping to gain insight, hoping for a new direction while waiting in the wind for their lives to change. So desperate and naive they refused to give up, but instead of helping themselves and sticking out a thumb, they just stood there and melted into the landscape. I look out the windshield at the clouds shifting in the sky horizontally trying to imagine what my grandma's or Crapwalker's or Jimmy Birchbark's soul might have looked like when it was leaving their bodies. The dowsing pendulum dangling from the rearview spins, circling always to the right. I ask questions in my mind that can only be answered yes. It amuses for a while.

Aubrey sings and strums his guitar as I drive, encouraging me to harmonize with him. Wish he'd stop bugging me to sing, can't he hear how nonmusical I am? My wrong notes ricochet off the metal of the car and back into my ears as if I'd grabbed a conch shell and overturned it spilling tone-deaf self-consciousness all over myself. I interrupt his crooning. "Did you know that when you hold a shell up to your ear it's not really waves that you hear but the sound of your own blood echoing in the hollow of the empty shell?"

He sets his guitar down at his feet, leans his chin on the tip of the head stalk and stares out at the rock. "How can trees, anything, grow in all that granite?"

"The rock makes me feel at home. You know when we were in Australia, in the outback? All that sand was unnerving like it could blow away somehow or dissolve in a rainstorm. Ever think there's something magnetic in the land you're from that pulls you back?"

"There's a place in Miami Beach near my grandparents'. Went there every chance I could. It's where I learned to surf. I was always happy there. No matter what kind of fucked-up madness was going on with my parents, the landscape was predictable. I knew what to expect and could anticipate and deal with it. The slope of the sand, how the waves would hit and react. Incredible. But if I only ever surfed there what would I learn about surfing?"

"Think we'll ever get back to Australia, Aubrey?"

"We can do whatever we want."

Such confidence. "What do you want to do when this trip is over?"

"But we just started. We're not even at the coast yet."

"I'm mean like big picture."

"You're going to make art I'm going to make music. When we have money we'll travel and hang out."

"Where will we live?"

"Wherever people like art and listen to music."

"I don't want to paint pictures of birch trees and pink flowers to match people's furniture."

"So don't."

"I wanna create something that matters."

"So do."

We find a cheap motel on the outskirts of Winnipeg with a rusting, semi-hazardous playground on the front lawn as its main attraction. Still, a bed's a bed, and a shower's a shower and we're grateful for them both. On a bus into town, Aubrey starts up a conversation with an Indigenous guy who tells us the best place to see live music is at a bar called Spirit Chaser.

The place is as dead as the Queen in February. Must be early. Station ourselves at the bar and it isn't long before Aubrey's guitar talk has the bored, bandana wearing bartender eating out of the palm of his hand. He agrees to allow Aubrey a non-paying gig as an opening act for the headliner, *Wendigo*. Flips his long black braids over his shoulders and points to a poster on the wall behind the bar with an emaciated man-like skeleton creature with its skin stretched taut over bone, face and fangs screaming into blackness.

Aubrey slugs his beer. Asks if I get the poster. I explain what little I know of Algonquin mythology. That the Wendigo is an evil spirit who possesses humans and hungers for human flesh but can never be filled up. The more it eats the bigger it gets and the more it needs.

"The more we consume the more we think we need to consume. I get it," he says.

"Think a person really can be possessed? Like by an animal spirit in a human body or vice versa, a human in an animal body?"

"Suppose anything's possible."

The bar begins to fill. Lights dim, music grows louder. The backdrop of the stage appears engulfed by a wall of flickering flames projected onto a scrim. When Aubrey walks the three short steps up onto the stage, I remind myself to breathe. He mouths *This is so cool*. Bandana bartender brings him a guitar and they become men moving among flames. He's so beautiful standing on stage with that guitar.

Bandana Boy tries to engage me in conversation, but I falter and don't hold up my end of the bargain. He pops the tops off two more beers and points his hand, the extension of a huge bicep in a tight black t-shirt, at Aubrey and says, "Drinks are on the house tonight."

Sit at a table for two at the front right of the stage where I can observe the performance and the crowd. He's somehow swapped the acoustic for an electric blue Telecaster. The black walls around the room drip red paint down from the ceiling like blood. The Spirit Chaser logo, a red peace sign inside a red dream catcher, makes sporadic wall appearances and is emblazoned over the black T-shirted chest of every server. Bandana Boy leaps over the three steps onto the stage, grabs the mic, taps it a few times and announces, "Ladies and gentlemen!" Pluralizing *lady* was wishful thinking. "Spirit Chaser would like to present an early act for your listening pleasure, please welcome all the way from Miami F.L.A., Aubrey Santiago!"

Next thing I know, Aubrey rips out *American Woman*. Shameless. Playing *American Woman* in Winnipeg is like playing Van Morrison to a bunch of boomers. Smiling, I shake my head at him. He winks and hams it up on stage with exaggerated facial expressions and a lot of bouncing around. Tops it off with that stupid Warren Zevon song about grandpa pissing his pants. As the crowd swells in anticipation of Wendigo, I hear them murmuring, Who is this guy?

Aubrey slips through the audience, saying, "God, that felt so good. It was like I was a portal for this invisible current. It's such a rush. I fucking love it. I give to them, they give to me and we're both a part of something bigger. Is that what it's like when you paint or make art or whatever?"

I nod. But it's not really. It's different, a little quieter, a little less immediate in the feedback department. You never know if anything you do is any good. The soundman hops off the stage and slips a chunk of hash into Aubrey's front pocket. When I first met him, he compared himself to Orpheus. And he is. He's charmed the trees, made the rocks dance, turned a bar full of hard rockin' 'Peggers into best friends for life.

Next day, we drive. Our maroon Tempo falls in line again and again until we are behind a procession of beastly trucks bearing the earth's exploits, leading us across the prairies. Diaphanous petticoat clouds skirt the sky. Barrels of harvested hay, walls of wheat on either side of the strip of black asphalt that stretches out ahead like a video game without end. Eyes, glazed and cloudy, eyes, sick with motion, fueled by coffee and weed. The penciled-in vanishing point dot-like on the horizon line exists after all. All these years of drawing and now I can see it, drive toward it chasing the elusive something that is perpetually off in the distance.

Grasslands and wheat turn to trees.

Then the trees become our silent, expressionless audience with the experience and longevity to go the distance. They mock us and our weak constitutions, spitting sap in our faces as we drive. It's as though they have lined up early to witness this little motorcade, to chide us, *You're halfway across Canada and exhausted from the drive. Pathetic! Our dear Terry ran as far on one leg. Shame on you, you good for nothing layabouts.* More trees grow rapidly out of nowhere and our audience increasing, watching, scorning us and our squandered talents. Kamikaze insects dive bomb the windshield, splatter themselves like bloody raindrops as we jettison across the pavement, a Jackson Pollock in real time across our eyes. Is this real? Am I outside myself or is this happening? Stare down at my hands locked in place on the wheel, hands controlled by the road. And just when I think I'm about to crack, it's goodbye Saskatchewan. The road curves into Alberta, an orange sign with a bucking blue cowboy silhouette. I pull off the road. Aubrey takes over. Fall asleep in the passenger side.

On our way into Lethbridge Aubrey asks, "Shouldn't we call your brother or something?"

The last thing I want right now is to deal with Stanley.

"C'mon. How often do you get the chance to see him? He's your brother! I wish I had a brother."

"He's not really…" What to say? How to say it? He'll have to experience Stanley for himself.

We meet him and Hazel at an off-campus pub that reeks of fish and stale grease. When he was younger, Stanley's T-shirts used to sport superheroes. Now they have prehistoric gags like the one he's wearing today, a black T with the white outline of a brontosaurus and a cartoon bubble that reads, *All my friends are dead*.

Over beer and nachos, the four of us epitomize awkwardness.

"Can you believe how stupid mom and dad are acting about this incinerator thing? Fuck. I mean can you imagine?" Stanley looks to Hazel for confirmation and with a smirk on his face, says, "They're always doing things like that." She plugs her pretty mouth with molten orange-covered nachos. Aubrey examines the foam on top of his beer. Stanley's hair is shorter now than when I last saw him a few months ago and it's turning a little darker, ashen. Makes him look older. Possibly even more nerdy. "Remember when they tried to stop the mall from being built on the fairgrounds because they thought it would wreck the downtown?"

"It did wreck the downtown."

"Like they could have stopped it. Pointless. Man, like every animal before it, will soil its den." He snorts a mean laugh. "Embarrassing. And SIN?" He shakes his head, scoops a couple of nachos into some salsa overfilling his mouth. Sour cream squirts out at the corners and his nostrils flare as he struggles to chew.

On our way to the car, Aubrey says, "What's with your brother?"

"I told you! But you were all *Oh you have to call your brother. I wish I had a brother!*"

"The only thing he wanted to talk about, other than himself, and ragging on your parents, was the Albertasaurus. He never once asked about me or you or where we're headed or anything."

"Where are we headed?" I sneak a look at his face then say, "That's Stanley. Other people exist only in the way that they are incidental accessories in his life."

"And Hazel? Can she not speak?"

A vintage Grandma Dorothyism pops into my head: "Totally. She wouldn't say shit if her mouth was full of it."

"Anyhow, glad I met him. I now know more about the Albertasaurus than I ever thought possible."

"Growing up with a sibling tends to be idealized."

"I guess. The way I imagined it, a brother would be an ally. When things were scary or your parents weren't there, at least you'd have each other."

I stop on the sidewalk. Swaddle him in my arms.

—

Calgary and Edmonton are glass and steel, cement and brick serving as weak substitutes for the trees and rock to which we've grown accustomed. Who cares about the Saddledome when there are mountains? Who cares about the West Edmonton Mall when there are glaciers and hot springs? People are stupid. I write so on the Tempo ceiling followed by *the lunatic is on the grass* in a scrawling cursive that would sour my dad's love for fonts.

In Jasper at least there's something to look at. Mountains loom along the perimeter reaching up like the sides of a castle. The town is protected by these guardians of stone that remind us we're nothing but specks in their grand shadows. Mist clings to eyeglasses, windshields, storefronts, Gortex jackets. We wander around watching tourists snap photos of the black cartoon bear sculpture, poke in and out of faux rustic post and beam plazas with gift shops, gear shops, restaurants and, hallelujah, laundry. Start a couple loads at the laundromat, dumping in mini-boxes of detergent, tiny balls of blue suspended in white powder, and figure we may as well use the coin-operated tourist showers as well.

Aubrey must have finished his shower early because when I come out the door, he walks toward me holding purchases. He's woven his way through *I love Canada eh?* T-shirts, stuffed beavers and bears, Mountie key chains, maple sugar leaves, moccasins and other handicrafts, clutching a book in one hand and a chocolate patty wrapped in waxed paper in the other.

"Wanna bite of my bear paw?"

I pull the brown circle with cashew claws still in Aubrey's hands toward my mouth. Chocolate, caramel, nuts ooze a sticky rapture in my mouth. He waves the paperback in my face.

"Check this out." Bright yellow letters scream, *Real Life Bear Attacks,* a taffy-coloured grizzly squats on its haunches, baring teeth. Aubrey flips pages, juggles his bear paw and shows me horrifying pictures. Points his sinewy guitar-playing finger at a photograph of an enormous, seven hundred and eighty-five-pound grizzly bear beside a mangled camper van. "Imagine what it could do to a tent."

All the way up the mountain curves to Jasper National Park campground, Aubrey reads gruesome bear attack stories aloud. Ill-fated moments of sleeping under the stars ending with partially devoured bodies, menstruating teenagers pulled from tents and overheard screaming *oww, owww, oh no, oh god it hurts*. Dirty campsites and gobbled up scalps, and my favourite, the young naturalist who had both arms chewed off and survived to write the tale with prosthesis.

Before nightfall it was all laughter and good times, the giddiness of a ghost story. Now that we're lying in the glow of flashlights sipping Jägermeister from its green medicinal-shaped bottle inside the pretend walls of a tent, fear wears the face of a hovering bear.

"What would you do if we were asleep and all of a sudden you heard scratch, scratch on the side of the tent?"

"It would probably be more like rip, rip," I say.

"What would you do? Like, what if you were building a fire and turned around and there was a bear standing right in front of you on his hind legs."

"Remember the scene in the *Karate Kid*? Daniel Son up on the beach stump doing the crane?"

"C'mon, seriously. What if we were on a hike, way out in the middle of nowhere, when around the corner there's a bear chewing on the neck of a mountain goat. That's what happened to the naturalist. What would you do?"

"I don't know." Would I scream and get aggressive, counterattack? Would I seize up like a rabbit? Go all metaphysical and float above, watching myself being partially devoured? "What would *you* do?"

"First, I'd slowly crouch down, then I'd start to back away while I was making deep, growling sounds, and I wouldn't look it in the eye, but I'd know where its eyes were. Then, if it started at me, I'd stand my ground, make myself as big as possible and stab it right in the eyes with my two fingers."

"Yeah, well, I guess that's a good plan too."

Our thoughts float in the dead air above our sleeping bags. Something big, which neither of us can control, but both of us suspect, is going to go down on this trip. I can't stand being idle in the tension. I growl like a bear, pounce on top of Aubrey and attempt to gnaw his ear off. That's when I see it. My Swiss Army knife open to the left of his pillow.

"What the fuck are you doing with that?"

He sits up, mirth drained and drawn. "We have to be ready. In case."

"In case what?"

"This is bear country."

"That knife, a bear has a whole fist of claws the size of that blade." Where's my happy-go-lucky, guitar playing, confident guy? His eyes are terrified. "Never mind. It's just weird sleeping next to a guy with a knife," I say to hide the fact that camping with him is turning out to be a turd spiral.

My knife.

"I'd never hurt you. I want to protect you, us." He pulls me to his chest, kisses the top of my head.

And so Aubrey sleeps with my knife under his pillow in case of a bear attack or something. And just like that I am no longer an I, but a we.

At the wash station in the morning a nature zealot accosts us. "You have to do the Tonquin Valley hike," she says decked in her North Face gear from the band around her greying hair to her worn brown hiking boots. Then she practically climaxes while describing the view from the lake and *oh the mountains*. It's as though she witnessed the birth of the mother of God. As though she's rehearsing for her water cooler talk when she's back in Toronto.

Before we head out along the trail, in accordance with bear country protocol, Aubrey devises a noise-making bear deterrent from a chick shake and a tambourine, attaching both to his backpack and in the jingle jangle morning I go following him. We're making an awful racket while trying to enjoy the peace and quiet of nature. And, in a couple of kilometers, Aubrey's back to his old self and we're laughing and singing and making fun of each other when we spy a Parks Canada map with a neon green laminated sign. In bold black: *Grizzly bear spotted on Tonquin Valley trail May 15th.*

"What day is it today?" Aubrey asks.

"May 15th."

We scream and run like idiots, tambourine in tow. Terror gives way to exhaustion and panting. We arrive at the trailhead willingly accepting that the only orgasm-inducing mountain lake the colour of antifreeze we'll see at close range in this park will be on a twenty-five-cent card at the trading post.

On the way to Lake Louise we hit a bear jam: a bunch of cars clogging the road with people hanging out of windows madly clicking cameras in an effort to capture the image of a bear at close range. Reminds me of the Japanese men who kept asking to take my picture in Australia. Will they brag to dinner party friends of their bravery, their proximity to danger, their conquest? Stalled by traffic and jackasses skulking around outside of their cars, and being bear voyeurs ourselves, we strain to see. A noisy, navy river bubbles along past a picnic area with a twin set of brown and yellow Parks Canada outhouses. Sitting between the water and the toilets, a baby bear stuffs its mouth with grass. Just a wee little cub all alone. His mom better come soon and save him from this crowd of hungry humans craving authenticity of experience. Black fur with blond tips glistens in the sun. A small taupe nose no bigger than a German Shepherd's sniffs the air and he cocks his head as if to ask us what we're looking at.

"Don't be fooled, Serena." Aubrey returns to the bear attacks book he has stashed like contraband underneath the passenger's seat. Reads the account of Judy and Al, weekend moose hunters. The bear dragged Al away from camp by his head. Judy recalled him looking like a rodent in the mouth of a cat. And then the tale of two teenage love birds whose musky scent of sex led a grizzly right to them where it fought and dined, but, unable to finish its meal, left them both partly consumed.

I pull off at a roadside viewing point to observe the valley of glacial lakes from a height. Aubrey stands at the end of the railing stretching his long slim body. The outline of his shoulder blades shows through his snug, blue-fleece pullover and makes me want to run my hands along his naked back. I grab *Bear Attacks* from his seat and walk to the edge of the vista on the opposite side of him.

"Hey," I call, waving the book in my hands. "Yoo hoo, look at this!" Aubrey, like a junkie watching his drugs about to be flushed down the toilet, stares at me, *you wouldn't*. I chuck the book as far away down the mountainside as I can throw it. It clunks and tumbles down the jungle of firs and into oblivion leaving a trail of upturned dirt. "Good riddance," I wave. A woman exiting a car gives me a dirty look. "It's biodegradable," I say.

We walk toward our car. "Had to be done, friend."

Aubrey puts his arm around my shoulder. "You did right."

As we spiral up Mount Crumpet, I figure we need to have the talk. About bears. "When I was at MNC, especially in the first few weeks, it was easy to get freaked out. They give you a self-defense class in the morning, then slip you an envelope that says you're on the male behaviour ward for the afternoon and set you loose. That first day, you walk the halls all by yourself. You hear moaning, screaming, banging and right around the corner, you can't see, but you hear panting, heavy breathing. You can't hide in a hallway. There's no option but around the bend. So, your mind makes up all kinds of crazy shit going on around the corner that isn't real. Course, after you've worked there awhile you figure out who the moaners and screamers are, which guys bang the windows and walls and that the heavy breathers are just lying on the floor around the corner beating off, and no one's out to get you. They're consumed within their own mind trappings. Just like we all are. But those first few days, all you know is administration gave you self-defense, that it's a male behaviour ward, and there's nowhere to go but into the heavy breathing. Makes you realize your imagination, your thoughts, are super powerful. Gotta remind yourself all that stuff that goes on inside your head, just because you're thinking it, doesn't necessarily make it so. Remember your rabbit story? Don't be a fear caller, don't draw the danger to you."

I'm one to talk. I'm one to be doling out advice about imagined fears. What a laugh. It's true, though, imagination *can* drive you mad. Wonder if imagination ever got the better of Crapwalker. Did he wander up and down the highway in mortal terror of something out to get him? Killing fear is like trying to grasp the future in your hand, it slips through your fingers like a mountain mist. You look in your empty palm and hardly know what you were afraid of in the first place.

August: Ten Months Before

A NIGHT IN THE QUEEN

The usual clerk in Patterson's feigns preoccupation by shuffling papers around the cash register so he can keep an eye on me while I shop. He's small. Not Guinness Record Book small, but small enough that if I was in a bar with Tracy and saw him I'd probably say, *Hey Tracy, check out the small guy*, as a notable point of interest. His doughy belly hangs out over his Harley Davidson belt buckle and his face has a disturbing absence of facial hair. Probably the kind of guy who watches pornos with friends, slaps legs when the guy comes and talks about motorcycles, calling the Asian ones crotch rockets. And they give each other nicknames like Shorty and Red as they drink their Labatt's Blues and stub out their Export A Greens into tinfoil ashtrays before falling asleep dreaming about monster trucks and masturbating in their mother's basements under Star Wars comforters.

I like to browse in army surplus stores, especially ones that display hunting knives. Though I'm usually imagining some future trek around the world while pricing their field gear, I inevitably wind up staring through protective glass at the steel blades. I'm drawn to their shine, or maybe it's their sharpness. I've wanted a Swiss Army knife for a while now. You need one for traveling. And, since staying in Mariposa much longer is akin to committing metaphysical suicide, a pocketknife just may be the perfect catalyst to get my shit together.

Tuesday. My second day off after four days of twelve hour shifts and I'm all shaky and dehydrated again. I look up into the jungle canopy of green rucksacks, rolled camouflage sleeping bags, strung together black combat boots and other assorted memorabilia of war and hate.

"You need help?" His girlish voice rings out loud above the din of what sounds like *After the Gold Rush* through the crackle of ancient speakers. "You see sumpthin' you want?" He stands beside me. His body odor wafts up from his pits like a steaming bowl of onion chowder.

Ask to see the Swiss Army knife called the Hunter. What on earth could I possibly be hunting for? Oh, I don't know, a life? He opens the case with a small brass key attached to a chain on his belt and removes the red knife.

"She's a beauty all right. Buddy o' mine took one of these here babies moose huntin' with him last season. I'd say they're right lucky. Didn't he shoot himself a big ol' bull. Used that there saw to cut off the balls. Though the knife woulda likely been sharp enough." He shrugs. "He's a real character, that one, keeps a jar of 'em in the bedrum."

I nod and smile. Take the knife from his hands.

"The wife don't think much of 'em. Course he tells her it's one of them there things that the China men use uh... Jap apro... you know, one of them things that make ya want to have sex all the time." He shakes his head and laughs. "I tells ya it takes all kinds."

There is something sinister about knives outside their kitchen context. Settlers of debt, exacters of truth. I dig my thumbnail into the side notch to extract the blade. It's not been out of its red plastic sheath for three seconds before I run it between my thumb and index finger and subsequently slice the former. Balls off a moose, thumb off an idiot. I can drop the knife and leave, or I can hide the bleeding evidence that is my thumb in the pocket of my jean shorts and make my way to the cash. I choose the latter.

Damn. I should've called my parents last night to tell them I was staying over at Tracy's. The truth, of course, is that I passed out at Tim's after partying my face off at the Queen. Again. Dave and Margaret are probably home right now cutting and pinning green satin ribbons to SIN pamphlets and worrying themselves sick. God, I hope they're out seizing the day so I can slink down to the basement and rot like the toxic garbage dump that I am. I still cannot believe that McLaughlin and Banbury have been encouraging Toronto to truck its garbage north for incineration in an effort to boost Mariposa's economy. I understand that it's 1994, recessionary times. Half the people I went to high school with are back living at home, working part-time service industry jobs despite university degrees. Muffinpump keeps pulling out the old *desperate times, desperate measures* line. He must be seriously myopic if he thinks that burning tons of garbage for peanuts in a lake district is the best financial stimulus. Anyway, it's a big deal around here, probably eased Dave and Margaret's transition into emptynesthood. Except, their nest isn't so empty now that I'm camping out in their basement, my sporadic presence a disappointing reminder of my failure to progress in life.

My parents' house is stucco. One of those fake Tudor jobbies. The front door is dark brown, has always been dark brown. Tried to convince my mom once to paint it red and though she didn't disagree that it would look nice in oxblood, she still painted it the same shit brown as always. Hellos echo, bounce off ecru walls and tan tiles that ensconce the foyer. Wonder how long they'll be gone? Drop my keys on the antique table in the hall. Don't know if it's actually an antique, just that it's been here since before I was born and has twisty legs. Mom calls it Jacobean. It's not from this world, that's for sure. Collapse onto my basement futon only to find myself unable to get comfortable because of the Hunter in my pocket. At least I've managed to do something productive in the last twenty-four hours. Taken the first step in my journey of a thousand miles.

The phone rings. It feels like the middle of the night. Clear my throat, gack into a Kleenex. Clock radio on the bedside table says seven fifty-five.

"What are ya up to?"

Tracy. "Sleeping."

"We're goin' to the Queen for beers and darts."

"I gotta work early."

"Come for a bit."

Can't. Can't afford to waste one more second of my life on this endless loop of debauchery. Hanging out at the stupid fucking Queen of Spades with Tim and Brian from high school, from the Royal Frenzy along with their slow rise to musical mediocrity. Tracy won't take no for an answer. Suppose I have get up anyway.

"What's gotten into you lately? You're like all gloomy."

"Objection. I'm not gloomy."

"Overruled. Y'are, depressed even. Ever since you broke up with what's his nuts and moved home."

"Your Honour, badgering the witness."

"Establishing grounds. Cross-examination of the defendant's deposition."

"I'm not depressed. It's just that…" Silence. "Maybe I'm having a spiritual crisis."

"Like a Saint John of the Cross dark night of the soul?"

"Do you have to be so Catholic about it?"

"Well, what the fuck's your problem then?"

"I don't know." And I don't. And I'm too tired and hungover to play dueling television lawyers and I don't know why I spoiled my relationship, or why I didn't go looking for gallery jobs and networking to find spaces to show my art, or why I didn't at least get a restaurant job and a sublet in Toronto, or why I thought life was going to show up at my door with a bouquet of cheques and a nice Chianti, or why I'm stuck in this perpetual cycle of self-loathing continuing to do the very things that cause the self-loathing. Probably I didn't think at all. Not since I've been hiding under this shadow as big as a bear.

Tracy says she'll call me back to read me my Miranda Rights. The stale water beside my bed tastes faintly of dust and chlorine. The phone rings again.

Tim.

Then Tracy.

Resistance is futile.

The back of my hair is lumpy with tangles. I drag my brush though and notice afterwards it's full of corn silk. That's how

Jinglenuts described the little circular mats of blonde twisted around the bristles. When I was a kid, I used to watch my Grandma Dorothy brush her long grey hair. She has a short old lady do now, but back then after brushing, she'd take a metal comb scrape it along the brush tines and throw the little puff out the window. *Maybe some bird will make a nest out of it*, she'd say. The mirror tells a worse story of last night than I do. My face is red and bloated. I am too ugly and vile to be seen. Must turn my face away from the garish light of day, from cold unfeeling light.

On the marble topped island in the kitchen is a note from my parents:

> Dear Serena,
> We've gone to the city today to participate in a province wide anti-incineration information session. We won't be home until quite late. Since you have the day off, I thought you might help us out around the house by doing a few little things. Please clean the bathrooms. Don't use the powdered cleanser on the brass faucet or in the white tub. Use the liquid. Cut the grass at the side and back of the house—please sweep up any grass that ends up on the Unilock brick. (Your father started to cut it at the front this morning, but I asked him to leave it because of his heart.) Thanks Honey! We really appreciate it.
> Love, Mom
>
> P.S. If you use the kitchen, please use the blue cloth to wipe the counters and the green one for the marble on the island. Also, if you are not coming home at night, please call us and tell where we can reach you in case of emergency.

Not entirely unreasonable. Was that note passive aggressive or assertive? I can't tell. She *had* to put in that bit about dad's heart. Ever since he had that slight blockage, a wake-up call, he said, Margaret has been tyrannical about their food and activity levels. Dave has to eat steel cut oats with crushed flax seed every day and can't lift a finger around the house without extensive discussion and monitoring. Might be the stress of healthy living that gets him in the end.

I rummage around finding a turquoise and red batik vest in my closet that I haven't worn in a while. Put it on and begin to feel human. Finger the amulets that dangle from the edge of the mirror, choosing the carved wooden Buddha necklace Jinglenuts gave me. It hangs down to my belly button and has a little secret baby Buddha nested inside with a tassel attached to the bottom. The second time we got together at his place, before it became our place, he made me an Indian feast, aloo gobi, saag paneer, dahl, rice, naan bread. The triplex reeked of spice, and I couldn't stop smiling thinking of spending the evening with my older, sophisticated boyfriend who studied religion and cooked exotic foods. We curled into each other on the Mexican blanket covered sofa when he pulled the necklace out of his pocket and placed it in my hand. Rubbing his thumb over the Buddha's belly he said this would bring us good luck in life. Then extracted the baby Buddha, rubbed its belly, said the inner Buddha assured us good luck in love as well. What a cheeseball. When I think about the way he used to look at me, the way he'd try to bore inside my soul with his eyes, I could just about throw up. What an arrogant poseur. To think he could know me.

Is it disingenuous to wear some spiritual symbol around your neck that you're not sure you fully understand? Probably. Not that it ever stopped anyone. I grab the Hunter and stuff it in my pocket. For courage. For safety. Gotta be as at least as useful as a Buddha necklace.

When I moved back here in the spring, I knew it was going to be hard. I also knew that if I held fast to the idea that I could one day free myself through travel, I would survive. Every penny I've saved, and being honest, that I haven't smoked or drunk, I've put towards my quest, the purpose of which is to experience life. Fill up my proverbial cup. Or maybe figure out what it is I should be doing, could be doing with my sad self. Or at the very least, to have a damn good adventure and get the hell out of this shit hole. And now, it's nearly September. I'm slogging through days, teetering on the edge of sanity, and still haven't made a move. It's like living up north or somewhere when everyone's going crazy on account of winter inertia. You can't go anywhere until the ice breaks, so you just go to the bar and drink with folks you've known for years. Where should I go when the ice breaks? Borneo? Belize? Argentina? Europe? Na, everyone goes to Europe. What about India? Australia? Used to have a pen pal in Australia. She'd send me postcards of kangaroos and koalas. Surfing Santas and picnics on the beach at Christmas.

It's probably a good time of year to go and speaking English would make travelling by myself easier.

Two black-shingled faux spires of grey stone flank either side of the entrance to the Queen and has always reminded me of the Friendly Giant's castle. Makes me want go inside, curl up in an armchair and play my recorder. A *ye old pub* shingle with a robust Queen of Spades hangs out front overshadowed by the neon Coors Light and Canadian signs flickering in the window. One side is carpeted with a black and red card motif and has beat-up couches and coffee tables, pool, darts, and board games. The other side is tall tables and stools by the front window next to a stage. If you walk past on the street and look in, you'd see the back of the band and the faces of the people watching. The bar itself is dark walnut with hearts, clubs, diamonds and spades cut out of the wood around the edges. Tracy spies me through the window and waves.

As I cross the threshold, I feel apparition-like. As though I've been thrust into someone else's life. A Doug Henning illusion who's materialized in a puff of smoke. Here I am everybody—ready to perform!

Tracy, holding a smoke in one hand, rushes over to give me a peck on the cheek. Makes sure to keep the hand with the cigarette high and extended so as not to ignite my hair. She loves her dramatic accessories, long cigarettes, short skirts, tall boots, tight shirts—sequins, all serving to underscore just how dreadfully out of place I feel in this place, this town, this life, these people, my friends. Tonight, she's got on black leggings and a billowy white tunic cinched at the waist with a braided belt the same leather as her cowboy boots. "You're here!"

Welcome to the world of illusions.

"But you have to work at that awful place tomorrow. We were just talking about you. How do you stand it? Washing and feeding all those gross men. You should work at the A&P with me." She hooks her arm in mine, leads me to our table. "It's so easy. Someone says, *I'd like 300 grams of shaved ham,* so I stick a fork in a bin, plop it on the scales, print out a label and voila, done. Once in a while ya get an old bitch lookin' for a fight, but so what? I get a smoke break every few hours. Life's good, eh?"

Tracy's right. The A&P would be easier emotionally. Glad to see her degree in psychology from Carleton is paying off. But money's good at the MNC and right now money means freedom. Maybe money always means freedom. But it's not only money that keeps me at there. Some places are built on mines or steel mills and that experience becomes part of the subconscious of the town. It's the same with Mariposa, only we've got the MNC, popularly referred to around here as the Wink Ward though I don't feel like people really mean it as nasty as it sounds. Just kind of ignorant like the politically correct movement hasn't quite infiltrated the nether regions of the province yet. And you know how people have to lump other people together in categories to make sense of their own damn selves. Maybe it's just the way people around here have collectively decided to deal with having an institution as the main source of employment keeping the client's separate and distanced from themselves so they can live with their consciences. Makes people grateful for small mercies. I don't know. Guess it's better than them saying retard.

Someone from the table hands me a glass of beer. Tim. His dark wavy hair is pulled back into a low ponytail, his plaid flannel shirt has the sleeves ripped off.

"Cheers," he says.

There is warmth and familiarity in his gaze. I trill my fingertips down the length of his arm to his hand. Squeeze. Can't keep doing this. Rotting away in Mariposa. Fooling around with Tim. It's bad enough my body has been wandering around all summer without me. And yet, somehow, I can't seem to stop myself.

We drink and smoke and shoot the shit and the conversation as a perverse sidebar of interest turns to my job. Brian, the bespectacled bass player in the Royal Frenzy, and Tracy's ersatz boyfriend, pats his green spikes and asks, "How are the Winkies? Tell us about the guy with the huge cock."

The beer has boosted my spirits and I aim to entertain.

Another band mate says, "How big are we talking?"

"Dude, he has like elephantitus of the dick or something," says Brian.

"It's not elephantitus," I say. "It's just a freak of nature. There is guy out there with elephantitus of the nuts, though. His scrotum is so big he has to be steered around in a wheelchair with a special sling to accommodate his bag."

Everyone groans. Brian and Tim cross and uncross their legs.

"So how big is the cock?" asks Tracy.

I thrust my forearm across the table. "Nearly as big as a Christmas yule log."

They accuse me of exaggeration.

"I swear to God! You know how we bathe clients every day and lay out their clothes? He has a sign above his cubby that says do not put Edgar in shorts. Last week it was so hot and the only pants he had were these thick fleece track pants, so I grabbed a pair of super long Bermuda shorts from one of the tall guys and dressed Edgar in them, they went down way past his knees. Problem solved, right?" I shake my head. "I see him strolling around the exercise yard, the tip of his dick poking out the bottom of his shorts."

Although my merry band of drunken accomplices responds to the tale with enthusiasm, as soon as the words leave my lips, I feel like shit. I picture Edgar lined up for breakfast in his little kid pajamas at the door of the dining room smiling and giggling when I creep up and pretend I'm going to tickle him. A sweet, slow two-year-old in a grown man's shell.

Brian pushes his round wire glasses up on top of his head. "Didn't he rape a guy? My uncle works there too and tells me all kinds of weird shit."

I nod, knowing I betray poor Edgar, though I'm enjoying being the centre of attention. I'm so weak. "It's true. He snuck into the bed of some real passive guy in the night. When he was done, the other guy needed twelve stitches."

"That's totally primal," says Tim. "Weird. I always thought rape was like a power control thing, not a sex thing."

Tracy swallows a mouthful of beer. "Probably is. Probably someone did it to him."

And she's right.

"Kind of depressing, Serena," Tim says.

I slap his shoulder like he's my hockey buddy, excuse myself. Looking in the mirror on my way out of the bathroom, I think of a snake swallowing its own tail, eternal, cyclical, inescapable. People say I'm beautiful all the time. I don't even know what that means. All I see is imperfection. I'm gulping like a serpent at my image when a girl bursts through the door. I pretend I'm studying some facial flaw instead of swallowing my face or my mind or whatever. I examine my sunburned nose and pale eyelashes. The ruse must have worked because the girl speaks to me as though I am normal. Maybe she's just loaded.

"Aren't you Serena Palmer?"

I nod. She paints her lips a shade that can only be described as peppermint peach.

"You went to Mariposa C.V.I. right? You're my brother's age. You go out with Tim Thompson?"

"Sometimes."

"He's so hot." She maneuvers around me to the toilet cubicle and closes the door. I turn away from the sight of myself. "How long you been together?"

How long has it been? The girl starts pissing.

"A long time, eh?"

"On and off since I was sixteen."

"Wow," she says. "Destiny."

God, I hope not.

When I return to the table, Tracy's talking about her dad. "I don't understand why," she says.

"How did he line up a gig like that anyway," asks Tim.

"Oh, he saw an ad in the News Packet and sent photos into a modeling agency called *Real Life Models* or something like that."

"Maybe he can introduce us to some hot model chicks." Brian refills his glass. Tracy rolls her eyes.

"Since Mom died, he's put on weight mostly around his middle. And he's grown this heinous white beard. I went to the bank with him the other day and two little kids kept staring at him. He loved it! He turns to them, says, *Ho, ho ho*. It's so embarrassing. Now he's working weekends as a substitute Santa at Santa's Village. It's enough to make me move back to Ottawa."

"Don't go!" Brian nuzzles her ear as he pleads.

"Parents do weird things," I say.

"Yeah," says Tim, "look at your folks. They're all crazy on the incinerator thing right now. They had us driving around on my Triumph last week dropping off pamphlets."

"It was hilarious. People would see this long-haired guy drive up on a motorcycle and they'd come running out of their houses all frightened. Then Tim would say, *Good evening, sir, have you heard about the campaign to stop the incinerator?* And pass them a SIN pamphlet. Priceless. But they've always been into that shit, this activism is nothing new."

Brian leans in close, asks Tracy to dance.

When they leave, Tim pulls me onto his lap and kisses my temple. "You're beautiful," he says.

"Shut up," I say.

Later, Reg offers us the back dressing room for after-hours partying. Brian whoops and calls for a round of tequila shots. I heartily partake, ignoring my previous call for moderation, and think no more of Inco. Tim plays his guitar all bluesy and Reg passes him a beer bottle to use for a slide, so he uses that for a while. Then he passes him a bar glass and he uses that too. Then a vase, then a shoe, then Craig brings him a toaster from the counter and Tim keeps a straight Mustang Sally face as if he's the most serious musician this side of the Delta, never missing a beat. You could love the guy sometimes, if you were drunk enough.

October: Eight Months Before

MID-AUTUMN NIGHT'S DAY DREAM

Down the 'Gold Coast', I cruise over to Magnetic Island in hopes of seeing koala bears munching eucalyptus leaves in their natural habitat. A guy eating muesli and yogurt in the hostel kitchen introduces himself as a doctor from Germany and invites me for a walk. Spend the day traipsing around the island listening to more information on koalas and rainbow lorikeets than I can possibly retain. By kilometre twenty I'm exhausted, though a swim in our skivvies on a jellyfish free beach helps to rejuvenate. And then we're both happy to say goodbye and I think, this not forming attachments is great. I could get used to bouncing along from one thing to the next, one person to another.

In Brisbane, I tour parks, museums, city beaches and art galleries with a chain smoking, dark-haired Danish guy uniformed in a white T-shirt and light blue jeans. Seems to always be guys I meet, guess more men travel on their own, and groups of females seem less likely to want to pair up with a single. The Dane and I talk about British colonization in Australia and British and French colonization in Canada, and the disgraceful treatment of Indigenous people the world over as we observe the cultural offerings of Brisbane. I don't often feel embarrassed by my heritage, by my country. I mean, even though my great-great-grandparents were born in Canada making me at least, like, fifth generation, I continue to reap benefits that the original inhabitants do not, and I have no idea what I'm supposed to do to change it. I feel guilt and shame about so many things and yet I think that feeling guilt and shame sometimes is not enough. And at the same time, I didn't do anything, and I have no other home.

It's not like I can scatter the various European bits of me back to where they're from.

The best art gallery we visit is divided in two. One side with landscapes and representations of daily Australian life painted by early English settlers and the other side, a blur of pastel dots that looks as though the Aborigine artists shook the contents of their heads out onto the canvases and their spirits helped organize the dots into the shape of snakes or lizards or kangaroos. Kind of like some Native Canadian artists with their simplistic forms, saturated colours, their nod to animal essence. I hate it when people call it naïve or primitive art. These paintings tap into something as old as dreamtime in a way that no colonial landscape or portrait ever could. I can feel it when I look at it. Compared to the Aboriginal works, the landscapes and sheep shearing scenes are like still deaths. I think of the dancers from my in-flight magazine. Art's when something seeps out from the confines of its form, reaches into the atmosphere gliding through the every-thingness into all it encounters reminding us that we're all kind of the same. That's how I want to paint. That's how I want to be in the world.

In Sydney, I seriously recalculate my funds. If I don't spend more than five bucks a day on food, I can keep on at this rate for at least another three months before I have to find a job. My *One Planet* guide suggests the best fun in the city is to be had at The Jolly Swagman Hostel in the *reddish* light district. When I arrive there, Josephine, a German girl around my age (Australia is full of German and Japanese tourists) is making cheese and pineapple sandwiches in the kitchen. She offers me one. After a steady diet of peanut butter, it's a tropical hi-five for my mouth. Together we wander the Cross, Bondi and Sydney Harbour. And standing in front of the Opera House, a landmark I've seen photographed a million times, I imagine I'm elegantly dressed and about to attend the show when it occurs to me just how far I actually am from home. Shielding my eyes from the fierce sun bearing down overtop my sunglasses I look out from the harbor. The wind off the water is warm and salt soaked. Then two sets of Japanese men ask to have their pictures with us. Josephine, taller than I am with brown hair down to her waist, could probably kick Mats' ass. They must suppose we're a couple of Amazons by the way we dwarf them. What a laugh to think we'll be forever immortalized in some Japanese guy's slide show as freakish Anglo-Saxons.

Josephine is on the opposite loop as I am, making her way north up the coast instead of south. She recommends staying in Coober Pedy on my way to Alice Springs. Says they have underground hostels called *dugouts* and that you can mine for opals. But first, to Canberra, the capital city.

On the Greyhound, I stroke my Patron Saint of Winkies medallion thoughtfully with my thumb. The time has come to make my Jimmy Birchbark drawing. His death mask is burned into my brain, and I need to exorcise it because it keeps swelling in my thoughts each time I close my eyes. I sketch his egg-filled fist, the strained look of asphyxiation on his face, eyes squeezing out of their sockets, the veins in his neck surging with angst and blood, an egg the size of an ostrich's lodged in his throat where an Adam's apple would be. The result is ghastly.

When I check into my Canberra hostel the man at the front desk examines my passport picture, runs his tongue along his lips and smiles. Says, "You look sweet sixteen and never been kissed." A guy behind me, also waiting for a room, laughs. I turn to look. It's Steve. He hugs me and kisses my cheek. Fuck! The clerk suggests we rent a bike for the day as it's a fantastic way to get around Parliament, says there's a bike hire just around the corner.

Steve's dressed in full Aussie attire: grey work socks slouched down toward the tops of his brown slip-on Blundstone work boots, baggy khaki shorts and a light flannel shirt with the sleeves rolled up. He tells me he's been travelling down the coast looking for me, that I'd mentioned stopping in Canberra. That us meeting right here, right now, at this hostel, is either fluke or fate. It's both creepy and, oddly, flattering.

We ride around the Capital on old yellow bikes, and even though our guided tour of Parliament is impressive with its

marble structure, representing the eucalyptus trees and other natural elements important to Australia, we are promptly bored.

"Well," Steve says, "this is lovely but I'm from England, so
all of this is, as they say in Americer, pretty Mickey Mouse. Let's
get a cold drink." He points to the War Memorial. "I reckon
they'll have a café in there."

We grab our bikes and head over. Inside the War Memorial
at the Poppies Café, we each have a tall lemonade.

"How long you been here?" I ask.

"Got here last March, so nearly ten months. You?"

"End of September."

"You're a real virgin yet, eh?" He adjusts himself in his seat
as though he needs to accommodate a giant nut sack.

"Have you just been traveling around all that time?"

"Na." He shifts in his chair again, leans back and lets his
knees fall apart like he's never been more comfortable and confident in his whole life. "I worked at a Farm Stay helping out
with sheep North of Adelaide. Thought I'd take a look at
Melbourne and Sydney, maybe get a serving job at a bar."

I stir the ice round the remnants of my lemonade. "I've been
thinking about work too. My money's not gonna last forever.
I'm not sure where I want to be yet." Or who I want to be with.
"Thought I'd do a quick tour and the right place would find
me." And the right people. My people.

He tilts his glass and lets the remains of his drink slither down
his throat. I imagine it like water crashing over rocks as it slides
over his prominent Adam's apple.

"And?"

"Thought I'd head to the Outback."

"Won't find much work there. What did you do back home?"

I never know how to answer this. "I worked at this hospital
place and helped take care of people who couldn't take care of
themselves." Does that cover it? "I went to art school."

"Wholly practical, I suspect. My sister's a nurse. Shitty job,
don't envy her. She shacked up with a Jamaican guy. Still in
Liverpool. Been meaning to call her actually."

"What'd you do before here?"

"You might not guess it to look at me, but I was an accountant for seven years."

"Really."

"Yup. Hated it. When I turned thirty last year, I looked around at my life, saw my sister going through all kinds o' bullshite. She has two kids with the Jamaican, gorgeous kids, both coffee-two-cream. Not for me. I didn't want any part of it. All the rushing and acquiring. Nope. I quit 'n came here."

"Will you go back?"

"No. Not going back. Not to Liverpool. Not to England." He looks around the café as if bored by it all. "I'm not that interested in the contributions of Australia and New Zealand in English wars. Anzac and all that. Astounding they would even be bothered fighting so far away. Wanna just go for a spin around the waterfront?"

"I'm here and everything. I wouldn't mind checking it all out."

"I'll join you then," he says. We make our way to the tomb of the unknown soldier.

Later, since we both have to eat supper, Steve offers to cook. We go to a grocery store, get some rice and peppers, which he calls capsicum, garlic and cheese to make a risotto. He pays for the food and swings the plastic grocery bag over his shoulder. I always wanted to go out with a guy named *Steve*.

After dinner, I retreat to my dorm room where I sketch another page. This time I draw a giant pile of cigarette butts spilled in the grass of a parking lot with some still smoldering. There's a knock at the door. Steve.

"Nothing doing here. Want to find a pub? My treat." He looks down and sees my black hardcover sketchbook and pencil in hand. "What're you drawing?"

I don't want to show him, but I do. I hold my sketch open to the cigarette butt page so he can't take the book and flip through. He looks puzzled. I stash it away, brush my hair, and explain while on the way to the pub, as best I can, about the clients I worked with and their lives, topping off the conversation with the story of the full ashtray.

"We took a bus full of guys to a carnival at a park. Some of them need individual escorts because of flight risk. It's not like they're gonna run off to start a new life of their own or anything. I mean really, where would they go? It's usually the picas hoping to feed their old nicotine addictions. So, me and this other staff guy double-team Maurice as we step off the bus, each holding a wrist. On the last step off the bus, Maurice dives down, throws his chest into the gravel, skids away from our grip and dashes across the parking lot as we chase him. I look behind me and see my partner, an old fat guy, hyperventilating, clutching his heart with both hands. And Maurice, two picnic tables distance ahead of me, is on the ground, his face immersed in the jackpot, a dumped car ash tray. There he is using his palms to scrape the butts from the mound and shovel them into his mouth while surging his head and neck up and down like a chicken pecking grain to help himself swallow the ashy, fiberglass wads."

Fucking disgusting is all Steve can think of to say. But I only told him enough to explain the picture. I didn't tell him what happened after we caught up with Maurice. Ken yelled, *You piece of shit,* between huffs as he staggered along. *You fucking piece of shit, you'll be puking all the way home.* He grabbed Maurice's shirt collar and yanked him like a marionette to his Velcro runners. A frenzied pitbull, Maurice chewed and chewed, butts falling from his mouth. He had to be handcuffed to Ken the entire time we were in the park. Sure enough, on the way home he vomited on the floor of the school bus. You haven't lived until you've seen and smelt undigested cigarette butts and chopped egg mingled together in *a yellow bile au jus* trickling up and down the black rubber ridged mat in the centre school bus aisle the heat of the afternoon.

At a traditional English pub not far from the hostel, Steve and I are the only customers except for a couple of burly young guys drunkenly arguing.

"G'day mate. Couple a schooners a Guinness, please," Steve says to the bartender. He nods to me as if for approval. He's trying so hard to assimilate. His face isn't too bad, but the gap tooth situation makes him look like a donkey—albeit a semi-attractive one. Anyway, it's nice to have someone to talk to, be with.

"What do we have here?" The guy in the purple T-shirt scans his glassy eyes up and down Steve, then turns to nudge his buddy. "I'd say we have a regular old POM."

The other guy, both are bigger than Steve and me, pushes right up, imposing himself on us. The larger of the two is red faced and slobbery like a cartoon bulldog in striped Rugby shirt.

"Yeah, I'm a Pommie all right," says Steve.

The bartender sets our frothing beers on the dark wooden bar. "You lot want to act like a matching pair o' arseholes, get yourselves back to the Uni pub," he says.

"Right, mate, sorry," says Purple T-shirt.

I follow Steve to our table as he carries the beer carefully out in front of himself trying not to spill.

"What the hell's a pom"?

"It's stupid. Some Australians call British people *Poms* or *Pommie*. 'Prisoner of Mother England' or some such. It makes no sense. They're the original prisoners from England. Ignorant pair of gits."

We settle into our beers, bridging the silence of not knowing with easy slurps. I like the way the foam lingers on the fringe of his moustache. He reaches across the table and fingers my medallion touching my chest. "It's like a child made it," he says.

"If you're not going to be an accountant, what're you going to do?"

"I've got a million-dollar idea. I'm going to make it happen, too, I'm superstitious, though. I can't tell anyone because it will water it down and give it less power. If I speak it out loud, I can see it vaporizing. Poof." He grasps at the air as if catching fleeting mosquitoes.

"Okay, well, what is it?"

"Weren't you listening?"

"I'm just shitting you. Whatever. Good luck to you. Maybe I'll be a world-renowned artist someday and you'll have one of my paintings in your living room."

A while later, Purple T-shirt comes by and says, "You a pom too?"

"Nah, I'm a Canuck."

"A what?"

"A Canuck. A Canadian. We call ourselves Canucks, like you call yourselves Aussies."

Steve says to him, "Are you an Aussie?"

"Is the Pope Catholic? Does a bear shit in the woods?" The bulldog interjects and slaps Purple's back, guffawing.

They clink our glasses and join us in our booth. Alcohol is a lovely solvent. Bulldog says, "We were arguing earlier about the ultimate carnivore. Who do you think would win a fight, a tiger or a bear?"

"Cat goes straight for the throat," says Steve.

"The bear has powerful paws that club the cat before he even gets to his throat," I say.

"What about a lion and grizzly?" asks Stripes.

"Hands down lion," says Steve.

"Male lions don't even hunt in the wild. The females do all the work. He'd be totally out of his element," I say. "For sure, the bear."

"Ooooo" says Purple, "the gender card. She has a point."

"A polar bear and an orca, eh, eh?" says Purple, pointing his thumbs and forefingers at us like cocked pistols.

"What about a fight between a shark and giraffe?" I ask. It goes on like this until our minds are at the bottoms of our glasses. Steve whispers to me while Bulldog and Purple are squabbling about *footie*, "I have a bottle of Jim Beam in my room. Fancy a drink?"

"You in a dorm?"

"Treated myself to a single. Coming?"

"Is a bear Catholic? Does the Pope shit in the woods?"

Steve laughs, loops his arm around my shoulder, and we stagger back to the hostel to swill Jim Beam in his room while sitting on the edge of a wire-framed double bed. The amber bourbon trickles down my throat, hot and sweet. Steve hoists his white T-shirt above his head, catching it momentarily on his goateed chin. On his chest, poking perkily out, are the longest nipples I've ever seen on man, woman or beast. They jut out perpendicular from his chest like giant erasers on the end of pencils. I try not to stare but have a moment of pause and sobriety as he struggles to drunkenly remove the rest of his shirt. My thoughts vacillate from *What the fuck am I doing, to Ah, what the fuck?* One minute he's got his fingers in me and the next, he's humping away like he means it and I look around a bit thinking I must be especially messed up or at least drunker than usual because I can't feel anything. And I can't exactly ask, *Are you in?* Slip my hand down between my legs and understand from basic positioning that whatever he has for a cock is actually inside me. And I can't feel a thing. He gives the old sighing grimace and pushes himself off, collapsing. When he disposes of the condom, I get a look at the nearly invisible culprit, a shriveled little button in a fur coat. Man, poor Steve. He can try to reinvent himself however he wants, this year a rugged Australian bloke, next year maybe a surfer dude, but anyway you slice it he's still an English accountant with giant nipples and a hard-on the size of my thumb.

He passes me the bottle for a final swig of Jim before passing out. I wake around four, parched, plasticine for brains, wondering where I am. And then I look beside me. And methought I was Tatiana and enamored of an ass. On the corner of the cheap veneer dresser sits the bottle of Jim Beam a mere ghost of itself and beside me an ass head complete with long donkey ears, big front teeth and braying snore. I do the pink panther creep stealthily gathering my bra, undies and shorts hoping not to wake the beast of burden.

Without opening his eyes, Steve says, "Where are you going?"

"Back to my room to get some more sleep," I say softly, hoping that will be the end of it.

"Disappointed. Was thinking we might go for another round this morning." Gross. He seriously has no idea.

"I've got to take an early bus to Melbourne."

"What? So that's it, aye? Just a drunk fuck?"

"I dunno, Steve. I gotta go. I'll see you." And, wearing my T-shirt with the rest of my stuff balled in my arms, I'm half out the cheery red door of his room.

He sits up. I hold my breath and squeeze out closer to the hall when he grabs my wrist through the remaining crack. God damn it. Why can't I say *Yeah, you were just a drunk fuck and a shitty one at that*. Why does hurting this dickhead's feelings, some guy I hardly know, make me squirm like a caterpillar with a pin stuck through it?

"I know a Backpackers in Melbourne. I'll meet you there in a couple of days." He lets go my wrist and scrambles around the room bare-assed, searching through his pack for a pen. Scribbles the hostel's name on a brochure for wine tasting in the Bourassa valley.

"Sure," I say, "great, I'll see you there."

"No kiss?"

Kissing him, while repugnant, makes parting swift.

In the early dark of morning with the sounds of responsible people starting their cars and heading off to work, I shower. Hot wet drips cleanse, would forgive almost, if not for throbbing temples. Rummage around my backpack, stuffing it all further down, trying not to disturb those around me, though I notice each turning body in a sleeping bag laden bunk as I make my hasty exit.

When I get to the Greyhound Station, I buy myself a huge bottle of water, a bag of roasted chicken chips and a ticket to Coober Pedy, bypassing Melbourne entirely. Weird how Steve just showed up at my hostel. Like, was he waiting around at the bus station and stalking hostels for days on end hoping I'd turn up? Shouldn't have told him I was heading to the Outback. Try not to beat myself up too much, just a brief relapse into my old ways. Damn that Jinglenuts. He always said, wherever you go there you are. He's not right. I won't let him be. The driver has navy shorts and socks pulled up to his knees. Hope they are part of his uniform and not a perverse fashion statement. Sling my pack into the belly of the bus and climb aboard for sleep asking myself what I'm even meant to be doing here.

At a dinner stopover in Adelaide, I call my parents.

"Not too much has changed around here," dad says. You know Sandy McPherson. You went to school with him."

"The Mariposa sanitation heir?"

Dad laughs. "I guess you could say that. His father, I think he goes by Bud, has joined in against the incinerator, which is just our luck because he has funds the rest of us lack."

"He's all gung-ho to support something environmental?"

"I can assure you it's not altruistic. McLaughlin's incinerator will cut into his disposal profits from running his trucks across the county to the landfill. Your mom's away at your grandmother's. She and that friend, that Jean woman, have been *dowsing*. Do you know about that business?"

"Divination? A little."

"Foolishness. Your grandmother has convinced herself she's going to keel over any day and has taken to labeling the contents of her condo with stickers and names on each of the important items."

"Think she's serious?"

"Who knows? You ask if she's read the paper today and she answers, *I love roses though pansies were mother's favourite*. It's hard to know with her what is real and what is imagined."

With any of us, I think.

"I suppose it *has* gotten worse lately, even since you've been gone. I took her over to see Doctor Stephenson and he put her on some new drug. It helps slow memory loss. But you know what she went through with Barnaby."

My poor, old, crazy grandma. The least I can do is send the woman a postcard.

March: Three Months Before

HONESTY IS A SHITTY POLICY

Wiping up and restocking the fridge in preparation of the busy night ahead gets me thinking about a conversation I had with Lisa a few days ago. She said that traditionally each person in her band has an animal totem that acts as a spirit guide. Do you choose the animal or does the animal choose you? I stack bottles in the base of the beer fridge looking up in time to see Tim walk in slinging his guitar case. Damn. He saddles up onto a barstool.

My palms sweat, hands tremble. "Hey. How's it goin'." Place a generous vodka soda in front of him.

He nods. Guzzles half his drink. Doesn't answer me or smile, just unwinds the black and white checked scarf from around his neck then guillotines the awkwardness with: "You're quite the fisherman. Reeling me in, throwing me back."

Tim's wasted. "This new man. Where's he at, eh?" Pushes up the sleeves of his black leather jacket. "Why do you think you're better than everyone else?"

"'Cause I am."

"Seriously." Slowly, painfully, very loudly, he annunciates each syllable: "WHY DO YOU THINK YOU ARE BETTER THAN EVERYONE ELSE?"

"Shut up. I don't. I don't. You should know that."

His eyes stare through me cold and hard, icy shards pierce. Downs the rest of his vodka soda in a single gulp. Hoists his guitar on the empty bar stools, flips open the latches to the case like he's about to pull out a shotgun. Keeps his hurt eyes on me as he grabs the guitar neck walking backward toward the stage.

"This one's for you," he says, pointing his finger at me.

If I had the ability to transmogrify and dissolve or melt or shrink into something as inconspicuous as some kind of hard-shelled insect with wispy little legs and scuttle under the sink for even just a half an hour, I so totally would. Honestly, did Tim really think that I was ever going to be happy getting stoned and lying on the dirty carpet of his basement apartment listening to *Pet Sounds* for the rest of my life? Patrons clap and whistle when they see him take the stage.

He reels them in with a riotous riff then belts out a heavy cover of *Second Hand News* flinging his guitar around his back at the end. Leaves the audience with turned heads and raised eyebrows. Stalks me at the bar until my face burns under his frozen glower. Pushes the bar stool aside, leans over and with his hands on my shoulders and then one hand around the back of my neck, pulls me to him, rough and demanding, his face in my face, his lips on my lips.

"Get off! Fuck off!" Fuck you, Tim.

He drops me, pushes me back against the mirrored liquor shelves knocking bottles over but nothing breaks. "You blew it," he says.

Lisa runs to the bar from across the restaurant and seizes my wrist. "That is bullshit," she says.

"It's nothing. He's gone. Don't worry about it," I say.

Never meant to cause all this hurt. Guess he was another casualty of the sloppy way I threw my love around.

Not telling Aubrey about this Tim thing would be a lying by omission, an equivocation. Tired of sending out valentine-shaped lies. I want everything transparent. Don't want misunderstandings, mistrust or half-truths lurking in the background of our lives. I'd want him to tell me if Gina jumped him, if he didn't tell me and I found out later from someone else, I'd feel betrayed. And for a very expensive minute late that night, Aubrey is silent on the phone. Guess I should have kept my big mouth shut. Honesty. What a joke. No one wants to hear the truth. Everybody already knows what he knows.

May: One Month Before

THE WEIGHT OF WATER

It's a torrential downpour by the time we get into Lake Louise proper, so we drive around admiring the quaint little mountain town and tucking images of soggy tents and wet sleeping bags into the backs of our minds. Stare wistfully at the Chateau Lake Louise and its spires of green weathered copper imagining downy, floral bedspreads and feather-filled pillows. Since we're here and there's a row of pay phones, I park and leave Aubrey in the car while calling my parents for an update. Watch him play guitar from the phone booth window as I dial, thinking about the rain pelting down on the car obscuring my view of him, and about how all the water that's ever existed has always been here, that every drop of moisture that ever fell was once drunk by dinosaurs. So really, the water we drink is dinosaur piss. And if it's possible, that all the water that's ever been here has always been here, isn't it possible too that the Dreamtime was real? That all our souls or whatever, have been around that long too and have just spent the last however many centuries hopping around from body to body to body?

Mom answers. She's thrilled to share that the Ace Fitzgerald benefit concert last Tuesday at the Lake Wissinotti Pavilion drew a massive crowd and raised thousands of dollars in SIN contributions. And because it was Ace's first new song in twenty years, and served as his big *leaving-rehab-come-back* debut, the park was filled with people ultimately generating loads of national media attention on the Mariposa incinerator debate. Dad was the MC of the event and Mom said he was a real card. Thankfully, I was far, far away and didn't have to suffer through one-liners like *composts have a good sense of humus*. Anyhow, sounds like McLaughlin is going to cave and stop the incinerator project. National news story and all, he won't be able to bull through. With all that negative media attention, he and Banbury will come off looking like a pair of grade A dick heads.

Our campsite is a blanket of sop. Penetrating through layers of forest loam and pine needles, the rain imparts a sponge-like quality to the dirt, causing the tent pegs to spring back out. It's hard not to interpret it as an omen for the night ahead. We rig up a secondary blue-tarp rain-shield, tying off to trees and the picnic table with yellow rope. And though we have a certain synergy between us, we're no Bucky Fullers. The best we can hope for is for sleeping bag-sized dryers in the comfort station.

On the Columbia ice field the next day, we walk on frozen water left over from the ice age three hundred metres deep. I could be standing on a wooly mammoth right now and never even know it. Cold air in my nostrils, deep breath in my lungs, genuine relief the incinerator business is coming to an end. It's a small drop, so to speak, in the world's watershed. Signs warn of death and injury, advise careful footing. Aubrey grabs my hand. Crevasses in the glacier are cracks in my subconscious. Blue to their depths like Windex. Wonder how long it would take for my body to die if I leapt down into one. There's something about these mountains, this ice that makes a person feel as insignificant as a trilobite in one breath and part of the everything-ness in the next.

It's foggy after all the rain. In spite of the expansive land, the smell of pine and wet soil, the weight of the air hangs low and boxes us in. Aubrey's grumpy and agitated. And here I thought I'd be the annoying irrational one. Says he hasn't slept much the last few nights and walks ahead of me on the trail.

I rush to catch up with him playfully jumping on his back.

"Holy fuck, Serena! You scared the shit out of me!"

"Sorry." And I really am. There's a rock in his hand. I realize now that he's in bear attack mode, plotting and scheming our preservation. But how do you question your lover's sanity without making him all defensive?

"You're gonna throw a rock at him and then what, flash him my Swiss Army knife?"

"No, I'm gonna hit him right between the eyes. Paralyze him." He throws the rock off to the side of the trail into the woods and looks at his empty hand as if he doesn't even remember picking it up. Shakes himself like a dog coming out of a stream. "I know it seems crazy, but sharks, like when I'm surfing, I know as long as I get shallow, or am on land I'm safe, a shark-free zone, but with these fucking bears, it's like they're watching me, laughing, waiting for me to let down my guard so they can attack. And there's no escape. They can climb trees, run super-fast, swim."

"I know what you mean," is all I can say, 'cause it's true. The spectral bear has been on my tail since the day I became self-conscious and learned to value the perceived judgments of others over my own.

I manage to talk him down, convince him to stop in Banff before heading west through the mountains. We pull into the park to register for a campsite and face a huge white and red sign shrieking, CAUTION, ATTENTION, ACHTUNG, along with various other equally alarming Asian characters underscored by the warning, COOLERS ARE NOT BEAR PROOF! Two mangled coolers hang by chains from the bottom of the painted plywood sign. The gate attendant takes our money and hands us a map and a pamphlet titled, *Safety in Bear Country*.

Aubrey leans overtop of me from the passenger side, craning his head up toward the window. "You had problems with bears this spring?"

"Always gotta be alert in bear country. It's been a cold, wet spring. Any depletion in the food supply causes bears to wander in search of alternative nutritional sources like…"

"People?" interjects Aubrey.

"No," she laughs, "like people's garbage." Drawing circles and curving lines on the park map in yellow hi-lighter, she points us in the direction of our campsite.

I sit on our picnic table watching Aubrey stalk the perimeter. He takes big steps while walking, bobbing his head like a funky cartoon turtle. When he finishes scoping out escape routes, he perches beside me on the bench, and taps a rhythm on the table-top with his hands.

"Maybe you should use your music to tame the savage beast."

He pauses for a moment, looking up into the arc of pine-needled branches that create a lacey pattern of the sky and says, "You're a genius."

Aubrey's guitar playing, a couple of beers, some hash and a small cup each of mushroom tea melt the remaining bear anxiety and we dance in the dirt surrounding the fire pit with bellies full of greasy grilled cheese. Later, we join a presentation in the amphitheatre by park staff outlining information on camping in bear country. I shift on my ancient log chunk in front of the amphitheater and lean into Aubrey's ear. "Ready to move from the psychic fifth to the mystical sixth?" He winks and sits on his hands to keep from tapping. The remaining logs gradually fill with people from all over the world who've come to experience the Canadian wilderness. Their different languages weave in among the old growth cedars that surround us making me feel as provincial and rustic as the logs. Soon, a uniformed Parks Canada ranger comes out from behind a large white screen carrying a mesh sack full of puppets and a tell-tale chewed-up cooler.

Ranger Dan strokes his fuzzy mustache and starts *good evening folksin'* us. He tells us that a bear can smell a soiled maxi-pad from fifty metres away. I'm imaging how he might have tested this when he advises us against copulating while in bear country. Sneak a look at Aubrey's entranced face, watching the ball in his throat gulp up and down as he swallows. Great. No more sex. The ranger points at his busted-up cooler and notes that *a bear will do just about anything for a pritnear defrosted hamburg.* An assistant promises a puppet show upon the conclusion of the impending film, a nature flick tracking a variety of bears as they make their way through the Rockies.

The picture on the white screen flip-flops snowy granite into black brush strokes and rainbow rings reminding me of a school projector film. Watching movies, TV, and plays while stoned is totally trippy for me. Like, interactive almost, as though the picture takes place through me. On screen there are coastal mountains, valleys lush with firs and grasses, water and wild flowers, small creatures darting cautiously about. The camera zooms to a nearly still shot, practically a Robert Bateman print: bear in a waterfall, salmon in mouth, a burst of pink eggs up through the spray. Then two young black bears loll and bat each other. By bear scene three, I'm fully engaged as though immersed in some kind of virtual reality moment. At the base of the mountains, a golden grizzly lopes across the Canadian veldt and I see myself on screen in baggy arsed quick-dry MEC pants, feel the sun, the wind, the ground shaking beneath my sturdy hiking boots. I'm running now, anxiously looking over my shoulder. Running past a bright patch of cedars, past forested slopes and waterfalls. Running, running, can't stop running, almost tripping while the shadow of the bear gains ground. Dart across the screen, jump rocks, charge through tall grass, move forward till my lungs hurt while the bear is nowhere to be seen, yet, the shadow follows me. Gasp, startle myself and Aubrey. He looks at me, sets a hand on my knee. The spell broken, I shrug and turn back to the screen. The golden grizzly meanders along a meadow. The camera zeroes in on a close-up of the grizzly's mouth foaming green saliva from freshly eaten grass. Looks like one of my former clients who's gorged himself on lawn. Fuck. I'm no different than those guys: creating my own universe, dropping in and out of reality on a whim.

Take Aubrey's hand and like an ordinary sane person, watching as the rangers begin their puppet show. A raccoon and porcupine leave meat on their puppet picnic table, sleep with toothpaste and shampoo inside their tent, and throw garbage around their pretend campsite.

August: Ten Months Before

PUDDLE O'MUCK

Screw it, I'm not going to work today. Oh, but I can't not go. The guys are expecting me. C'mon, none of your *clients* will even notice. *Clients* is so phony, as if they're visiting a day spa. I need to quit. I don't want to let everybody down. You're not that important. I can't quit. I need more money. Have to get airfare, a work visa. I don't care. If I don't get out of this place soon, I'm going to wind up like a Vesuvian relic, trapped in Mariposa forever. Only instead of being petrified mid-run, I'll be a sphincter-lipped old hag getting wasted at the Queen, wrapping up shaved meat at the A&P and painting pet portraits on commission until my ovaries dry up. I'm giving Natalie my resignation letter today and booking a flight to Australia. I have to, I just do.

Throw my kryptonite bike lock, a gift from Jinglenuts, into my knapsack along with a bagel and a Nalgene full of water.

The early haze of morning swells up from the sidewalks and each breath earned through exertion cleanses, absolving me somehow. The wind at my back as I coast through the last continuous hill on my bike before the wind lifts me and I pedal hard. In this late summer air, all things are yet possible. Moving fast and faster through town, I pass the limestone, blue-shingled Catholic Church, the Davis and Sons Funeral Home with its Astroturf front steps, the glossy, white brick library, the red brick Opera House with twin spires, the Canadian Tire (a rock smashed through its triangular strawberry sign), the Pandora's Boxx Club proffering *girls, girls, girls*. Then round a corner and pass the cop shop with *I smell bacon* spray-painted on the north side until, finally, I sneak through a red lighted intersection and turn left into the Mariposa North Centre.

A bunch of early risers able to dress themselves are out on the front lawn wearing Velcro sneakers and furiously waving at me. Consistent as the sunrise, Willie's out there too pumping his one arm madly. Willie the one-armed-waver. Only in Mariposa. Used to be, up until about ten years ago, there was a school program here. Eventually any high functioning client was shipped out into the community to work and live in a less institutional, group home setting. Anyone left is either low functioning or has a serious behaviour problem.

Large oaks line the winding driveway from the road to the original red brick building and if you didn't know any better, you'd think you were at a fancy hotel and might even be tempted to stay awhile. I've seen photos and paintings from the 1870s of Victorian ladies with parasols picnicking on the grounds before the hotel developer went broke and the Ontario Government stepped in. Started out as a boarding school for the *feeble-minded* with stays of five years or less. For a while it was a working village with inhabitants learning skills like farming, cooking and sewing. Then families started abandoning kids at the front gate in the dark of night, and others were never collected, so their five-year stays became indefinite. A blue and white Ministry of Health sign covers the old stone Asylum for Idiots plaque, but a dead albatross by any other name is still a dead albatross.

Marty's smoking on the front steps of the admin building.

"See ya at lunch!" I shout and ride past.

I'm already ten minutes late and Natalie's been known to scold for less. Can't believe how much the staff gripes about her. If she were a he, everyone would grit their teeth and say, *He runs a tight ship,* but because she's a she they say, *Oh what a bitch she's making us sign in and out* and actually do our jobs for once.

Behind administration and the original asylum are a bunch of modern buildings called cottages, each linked through a series of underground tunnels for the easy transport of food, laundry, stretchers, and wheelchairs. Also useful for, if you believe the nasty rumors and innuendo around here, raping and sodomizing clients. My cottage, Shaw, is named for a doctor prominent in the eugenics movement of the 1920s and caters to low-functioning behaviour-disordered men. When you first walk in, it feels like it should be an arena or something because the lobby is tiled in glossy blue that switches to Plexiglas midway between floor and ceiling. Except it's missing that sweaty skate smell and a different odor lingers, smelling less of toil and more of cover-up. Until I started working here, I never knew why hospitals and places like this always had that *l'eau de urinal cake* reek. Turns out, there's an air deodorizer specifically for institutions called ADA that is delivered via potent drops of golden liquid from a small glass bottle designed to conceal, I suppose, the stench of desperation.

Lillian bunches the Winks into lines, two for the tubs and two for the showers. There's something about the depth of blue in this bathroom tile that makes it feel intensely impersonal. We don't drain and refill for each guy as per Natalie's instructions. It's a waste of water and we'd be here all day. We keep the tap running and figure it's sanitary enough. And I'm sure they're all supposed to have their own washcloths and soap as well, but how are we supposed to implement that kind of personalized service with a system and room designed to process small herds rather than individuals? I model my bathing technique on Lillian's, who, for all her faults, would never leave a fella unclean. Whatever we do has to beat Tom and Stuart's car wash method. It's the ultimate in no contact. They have sticks with pink scrubby puffs dipped in soap that they maneuver up, down, around and through each guy before hosing him down with a sprayer. It's an odd collection of naked bodies, cold against an icy backdrop, pure though, just hanging out together, perched on stools and benches, unashamed.

Gary, buck-naked, sees me and starts to run. His clothes are down the hall in front of his door in a heap. "Slow down. I'll open your door in a second." Lillian must have locked him out. Not to be mean, she's trying to follow Natalie's directions. Sometimes I could care less about following Natalie's dumb rules. Poor Gary. He was given his own room in the old days for a reason. He won't let anyone in and hates to leave it almost as much as he hates wearing clothes. According to his file, the guy's profoundly autistic. I get Natalie's point. He stands naked and rocks in his room all day long, it looks bad. But when they lock him out, he stands in front of the door and does the same damn thing only he's all bug-eyed and anxious.

He waits for me by his room, rocking, his dick swaying back and forth between his thighs in opposite rhythm to his hips. Swipes at my keys, grabs my wrist, yanks me toward his door so both my feet leave the ground. The keys fall. He picks them up and motions them toward the door but can't figure out how to insert the key into the lock. I open the door. He pushes past, shoves me into the door jam, resumes rocking. The whites of his eyes are bigger than ever. He turns his face toward me and blinks twice. Gratitude?

Gary kind of reminds me of this guy who walks the highways surrounding Mariposa from Hawkehurst to Ravenstone. I've worked in highway burger joints in both locations and watched him walking and talking to himself on the shoulder while I squirted mustard and ketchup circles on greasy meat for cottagers on their way to vacationland. When we read *The Old Man and the Sea* in grade eleven I couldn't believe how much the description of the Old Man matched Crapwalker. He has crispy reddish brown cheeks, lips like beef jerky, and you know all that sun can't be good for him and you want to help but you know that his compulsion to walk without sunscreen is the least of his worries. Instead of floating around the ocean hoping to catch the big one, this guy is seemingly directionless on a perpetual pilgrimage to nowhere. You might think he meanders. He doesn't. He marches with great strong strides. Like he's late for a meeting or surgery or something. Arguing mercilessly with himself, lips flapping like a whippoorwill's arse in a windstorm, all the while swinging his arms frantically, scissoring his legs back and forth while his too-big parka the colour of a seagull's back shifts up and down with each step.

Maybe he doesn't fit into his jacket like he doesn't fit into his skin. It's almost as if on some night when the veil between this world and the next was thinnest, two souls or spirits or the essence of that which makes us human got caught inside Crapwalker and couldn't decide which would stay and which would go. So now, there's this guy in Velcro shoes, an oversized grey parka and stringy mop hair doomed to argue it out in perpetuity while wandering up and down the highway and through the streets of town. We don't talk much about mental illness around here. We just mop up after our clients and laugh about an old man frothing out a continuous stream of obscene invective while cars with boats, and cars with ATVs, and cars with Seadoos, and Ski-doos whiz past into town to exploit the water and the people of Mariposa as the sun beats down on the fur-lined hood of his parka in the hottest part of the day.

I meet Marty at the archives at lunch. He's waiting for me, hands shoved down the front pockets of his jeans. Lean my bike up against a skinny willow. He stoops to tie his black Converse high-tops and grins up at me, seeming a little nervous. Staff aren't normally permitted in the confidential archives, but he has a key. We're giddy with deviance. He reassures me we won't get caught and as he does, his arm brushes mine. The touch surprises me. He grabs my hand and leads me down the dark stairs into the basement. Cool, damp air laced with earth and mildew. Marty stops abruptly at the last step and reaches for the light switch in the underground hallway. His sudden stop causes me to tumble up against his back, our bodies grazing in a way that doesn't quite feel so buddy-buddy all of a sudden. A weak bulb dangles from the room's centre, casting a faint orange glow and illuminating the crowded space like a torch hung from inside a tent. Shelves heave with MNC history. Framed photos, books, awards, medical implements. You'd think someone would have created a proper museum display of all this stuff. Baby cages, cribs with steel lids. Forceps, the cause of many an accidental brain-squishing. Electric shock machines with buckles and leather straps and an assortment of other restraining devices that would look more at home in a stable with bridles and tack.

On a side table, like a prized sculpture, sits an infant's cloverleaf skull in a jar. At the back left of the room on a shelf more prominent that the others, is a sepia photo of a doctor wearing a lab coat over his suit, clip board in one arm, the other draped over a client in a pinafore dress. In hand-lettered gold on the

bottom of the photo is *Dr. Charles Shaw, 1923*. Next to the picture is a leather-bound book titled, *Policies and Procedures in a
Hospital for Subnormals, by Charles Shaw M.D.*

"Hey Marty," I whisper and grab his elbow. "I think I'm
subnormal."

"Yeah," he replies distractedly, close enough that I can feel
the warmth of his breath on my cheek, "definitely subnormal."

Aside from this exchange, we do not speak. The breath on
my cheek, the arm touch, my body bumping up against his on
the stairs, the hand holding. Is he thinking what I think he's
thinking?

We shuffle around the room contemplating the wall-mount-
ed photos of the halcyon days in the fifties and sixties where
MNC earned prestige as a school for the *trainable retarded*. A
Down's Syndrome choir wearing matching red plaid vests and
kilts stares back at us from a photo on the wall with first place
medals around their necks. Marty moves closer, wraps his arm
around my waist, pulls me into him with uncharacteristic confidence. Then his lips are on my neck, my mouth. His hands are
cool against my stomach under my T-shirt. I press myself against
him kissing, breathing in his toothpastey smell. His hands search
the back of my shorts then along my thighs, then inside my
shorts, then he pulls away unexpectedly and apologizes. Says,
Sorry, I don't know what I was thinking.

As though nothing monumental has passed between us, I ask,
"What else is here?"

Marty points to the top of the file cabinet where sits an
archivist's scrapbook, black and layered in dust. The photograph
on the first page is of the original Asylum for Idiots with a typed
caption. *Between 1876 and 1950 nearly ten thousand people, mostly
children, were admitted with intellectual and other disabilities.* Deaf,
dumb, blind, epileptic, cerebral palsy, you name it. All manner of
imperfections could land a kid here. He creeps up behind me as
I'm flipping through the scrapbook, puts his hands on my hips.
Burrows his face in the crook between my jaw and shoulder,
kissing my ear. Move my head out of lip reach. Let him lean over
my shoulder so he can see the *Four Types of Mental Deficiency* and

the accompanying four pictures. Pointing to each black and white image of a long-dead human being, I read the subtitles: *Idiocy—mental age of less than three. Mongolian Imbecility. Imbecility—mental age between three and seven. Moron—mental age between seven and eleven.*

He rests his chin on my shoulder as we read the next page on eugenics, which claims morons as the cause of criminality, vice, and pauperism. "Weird," says Marty, "it's like they thought being born with some kind of brain damage or chromosomal disorder was a flaw of morality that could be corrected."

Half an hour left to go in my shift. The baked beans served for dinner are not digesting well. A slow bowel growl resonates around the common room followed closely by shuddering sphincter eruptions. Dennie farts so loud it propels him from his chair and sends him running for the toilet in a pants pulled down kind of panic. Tom and I laugh. Bill leaps up, heads down the hall toward the bathroom tugging at his shorts as he trots. Too late. Runny shit trickles down his bony ass and legs onto the hall floor like a trail of blackened baked beans put through a blender. I return with a mop and pail to find Jimmy Birchbark sitting on an orange rubber chair in a puddle of his own filth. The reek of liquid manure all around me, I slop the grey strings on a stick through the mud. Tom puts Jimmy in the bath, then follows in my mopping wake with sprinkles of ADA.

October: Eight Months Before

MINING, DIVINING

Coober Pedy is about 850km from Adelaide, a distance increased, the ticket guy warns, by many stops along the way. A distance, I hope, that will propel me far, far away from a certain dorm room in Canberra. Board around four for the milk run and a cheap night of sleep. The driver shoves a VHS tape into the TV. It's a movie about a guy who finds out he has cancer right after his first son is born and starts filming all the mundane bits of his life so the kid will know him after he's dead. Like anyone wants to bawl on a bus full of strangers. My trusty jar of peanut butter is getting low, but I manage to eke out a couple more sandwiches. I seriously need to find some fresh fruit somewhere as my teeth are about to fall out on account of the scurvy.

The trail from city life to almost instant desolation is swift. It's the edge of the Outback, nothing but red sand and sporadic gas stations. The driver interrupts the movie to offer scattered commentary.

"A road train is about to pass. These are transport trucks carrying three cars worth of goods and fuel. They're difficult to slow and will crush anything in their way." Speaker clicks off.

A deafening whoosh passes. The speaker clicks on.

"Lots of dead roos and cattle at the roadside. In periods of drought slight puddles form on the pavement. Roos will run for hours to sip at them. Cattle too. It's simply too large a territory to fence. That's why cars in the Outback have roo bars on the front grill." The speaker clicks off.

We pass a herd of scrawny cows, hipbones protruding. What in the hell do they eat out here? There's not a blade of grass in sight. What could grow in this dusty earth? A white and brown spotted cow lies still on the roadside, thin skin melting into eye sockets. What's wrong with people? Cows don't fucking belong here.

Doodle and sketch a bit to avail myself the waning light. I've drawn Tracy's dad dressed as Santa Claus waving from a giant cigarette boat as he roostertails past the town dock. The bus groans, chugging as it slows, and pulls into a little white hut, a gas and groceries shop. A backpacker waits by the Greyhound shingle, both are covered by a film of red dust. Three overweight people, maybe Aborigines, two women, one man, stumble drunkenly around the outside of the shop. Inside is a drinks cooler, dusty cake mixes, soup cans, jars of vegemite, peanut packs, chip bags—nothing that isn't well preserved. A spotlight illuminates the powdered earth outside the shop and as I line up to pay for my mango juice, I see through the window, behind the cashier, the bus driver and another uniformed man in short pants shouting and chasing the Aborigines whose teeth glow white in the artificial light. Where did they come from? I can't see another structure around anywhere and there is nothing to obstruct my view. The bus driver grabs the woman in the yellow sundress, her pendulous breasts swinging, and screams in her face with his index finger thrust toward the clouds in judgment. The driver boards, clicking on his speaker explaining in unnecessary detail all the problems the drunken Abos create. It's the Wink Ward mentality all over again.

And so, Dorothy's dowsing is freaking out my father. I remove my Jimmy Birchbark necklace and allow it to twist and circle as I suspend it from the leather lace until it eventually comes to a neutral position. Will I return from where I'm going, safely? Circle, circle no. Will my Grandma be okay? Circle, circle yes. Circle, circle no. Return the necklace to my chest.

Finally finish *Frankenstein*, my light the only one on the coach still lit. Wonder if all Mary Shelley really wanted to say was that if we stopped discriminating between everything and everyone and just loved instead, we could avoid a lot of monstrous acts. Before I click my light off, I draw one last thing. A bird's eye view of Mariposa with a mighty dowsing pendulum swinging in concentric circles around the sky linking my parents' house, the opera house, my old high school, Lake Ossawippi and Lake Wissanotti, The Queen of Spades and the MNC.

Morning. Still a whole day of adventuring ahead. Haven't been off the bus for an hour and already I know this is no place to find a job, no place to find a place. Maybe that Steve guy was right about there not being work. Ugh. That Steve guy. At least I've managed to evade that bad decision.

Coober Pedy is Mars on earth: hot, dry and red with dusty hills and craters. If you took a picture from outer space, you'd probably see eight or ten silver roofs glinting out from the rusty sand like flashes of opal in a rock. Most places are caves carved into the side of a hill keeping them cool and dark in the treeless heat. Check into my dugout hostel and add *Frankenstein* to a pile of discarded novels exchanging it for another. And believe it or not, it's *Haunted Summer* by Anne Edwards: the fictionalized story of the writing of Frankenstein. When I ask what there is to do in Coober Pedy, the woman who takes my money points to a humble row of opal shops. At least there's a bus to Alice Springs in the morning.

Bright blue-sky, white clouds, streaks of red earth, the opals themselves echo the landscape. Who would have thought that under this rusty dirt rainbow-stones lie in ribbons like giant chunks of mother of pearl. When I sign up for a tour and a chance to mine my own, the woman in the shop hands me a pamphlet outlining the mystical properties of the opal. Apparently, they enhance imagination and creativity, release inhibitions, improve memory and can even aid in astral projection, which just may come in handy someday. All round, it's an auspicious start. Maybe I'll dig out a gazillion dollar winner and solve all my problems.

While waiting for my tour to begin, I sit on a bench outside the shop and draw a punky picture of Tim's band. I make it like a Sex Pistols' postcard photo from the seventies in grey scale, black and white. Sketch two red nailed women's thumbs holding it as though it really is a postcard. Then on another page, I do a revised version of this horrid bronze sculpture in Wissanotti Beach Park. I've been thinking about it since the Aborigine incident last night. The actual statue is enormous with Samuel de Champlain on top, and a second lower tier depicting Native guys in loincloths and head dresses at the feet of a cassock wearing Jesuit priest who holds a cross up like he's conducting an exorcism. I recreate the scene inverting it. Draw a clothed Native guy on top, Champlain and the priests on the bottom in skimpy Euro-Speedos. Stick a pipe in one of the priest's mouths and a roach clip with a feather in his hair.

A white cargo van pulls up to my bench for the opal tour. The back door opens, and an English girl invites me aboard. As we tromp through the depths of mines, I'm reminded of the subterranean tunnels of MNC. That place is like a bad stink trailing around after me. The guide gives us each a mini hammer and leads us to the inside of a cave.

"This is all a bit of a lark. Can't imagine they'd give us the choice pickings," the English girl says.

Pick up my hammer anyway tapping away at the tawny side of the cave next to her. Suddenly, a huge chunk of the wall falls out and she shrieks as though we're in the middle of an *Indiana Jones* style avalanche. Echoing screams dissolve into maniacal laughter when she realizes the over-reaction.

"Providence," I say, encouraging her to whack the chunk. It's nothing but rubble. Guy from Sydney finds a speck of opal and the guide compliments him. He stands a little straighter, a real prospector. I chisel out a line along the bottom edge and sure enough a little flake of opal comes out. It's nearly white.

The guide looks at it. "That's a fine piece of opal. Not much colour, very thin, not worth a whole lot but it'll make a nice piece of jewelry."

We return from the mines where I show my little flake of opal to the woman in the shop. She smiles and tells me white is good for stimulating memory. Perfect. Now I have something special to send Grandma. Buy some wire and jewelry cord to make a necklace while on route to Alice Springs. Figure I better eat something before another long bus ride, so I rustle in my knapsack finding just some crusts and peanut butter dregs. A meager grocery store yields a small piece of very expensive Havarti and a scandalously priced tomato.

"Guess things cost more up here," I say to the checkout girl.

"That's nothing," she says. "You should see prices in the Alice."

March: Three Months Before

S.I.N.

The morning we are supposed to board the coach donated to the cause by the Sanitation Czar, Tracy picks me up in her Dad's French vanilla Lincoln Continental.

"I don't know if I want to do this granny thing," she says.

"You've got the car for it."

"I feel like an imposter. I don't really care *that much*."

"It's for a good cause. Mary's coming. We'll put on some crazy granny costumes and sing some stupid songs. It'll be an adventure, a last hurrah moment to remember me while you're away in Ottawa."

She's not convinced. "C'mon, I have weed."

We collect Mary at her parents' marina and detour to my grandma's condo where we rummage through bagged up clothing and shoes, pillage scarves, hats, broaches and various undergarments. I'm the first to pull on an enormous bra and girdle, stuff it with washcloths and pillowcases. The others follow suit, rendering us Rubenesque in our sixty-plus physiques. It isn't long before Tracy's into Dorothy's cosmetics and provides enthusiastic makeovers. The make-up is mostly ancient, great round trays of peachy powder with accompanying puffs, twist up rouge batons, tubes of ruby lipstick flattened into cylindrical knobs. We're a trio of hookers on a day pass from a brothel for the aged.

To Tracy's delight, I produce a bottle of sherry from a box of unfinished liquor. Mary looks disgusted.

"Mary," I say, "I totally understand if you don't want to drink, no pressure. But I feel this occasion calls for it."

"Can we smoke in here?" Tracy asks.

"On the balcony." I pour sherry in two fancy floral teacups I've unpacked from newsprint and rinsed. If Grandma's watching, she'll be sorry to have missed the fun. The patio chairs on the balcony are stacked and melded together with a layer of dirt and snow so we stand and smoke and sip our syrupy sweet booze in winter coats overtop of granny brown girdles in the wind of the fourth floor.

"Do you think it's safe to smoke-up in front of Mary?"

"What's she gonna do?" Tracy flips her Zippo open, lights first a cigarette and then my joint under a cupped hand in the breeze. "Call the cops? Maybe they'll send Ritchie over and he could join us. By the way, Tim feels real bad about the other night."

I roll my eyes at her sideways, giving her a dirty look.

"What? I was over at Brian's and he popped in for drink. I'm not saying anything! Just giving you the head's up that he's looking to apologize. He was hammered, barely remembers. C'mon." She tugs at my sleeve. "He loves you."

"Brian loves you. Why don't you move in with him have a whole litter of kids? You'll be head cashier at the A&P in no time."

"Touché. Anyways, why aren't you on a plane back to what's his nuts?"

"Come smoke this fatty with us," I call to Mary, poking my head through the sliding glass door, ignoring Tracy's comment even though it sticks under my ribs like a pin in the side of a voodoo doll. Mary sits on the pink satin chesterfield crossing and uncrossing her legs, fiddling with large clip-on pearl earrings from my grandma's stash. By the look on her face you'd think she was waiting for a pap smear.

"Seriously, Mary," I add, "it'll make the bus ride to the city a lot more fun."

Tracy points a finger in my face. "You don't have a ticket because you're chicken," she says, then squishes the butt of her cigarette into snow covered Astroturf. I shrug, she looks at her watch. We slug the remains of our tea-cupped sherry and I stash the bottle in my black patent leather handbag with the big gold clasp.

Dad stands in front of the bus presiding over his flock with his megaphone herding the huddled masses, herding the madding crowd, herding a bunch of lame ass Maraposians up the stairs. His eyes spring out like a shocked cartoon character when he sees us. He shakes his head. "You better talk to your mother."

Mom laughs when she sees us. There's hope yet. Once the coach is in motion, my fearless father leader resumes his position of glory and raises the megaphone to his lips. The noise deafens and reverberates around the bus. Grannies and their consorts shield their ears while my mother tries to shout over top of the megaphone to get his attention, telling him to shut the damn thing off but all she succeeds in doing is contributing to the cacophony of sound screeching, *Dave, Dave, Dave.* Mercifully, he abandons the megaphone and reverts to rhythmic chants about precautionary principles. *It's not enough to assume there no ill effects from burning toxic garbage. Prove it! Deal with your own stinking waste, Toronto. Down with Banbury! Down with McLaughlin! Down with incineration! SIN! SIN! SIN!*

As Dad leads the bus in a round of *If Had a Hammer,* I sit in the back two seats with Mary and Tracy passing around the sherry. Even Mary, in the spirit of the day, accepts and swigs. When Dave begins his next doctored ditty, *Where Have all the Flowers Gone, Covered by Incineration Ashes Everyone,* I slink down on my seat with the bottle of sherry and declare humiliation.

"Oh, you think *this* is embarrassing," says Tracy, "*my dad's* the fucking town Santa Claus."

Queen's Park is more of the same. Dad has printed large caution yellow signs for each of us bearing both the SIN logo, a black-circled building with a belching smokestack, and his company logo. He makes good use of the megaphone, demanding of the Chief Medical Officer of the Provincial Legislature, who is nowhere in sight, *What gives you the right to ignore the concerns of the people you were elected to govern?* Tracy takes hold of me, starts a can-can line linking arms with Mary, my Mom and the others.

By the time we slump back into our seats our intoxicants and made-up faces have begun to fade. Tracy's mascara has racooned her eyes and she's slopped dark sherry down the front of her yellow polka dots. My stuffed boobs are lop-sided. Lipstick bleeds from the corners of Mary's mouth. "Look at us," I say, "we're the *Golden Girls* in the lost crack whore episode."

"Speak for yourself, sweet tits." Tracy stands on her seat, swings Dorothy's long white beaded necklace like a lasso over top of mine and Mary's heads. "SIN! SIN! SIN!" she screams to a bus full of raucous applause.

SHIFT

Aubrey wakes me in the morning with a plate of eggs and toast and a hot mug of mushroom tea, which is a lot more palatable with a spoonful of sugar than chewing a wad of fungus straight up. I look forward to feeling different, to my impending altered thoughts. Whether they free me from my Bardo or not, I believe somehow these drug induced blips of delusion will bring me nearer to a life resolution of sorts.

"Think we're getting any closer?" I ask.

"All I know," says Aubrey, tipping up and draining his mug, "is that I'm seeing shit I've never seen and I like it."

"Me too! But there's this little part of me, maybe left over from health class, that keeps saying, maybe we're clouding our minds instead of opening them. You know?"

"Of course. But it's undeniable, when I'm high I feel greater than my self, connected to everything beyond my physical being in a way I'm unable to reach when not. I don't see how what we're doing is any different than what people have been doing on mystical journeys for centuries. When you finish breakfast let's go check out those hot springs before we pack up and move on. They're supposed to be amazing."

In a fog of sulfur steam, people cling like soaking wet snow monkeys to pool edges, red faced and sweaty. Tranquility lingers low around the pools, a hush of barely murmuring voices. Lights like fluorescent growths of lichen radiate in patches on the tiles and I slip in around them discreetly, toes first, barely making a ripple on the water's surface so as not to draw attention to myself. Aubrey cannonballs over top of me and nearly hits me in the face with his foot. This sets off a chain of snot filled hysterics that have us submerging our faces to quell the laughter and avoiding eye contact for a least half an hour in case we begin again. Serenity seekers are not impressed and soon we have the whole pool end to ourselves. Our laughter finally contained, we paddle around a little and I'm reminded of our first meeting in that pool in Alice Springs. I throw my arms around his neck, my legs around his middle. He waltzes me through the shallow water until I float by sculling underneath my back with cupped hands to keep my body level with the surface.

Aubrey stands at my head, grips either side of my neck on my shoulders immobilizing my head like a lifeguard or massage therapist. He walks around the hot springs pool with my floating body following his elliptical path. As he walks, he crouches under me massaging the muscles along my spine. In the relaxed state of my body, the altered state of my mind, I hear a benevolent voice. See a face looking vaguely like Byron Williams', then not, then like a yellow happy-face icon, then like a smiling Buddha. You've *done it,* the disembodied, ethereal voice says. Oh, great voice, I want to believe you, but I don't understand what it is that I've done. The giant smiling face just smiles, its apple cheeks look like they might burst from glee. *Don't be so coy*, Serena, it seems to say. But I don't know. All great and knowing face, tell me, please. The face laughs.

"What's so funny?" asks Aubrey.

I didn't know that I was laughing.

"Fuck it," says Aubrey, lying in our tent on the coast of Vancouver Island after days of driving and a week of cold ocean surfing. "We've got to finish this journey. Let's go north to the Yukon. We've come this far."

From the trunk, I produce the dowsing rods. "When in doubt, ask the universe." I walk with a rubber handled copper rod in each hand like I'm holding two mini hockey sticks out in front of myself. Okay, grandma, now's your chance, gimmee the big finish here. Nothing. Walk toward the ocean expecting the rods to waver, to cross, something, anything. I turn and walk another direction. Nothing. I fake it. "Look, Aubrey! You're right! It's fated. To the Yukon we shall go."

"Nice try. That's south."

Stupid things. Didn't want my dad to be right. I really wanted the dowsing rods to pull me in some direction, so I didn't have to make, and take responsibility for, the decision myself. And why haven't I heard from grandma? Or have I and am just not intuitive enough to interpret the message?

"We're gonna be camping," I say. "You all right with the whole bear thing?"

"I'm over it, babe. I've made peace with the forest sharks."

Don't know that I'm convinced. Suppose it's worth the risk. Maybe dowsing is bullshit. Maybe Aubrey's full of it too. We're all full of it, a bunch of liars covering up for being scared, plastering layers over our vulnerabilities. There may be no safety in bear country, but we all are safe. Transmigration here I come.

So, we head north to the Yukon or wherever the rainbow leads us. The coastline with its rugged trees is novel at first then blurs into highway tedium interrupted mercifully outside of Whistler by a series of red plywood hearts increasing in size. The largest, nailed to a tree on the edge of the road, has a pink painted arrow urging us to turn right off the main track and into unmarked territory, onto two stripes of matted grass a tire's width apart. A further heart, deeper on into the forest says, *summer love*. Forty-five minutes this side of nowhere a sign the size of a table-top reads: *welcome to the summer love rave*.

A girl in cut off jean shorts with high Joni Mitchell cheekbones and black hair down to her ass leans on the open window. Patchouli wafts in.

"Heeyy, welcome summer lovers. I'm Miranda, twenty bucks a head."

Aubrey and I look at each other. I nod. We need to save our money for gas and food. He shows her the brown Winnipeg lump and says, "Would you take a chunk of hash for the both of us?"

"Umm. Just a sec." She calls for Hugo a couple of times, but no one comes. She turns back and asks to see the hash. Picks a

morsel off with her fingernail, eats it and looks us over thoughtfully. "What the hell. Okay." Miranda reaches into her tight
front pocket and wiggles out an embroidered pouch. With a
hooked finger, nails painted lilac, she coaxes out from the sack
two heart-shaped candies, tablets, I guess. "E?" She holds them
in her palm for us to take.

Aubrey plucks them from her hand, allows me to select one,
then taps mine with his and says cheers as we place them on our
tongues. A shaggy guy with sun-kissed waves of brownish hair,
sloppy blue shorts and a plaid flannel shirt with the sleeves ripped
off, runs over, scoops Miranda up off the ground. He smells of
sweat, not B.O. but clean, wet sweat. I can smell it from the car.
She laughs as he spins her into a twirl of silky straight hair and
toasted brown limbs. Hugo. An Aussie.

"Better get your gear set up now before the E kicks in," he
says with an accent that makes us smile. Sets Miranda down and
gestures with both arms as though landing a plane the direction
in which we are to park the car.

Through the parting of trees lies a field of colourful tents
arranged in a horseshoe around a stage. We heed Hugo's advice
and immediately set up our tent in the timothy hay a few metres
from another couple with a yellow dome. The sweet scent of
fresh grass is all around us as we break the stalks and trample it
flat, the electric hum of afternoon cicadas sizzling in the air. As
the sunny day darkens into Saturday night, the field swells with
people jostling between tears and laughter. Shrill with dampened
inhibitions, the voices echo madness in the quiet of the forest like
a secret witches' coven, intoxicated and sublime.

We dance like my former clients with their tongues out in
the rain, reminding us all that our collective façade of normality
is exhausting, though even in my heightened condition I'm
aware this state is one of pretend. A real MNC client can't pretend anything. But what a wondrous state it is. I've never been
so unguarded. All of us here are unguarded for the fearful cannot
feel a love like this. A tangle of arms, of legs and torsos entwine
and throb to the beat, to the rhythm of the stage. We are primordial goo, writhing together, amoebas under a microscope, all of

us participants none of us spectators in this dance, we are one heart pumping for the whole world. Our eyes, Aubrey's and mine, our selves are so connected, so much love radiates between us I could open my cage of ribs, take my heart out, serve it to him on a silver platter. He presses into me, I into him, we two kissing and unkissing rippling together across the grass in gratitude, in beatitude, in acceptance of the oneness of god's love.

By noon, most of the revelers have recovered and emerge from nylon and polyester cocoons depleted, stumbling around, foggy headed, rough or retching. We chat with Miranda and Hugo by the water table in front the stage, empty now except for a knocked over lawn chair, an upturned stool, drained and scattered beer and vodka bottles. Aubrey tells them we're heading north to the Yukon, Miranda claps her hands, gives a little jump.

"You have to go to the Great Bear Rainforest. My grandparents are Nuxalk. I used to hang out with them near Bella Coola, they got these giant fucking trees, man. And spirit bears. Gotta see those fuckers, they'll blow your mind."

This new direction to our journey takes us off route from driving straight up to the Yukon via Prince George, to backtracking along the coast and negotiating a tangle of back roads. Some paved, most dirt or gravel. As we near the Great Bear Rainforest, nestled between the Pacific Ocean and the mountain range, we see pockets of clear cuts. It's as though a nuclear bomb exploded and left a red and brown circular burn in the Amazon of the north.

While Aubrey drives, I read aloud the Parks Canada literature which explains spirit bears are not albino but are a subspecies of black bear that are actually blonde. They're created by a recessive gene both parents must possess, causing one in ten bears to be born blonde.

One foot on the dock of the outfitter's at the water's edge, one in the centre of the rear cockpit of the rented orange tandem kayak, I check in with Aubrey. "Are you okay to do this, you know with your bear thing?"

He karate chops his right hand into the palm of his left. "Gotta do it. Nothing to fear but yourself, right?"

Wordlessly, we paddle through silent water, weaving under trees and dangling mosses and vines. Think of the park ranger in Banff saying a bear's nose can detect a piece of chewing gum in glove box. If a bear's around, it already knows we're here. Seeing a spirit bear is unlikely, but something in me knows better and so we paddle. We follow the curve of the land, close as we can from our kayak and look up into hills of rich, dark soil the scent of sulfur, bacteria and rot rife with each inhalation. There are things at work in this forest that I scarcely understand.

Then, on the edge of the shore, we see a small black cub digging for roots. Further up the hill in among the trees there is a full-grown vanilla furred mother. It stops, freezes, catches our eyes. Its head follows the boat, synchronizing with us. Watches us as we float with snout raised, ears flattened.

Aubrey whispers, "It's you Serena. There you are, pale and precious and rare."

The bear turns from us, and with her cub, the two retreat from the water, fur and fat undulating in waves along their backs as they tromp down the backside of the earthy hill.

We gravel road it again for a few hours before camping overnight and loading up on food and water in Prince George, heading out north the next day to a Provincial Park in the mountains. Aubrey's stiff jaw betrays muffled tension. He's determined to go through with it. I couldn't stop it if I tried. The terrain is rough, the campsites rustic and sparse. Wood platforms are built for tents in lieu of flat, soft ground. Around us, nothing but mountains, rocks, trees and sky.

As evening falls, he scrubs and burns all traces of our dinner stew from the dishes, from the picnic table and from the campsite lest a bear be sniffing downwind. When night seeps in, I lie with hands crossed at my chest, corpse in coffin style, on my sleeping bag in the tent. Thinking I'm asleep, Aubrey mills around the campsite drinking Kokanee and muttering death threats to any would-be bears. I drift asleep eventually but wake a few hours later to his shouting.

"Where are you, you fucking bastard!"

The night breeze ripples the nylon flaps, scurries between the bottom of the tent and the wooden platform.

"Show yourself!"

I unzip the mesh door to witness a bout of full-blown bearanoia.

As soon as you try to exercise control over that which is not yet formed, you're fucked. How do you explain that to someone deep in the act of? Guess the best you can hope for is to help them see themselves: "Hey, Tripper. What's goin' on out here?"

He holds my knife in one hand, wood-chopping hatchet in the other. I see a caricature of a bionic lobster looking over at me, the clear whites of his eyes shining like tribal beads in the full-lighted moon.

"I'm gonna beat this fucker at its own game. I can hear it. I can smell it." I pull on some warm clothes and step out. He paces in front of our tent like a worried dog. How did I become the voice of reason here?

Traces of foreign humans interrupt the black silence of wilderness that surrounds us, bone-crunching gravel under tires, the dying of an engine, headlights beaming streams of yellow onto our site. Two gun-toting park rangers in brown and tan uniforms climb out of the old green truck. They seem surprised to see us.

"Evenin'," says the young guy holding out his hand to me. "I'm Ryan, this is Ted." The skinny guy nods at me. Aubrey drops his hatchet on the picnic table bench to free a hand for shaking. "Don't want to alarm you but a problem grizzly bear has been spotted in the vicinity in the last twenty-four hours."

"*Problem grizzly* bear?" says Aubrey.

Sitting on the edge of the table, Ted adjusts his shotgun. "Bears got all kinds of personalities; you got yer Mr. Rogers bears and you got yer Charlie Manson bears. This one's got Charles Manson written all over it and a taste for human garbage to boot." Ted tugs open his utility belt to remove a mini- flashlight, the rip of Velcro echoes. In the absence of other noises, it sounds out of place like the drop of a glass on the stone floor of a church.

Ted apologizes, shines his light around the corners of our camp-site. "Wanted to make sure you haven't seen any unusual bear activity." Looks into the distance and sniffs the air.

Aubrey hands them each a cold beer. They look at each other, Ted checks his watch, says, "It's 'leven o'clock." They twist off the caps and skip them into the fire.

The flush of agitation from Aubrey's face begins to pale, his oscillating pupils settle. He seems relieved by the company or maybe it's the guns. With me they have the opposite effect. Maybe it's the Canadian in me. Aubrey mimes the action of lighting the pipe without the rangers seeing him, wanting me to rummage around in the trunk and get our gear. Plucks his guitar in front of the fire and I know he has begun to woo them, through Orpheus ways, hoping they'll stay as long as possible.

Ted kicks the tires of the Tempo. "You guys got one of the most remote drive-in camp sites, nice." Casually, I puff the pipe and pass it to him. Aubrey smiles and strums his guitar.

Ted takes a massive haul, exhales. "May as well, have to be up all night anyhow, don't want any accidental maulings. Likely won't see 'im. Would've waited 'til morning but now that we know you folks are here, wouldn't be right to walk away."

"How long you been playing guitar?" Ryan asks, his voice dripping with admiration. "I play a bit myself. Drum sometimes at Pow Wow." Aubrey passes the guitar to him, shows him a lick or two.

"Are both those shotguns?" I ask.

Ted's pleased by the attention, however feigned the interest may be. "One's a shotgun, one's a tranq fulla dope darts."

"If you see the bear, which are you supposed to use?"

"One we're after is a boar, a male grizz approximately 800 to 1000 pounds. There's a sow roaming these woods too but she's not been any problem. Ideally, we tranq it but bears are tricky characters, can run up to fifty-five Ks an hour. So if push comes to shove, I'd shoot 'im." Aubrey stops playing. Ted swills the rest of his beer. "Wouldn't bother with a shot to the head. Bullet could ricochet right off that thick skull. Forget the heart. Can still function even with a hole. Gotta go for the spine, cripple it."

"Really?" I look to Ryan for confirmation.

"Don't ask me. I grew up downtown Vancouver. Ted's your guy. I study botony at UBC. This is my summer gig, field experience and all that." He turns back to Aubrey, asks something else about music.

Another beer or two later, Ted catches Ryan's eye and nods toward the trail leading down the mountainside from our campsite. He shines the flashlight down the path and motions for Ryan to pick up his gun.

"Thanks for your hospitality, but we've got a bear to catch." In the orange haze of the fire, I see that Ted is slightly older than Ryan and maybe just a little older than us.

"Mind if we tag along?" asks Aubrey as he eyes the guns.

The rangers look at each other and shrug. Ted says, "Don't see why not. Like I said, we probably won't catch him, let alone see him. May as well pass the time. You gonna bring some beers and that pipe a yours?"

Aubrey stuffs a daypack with cans of Kokanee, swings it over his back. The fire crackles in sections, smolders in others, it will burn on like that for hours. The smell of ash rises in the air and settles in my lungs. I could wait here staring into the flames, conjuring bear images from beyond, I could fall asleep in the tent, run into the car if the grizzly sniffed me out. But what the Christ kind of story would that be to tell?

We step from the cleared campsite falling in line behind one another onto a roughly hewn trail. Ted leads the way followed by Ryan, then me, then Aubrey. With the moon hovering, the glow of the fire pit behind, it seems as though we could be leaving the earth's surface, entering some dark underworld, though the smell of loam and rusty pine is grounding. As we head deep and deeper into the wild, the path begins to thicken, as if the guy who started trimming branches just gave up and turned back. But we shall not be thwarted with such ease: we've got bear on the brain. All thoughts have turned to us and them. Like the Peruvians in Tucume, we relentlessly pursue our phantom terrorizer. We climb over fallen cedars and attempt civility by holding branches so they don't spring back and hit the next guy in the face. Ted pauses to adjust the strength of his headlamp and judging by the length of time, we're about two kilometers down the trail.

Then Ted points. "Bear activity. Look at these torn up roots."

Sure enough, the ground looks as though it's been tilled. He offers his flashlight to Aubrey, takes a big swig of Ryan's beer and points to a tree nearby. "Signpost number two. Look at the claw and bite marks. Yep. Scat too. Crazy Charlie's been here."

Aubrey's feet shuffle audibly on the forest floor. My adrenalin surges: no matter how many times I try to stuff it down, to placate my fear, *there's no problem* my mind repeats like a mantra, *there are four of us, we have guns.* My body won't listen to my brain. Blood thumps in my head like waves crashing against the hull of a doomed ship.

Though no one has spoken, Ted shushes. We continue walking, Ted stops abruptly. Shines his headlamp at the ground. About twenty-five metres ahead there is an enormous open-mouthed bear crouched on all fours with oak brown fur, ivory teeth in the fog of false light, a bristled hump on his back, the smell of sweat-soaked brute all around. The Charles Manson grizzly. His ears flatten, he rears on his haunches, thrusts his snout to the heavens. He must be ten feet tall. Claws like steak knives on the end of huge, furry boxing gloves. He doesn't growl. He snuffles, drops to all fours and charges.

"Holy fuck," screams Ryan as he sinks to one knee and struggles to load his tranquilizer gun. Shots ring out from Ted. Bang. Deafening echo of destruction. Bang, desperation, self-preservation. Bang, bang, bang. The charging bear tumbles head over heels somersaulting toward us. Greatness topples and death splays out upon his back, legs flopped open in an undignified heap. Don't die, my mind whispers. The bear answers, *How could I die?* Don't leave, I whisper. *Don't be silly,* he says, *where would I go?*

The guys approach with silent caution. My feet are glued to dirt that covers the corpse of everything that ever lived. I move my lips to speak, stutter incomprehensible word-like sounds, cry like a stupid girl. Aubrey pulls my face to him and I hear his heart knocking against his chest. Slowly, we move closer to the kill and see our bear's black gums, his long yellow fangs, his dark eyes still open like a stiff on a morgue drawer in some crappy cop show. His fur seems more cinnamon in this light than brown. Pools of black ooze at each wound's hole and puddle in the soil beneath our feet.

"And so she goes. Sorry, old-timer," Ted says, taking his pulse. He pauses a moment or two to record some information into his pocket spiral notebook. Ushers us quickly back to the campsite.

"We'll be back first thing tomorrow to haul the body out. Gotta take it to the ministry for some forensic work." They hop in the truck and disappear.

Rangers and conservation authorities descend upon us the next day in a swarm of kahki, brown and army green. ATVs and trucks, chainsaws, tools and body bags. Cigarette smoke and deep voices go on about their day as if innocence had not been murdered here last night. And we sit at a picnic table watching, drinking Red Rose tea out of black speckled enamelware, complicit.

Ted plops down beside me at the table. Rests his forearms in front of himself and lights a cigarette. Offers me one. I take it and move over enough to make space.

"That bear must be close to eight hundred pounds," Aubrey says. "How the hell are they gonna get it out of here? Will they have to use a helicopter of something?"

"If he were alive, yeah, but at this point we'll just quarter him and drag 'im out section by section with the ATV. There's a proper trail about five feet from where we found 'im. Guess we got a little off course in the dark last night. Funny how that happens. May never even have seen the fucker had we not done the bushwackin'."

He stubs out his smoke on a rock, flicks it into the fire pit. Says he'll pop by later with Ryan to further debrief and winks at us. The first ATV crests the hill into our campsite. I can't stand watching another minute so I grab the sleeve of Aubrey's coat and pull him with me toward the car and drive us both to Lake Babine for the day.

Early evening brings Ted and Ryan back around. Ryan slings a soft cooler bag from the bed of the truck over his shoulder. Ted repeats the action with a second bag, sets it on the picnic table and unzips the top.

"Cold beer?" Ted presses a can into each of our hands.

Ryan stokes the fire. Aubrey stretches his legs out on my grandma's wool blanket, leans back against a large log and fiddles away on his guitar. Ryan returns from the truck with a set of bongos and soon the night air is filled with wood smoke and the repetitious rhythm of Ryan's hands slapping skins.

Ted sits on a rock and tosses a spent butt into the flames. "We have a couple of things for you guys. If you're interested. You go first there, young Ryan."

Ryan digs into the breast pocket of his flannel coat pulling out a palm full of rolled joints or cigarettes or something, then produces a two litre plastic pop bottle from his cooler bag that's filled with mucky brown liquid.

Aubrey and I look at each other, clueless.

"Ayahuasca," Ryan says, like we should know what that means. "My buddy just came back from a research trip in South America, somewhere in the Amazon. It's really big in Brazil and Peru right now. People there call it vine of the souls, gatekeeper of the spiritual realm. My Buddy's got connections to some Peruvians downtown. It's made from a plant that when the stems and leaves are brewed together becomes psychoactive. You drink it and it's supposed to take you out of this world. Heard of peyote?" We nod. "Like that. So you drink this brew, then you smoke these but you're supposed to blow the smoke in each other's faces, don't inhale, puff like a cigar. I've never done it myself but since I was gonna be out in the boonies all summer I thought I may as well give it a try. Then Ted and I got to talking and we figured safety in numbers."

Ryan pours us each a paper cup full of grainy liquid. The taste is not unpleasant, sort of fruity and charred and it leaves a leaf-like residue on your tongue and in the cup, like the sludge at the bottom of a cup of loose-leaf tea. He passes out spliffs and lights his own. Last week I was a bear in a Bateman print, tonight I'm gonna be a Dali.

Ted downs his cup and with one of the joints hanging out of his mouth, purposefully unfolds a package wrapped in newspaper. I let the smoke and juice settle in me and stare up to where the stars seem pinpricks in some permeable membrane I keep trying to peek through.

"Guess what I got here?" Ted asks. He opens the paper and shows around a large grey-purple veined lump. "The heart of the grizzly we shot the other day. When Ryan told me about that super juice he got, I figured we ought to make a ritual or ceremony or something for all of us together. That's how this shit is meant to be consumed. And we shared a pretty critical moment. I mean it's not like I go around offing bears all the time. Fuck. I hate killing things. But I'd rather kill something and save two or four or more lives, no? Anyhow, we need to honour the spirit of the grizz. We were all present. Ancient Indigenous custom dictates that we eat the heart of the animal we've killed. We need to show respect."

We all stare at Ryan. He plays his bongos, doesn't look up. Can't tell if he's entranced or ignoring us on purpose. Aubrey who's been finger picking, sets his guitar aside.

"Not just respect," Ted continues, "but, so that we take on the strength of the animal, make it a part of us. Some tribes would eat the heart of the enemy. The killer in you is the killer in me kind of deal."

Ryan slaps his bongos once hard and stops. "No one does that shit, Ted." He resumes a steady rhythm, increasingly faster paradiddles.

"You ever seen a heart?" Ted flops the fist of muscle onto a cast iron frying pan. "Shit." He pats himself down. "Forgot a knife."

I pass him my good ol' red Swiss Army knife. He uses the blade to saw through the fibrous flesh, cutting it into four. It falls open into the wide pan. Ted crouches by the fire, finds a flat piece of smoldering wood on which to place the pan. Blood and fat drip and crackle.

"Ryan! Want some ketchup for yours?"

"I told you I'm not eating that, Ted."

The heart sizzles in the pan, its juices bubbling as it heats through. Ted stabs a quarter of the heart with the tip of my knife, holds to my nose. "Ladies first."

The piece drops into my palm and I juggle it back and forth until it cools, raise it to my lips. It's tinny, like when you lose a tooth or bite your cheek, it tastes of your own spilled blood. I manage to chew and swallow some. Throw the last bite, when Ted's not looking, into the fire.

He asks me how it tastes, wipes juices from the corner of his mouth with his shirtsleeve. "Offal," I say and laugh to myself.

"Aren't we supposed to cook a hundred metres from our campsite?" Aubrey's jaw pumps mechanically as he chews his piece of heart.

"Don't worry. We got back-up." Ted points to the two guns stowed under the picnic table.

Suddenly I'm hyperaware of the feel of the inside of my mouth, warm and wet, the smooth ridges of the insides of my teeth against my tongue. I'm at once centered and elevated. I attempt to slow the rampant brain activity with a drink from my water bottle, though stopping the flood of thoughts proves futile.

Jason and I tried to meditate together once. He said picture a box inside your mind. Inside that box is another box, and another and another until inside the last tiny inner box there is a key. The key was supposed to unlock something, I can't remember. Was it supposed to unlock a door? Inside my head there are doors. Door after door after door, flinging open one after another as I race through. I'm in a building. A building like the MNC. A hospital with corridors, double white doors as though constructed of giant feathered angel's wings that flap together open and shut as if they've been waiting twenty-one years to welcome me.

Ted stands, rocking between the balls of his feet and heels in front of the fire. He nearly loses balance once and I see him walk through flames in my mind. See a mammoth snake lying coiled in the coals, bursting into a hundred tiny glowing vipers. Aubrey's fingers fly up and down along the guitar strings, a maniacal muse of the spirit of song. The steady drumming of the bongos accelerates my heartbeat, tribal and wild. Can feel, can see my blood pulse through my veins into my hands. Nausea looms, I ache for darkness, to be hidden in cool solitude.

No one notices as I slip away from the fire. Leaves of emerald glass drip shiny drops from the bottom tree branches, creating an archway over the forest path. A knotty twisted branch morphs into a curling finger: *come this way Serena.* Then a whisper in the breeze: *come this way.* So I do. And then I'm running, running. Running wild with abandon, stopping only once to scratch my back along a tree. Drop to all fours. Dart between trees, deeper now, farther, jumping branches, climbing over logs. I'm no longer on any known trail but am one with the forest floor. Through ancient memory, I divine my way, weaving around trees to avoid collision. Digging at the ground, standing tall on my haunches unrestrained, sniffing and bellowing with the strength of my spirit into the blackness. Loping on all fours amid the rotting humus. Heading for solitary darkness, a womb, a cave. Thoughts of warmth. And then, no thoughts at all.

August: Ten Months Before

CHOP WOOD, CARRY WATER

Another week and still no flight. No letter to Natalie sent. Tonight, instead of going directly home, I veer off at the top of the hill near our street and coast down to a dead-end boat launch at Lake Wissanotti. Sheltered from the street by giant overhanging cedars, it's the perfect place to postpone life. It's not that I'm avoiding Dave and Margaret, just that I need to decompress a bit from work before attempting to perform a caricature of a pleasant dinner companion. Sitting on the grassy bank, I fire up a butt, watching the water trickle out of the culvert pipe pooling into concentric circles before it eventually becomes part of the lake.

When Tracy and I were in grade four, we watched a National Film Board presentation called *Paddle to the Sea.* It's about some kid who carves a wooden guy in a canoe and drops it into Lake Superior. The whole movie you're supposed to learn your geography by watching this boat travel via current through the Great Lakes water system to its final launch into the ocean as it sails past Newfoundland and into the North Atlantic all the way to France. Trace and I loved the idea of dropping something in the water and having it whisked away by forces greater than ourselves. We'd save our apples from lunch and race them through the gutter from the top of the hill down into Lake Wissanotti. As the spring runoff water swept them along, we'd try to outrun them, and each other. Would try to pick them up and bite them before they shot out of the culvert into the lake.

The rusting, blue metal garbage can at the water's edge overflows with beer cans and liquor bottles. It's not exactly a secret hideout. I used to come here to drink with Tim. We fucked here in the beginning too. Waist deep in water on a hot July afternoon, stoned and drunk, my bikini wasn't much of an obstacle. He lifted me, entered, thrust a few times, pulled out and groaned. I guessed it was over.

What the hell was that with Marty? Tim, we're usually so drunk we just pass out naked in his bed. Feels like they're both trying to stick their claws into me, trapping me here. And with Jason? Well, it's always so unselfish in the beginning when both sides want to please. Then something happens when people think they aren't getting what they deserve and the newness has worn off and everything takes more effort and misguided bitterness and resentment about who did what or didn't do what sets in and by then who even wants to bother.

The house smells of something dead roasting in the oven. Mom smiles, says, "You're home late," and places a bottle of low fat Italian dressing on the table. There is a spot set for me.

"Sorry. Hope you weren't waiting."

"Of course we waited."

The prodigal daughter returns. I pinch a radish slice from the salad. "Can I help?" The Mariposa News Packet sits beside the teak bowl on the island. My dad insists on reading both the News Packet and the Times Herald. Says that the News Packet is for entertainment and the Times Herald for news. A huge picture of Gerry Burton, also from my grade at school, holding a hammer and a toonie on the front page. The headline reads, *Local Man Proves Toonie's Worth*. What a maroon. Sitting in his parents' basement trying to whack the centers out of the new two-dollar coin.

Mom calls Dad away from the television.

"Where have you been?" Mom scoops a blob of skin flecked mashed potato—extra heart healthy fiber—on my plate. "We've been worried."

"I don't know, Mom. Just out with Tracy and stuff. Sorry, I should have called," I say. Bite my saucy chicken leg and avoid looking either of them in the eye.

"How was the world of work today?" Dad changes the subject.

"The usual: snot, piss and shit."

He frowns. I know I'm supposed to be polite, but maybe I just want them to be uncomfortable with the collective complacency everyone has about what goes on out there. Like somehow, it's okay.

"Will you stay on there this fall?" He sets his fork down.

"I'm going to Australia."

"Australia?" He nods to my mother.

"Australia's a long ways away," she says.

"So, you're quitting then?"

I nod.

"Business." Dad wags his finger at me. "I always said, go into business."

"I know business grads who have their walls plastered with rejection slips. No one I know has a *decent* job. Tracy's at the A&P, Marty and I are at MNC. Gerry Burton's hitting toonies with a hammer in his basement."

He laughs and we eat for a while.

Then Mom says, "Jason called." I stare at the grease pooling under my chicken part. "He asked how you were. He said you still owe him for the utility bill."

Push the fork into my potatoes. Dad says, "I only studied business myself to start the printing company. When that flourished, I was able to expand and develop a graphics division, then a sign department. I still have to make my birdhouses on the weekend."

"Why should I do something I hate just to make money?"

"Because that's what adults do."

Mom is silent. Her crinkled mouth lines show concern as if she wants to be on both our sides. "Speaking of birdhouses, dad has some very exciting news!"

Turns out some gallery guy from the McMichael is all hot for his folk-art birdhouses and wants my dad to stage a full-on installation this fall. He's pumped. I hear about his Dr. Seuss-inspired purple martin condo and a variety of other more aesthetically adventurous houses. Then his tone changes: "Look, dear," he says, "the trouble is, you approach life with the idea of the world as it should be, not as it is."

"Nobody wants you to do something you hate," mom says. "But you need money to live. There are many things in which you can find pleasure. Service, for example. There is pleasure in giving of yourself."

I paint a picture in my mind of Jimmy Birchbark stuffing his face and choking at the dinner table with ten-dollar bills.

Is it me? Am I the insane one? No. Insane is what I'd see in Toronto walking to and from the apartment I shared with Jinglenuts near Portugal Village. Old Portuguese women built like panini buns in striped housedresses, sensible aprons tied around tubular waists attempting to sweep every wet leaf from their porches even though the next hour would deposit more and then more still. And when the snow came, they'd be out sweeping with the same dirty wet corn broom. That's insane. Of course, Jason disagreed. He said the women were Zen-like, joyfully undertaking daily chores in the moment. I said they didn't look very happy. I said they desire perfection and therefore will suffer. Not to mention they seek external measurement of their worth by others, they've got a bad case of sweeping up with Joneses, I said. Suppose I was just being contrary. Or maybe we were both kind of right. And now he's trying to hunt me down at my parents' for fifty bucks worth of utility usage.

I call Tracy. She says I've got bigger problems. She says that Tim is telling everyone we're together and that he's going to ask me to come on tour with the Frenzy.

So here I am again counting the black dots in the ceiling tiles above my bed. I punch fluff my pillow, flip-flop in the covers. I'm an idiot. I thought Tim and I were doing the summer fool-around thing like always. Wish I could disappear, levitate from my bed and evaporate, transmigrate maybe. Jinglenuts would say that I can't transmigrate until I've ceased to desire. If desire burns when death, metaphorical or otherwise occurs, another flame is lit and on and on I'll go suffering for all eternity. The only way to halt the burning is to stop fanning the flames of desire. Guess I'll just have to stop wanting and be happy. Ha. What a laugh. Damn you Buddha and your Noble Truths. Now, how am I going to mop my way out of this pile of crap.

August: Ten Months Before

GRAVITY

Margaret knocks on my door at six AM. Must have set her alarm to catch me before work. Wraps her lavender robe tight around her waist and stands in the doorway. Earlobe length platinum hair is rumpled and perpendicular to her scalp in places. Pursing her lips, asks me if I'm able to visit Grandma today because she's been a little off lately, mixed-up.

Why the urgency? She's always been like that. Never stopped her from playing bridge or taking bus trips to Broadway shows or casinos. Margaret's face bears an accusatory squish of concern. Folds her arms over her chest, which I take to imply that I am selfish and irresponsible. Wish she'd spit out what she really thinks. Anyway, I *like* visiting Grandma Dorothy. She lives in a condo near the institution. Mom's right, though, I've been too busy lately trying to make myself invisible.

Marty waves me down from the steps of the admin building. Says, "Wanna go for lunch?"

"Ahhh, sure," I say, unsure.

Park my bike, take a deep breath, stretch my arms up toward the big ol' yolk of a sun rising over the water in the east and try to suck in the last five seconds of fresh air before I cross the locked door threshold. Ken and Candice are subbing for Tom and Lillian. It's hard to keep track of everybody when people are taking irregular vacation days all summer long. There's a conference underway led by Roseanne from the night shift. Ken's slumped on the couch watching TV and giggling along with the laugh track of a sitcom. The high volume echoes through the ward like the laugh track is in sync with my life.

Roseanne, wearing large, dangling cow earrings, peers out over her rectangle reading glasses and continues. "Edgar tried to sneak into Lenny's room again last night. We locked the doors for the safety of the others."

Candice raises her eyebrows at me, smirks.

"Also, be aware that Maurice and Bobbie have been hiding feces in their room under the door. We think it is to consume at a later date." Roseanne passes around the clipboard for us to initial. I throw it on the couch beside Ken, nicking his knee. I hesitate, thinking maybe I should apologize. He doesn't look away from the tube. Stretches blindly for the clipboard, pulls it to his lap and scribbles. Wonder how long he's worked on this ward? He's as institutionalized as any guy around here, and joy of joys, we're on cleaning duty together.

Ken's thinning white-streaked hair, Brylcreamed to perfection, makes me think he's fiftyish. The *piece de résistance* of his ensemble is the mesh back, foam front ball cap covered in little pins beside him on the couch. I sit down next to him to get a better look. There's a Canadian flag, a helicopter, a white rose, a bulldog, a John Deere tractor, a cat. If I get up and start cleaning, he's going to sit here and watch TV and there's no fucking way I'm gonna be his cleaning bitch.

"Ken, that's quite a hat you got there. You like pins, eh?"

"Sure do. I'm eclectic. Know what that means? Means I like to collect stuff." He slowly rises from the couch like an old man and plods along toward the storage cupboard. I am conscious of each time he lifts his foot from the ground, moves his leg forward and sets it down again. I should have gotten the damn supplies myself. At least Lillian is not decrepit. At this rate, cleaning the bathrooms is going to take all day and Ken doesn't seem to care a whit.

He stops after toilet number three, unfastens a pin from his hat. Places a gold, Asian-type cat in my palm. "My wife, she loved cats. Gave this one to me for Christmas last year before she took sick."

Stare at the kitty in my hand waving his one paw back and forth at me, tick, tock, tick, tock. "I like the way its paw moves."

Pins it back to his cap. "It's an original."

Start my next toilet. Ken's sadness floats around us in the room, smoke too thick to ignore. "Your wife make out okay?"

"Cancer took her, same as it done her mama ten years previous."

"I'm so sorry." What am I supposed to say to that? Wish I was the kind of person who'd drop her cleaning brush and give him a hug instead of continuing to mutely ream the dirty toilet hole.

Ken sniffs, wipes his nose on the back of his hand and resumes his chores.

For Christmas one year, Jinglenuts gave me *The Tibetan Book of the Dead*. Not exactly romantic, but it served to prove his intellect and, I suppose, he felt mine needed proving as well. I read it cover to cover because I still loved him then. There's a section about Bardo, a transitional existence, an 'in-between-state' when your body's died but you haven't moved on to your next life or next birth or whatever because you're unable to sort out your metaphysical shit. Starting to feel like my life up to this point has been, continues to be, a kind of Bardo. Makes me think, too, that maybe some of these boundaries we create about life and death, ourselves and others are really kind of artificial. Like, in here, it's all about survival, pretending that we're not all eating, excreting, humping, crying animals screaming for what we want.

The third time I almost died, I felt as though I was above myself looking down, like watching a movie of myself in an instant of my life. I was only three and could never have articulated it, but it was as though I could exist for a moment in the physical and metaphysical world at the same time. Looking down, I saw myself in a yellow party dress sitting at a kid's sized table eating cake with other children smiling, laughing, chocolate in our teeth. One kid has two party hats on his head like giant ears. I point and giggle, cake spilling from my mouth. Suddenly my eyes bulge and water, and I grab my neck. Jake Gibson's mom rushes over wearing a panicked face. Lifts me off my feet, slaps my back and a neon green Lifesaver hurtles from my mouth. The two of us crumple to the floor, she white as icing, me red-blotched and wheezing, tiny hands clenched at my throat. The party stops like a still shot, each child's face betrays ancient wisdom, a recognition of the gravity of what has passed.

Funny I remember the Lifesaver was green. I remember crying too, not because I was scared, though I was, I was more afraid that Mrs. Gibson would call my mother who would then scold me for bad manners. Turns out she did call, later, only to weep and swear up and down she'd never again bake Lifesavers into a cake.

Jason never tired of that story. He'd introduce me to people by saying, *I'd like you to meet Serena, she almost died once choking on a Lifesaver.* Mr. Graduate Student of Religious Studies, adept at stealing others' Zen quotations and working them casually into conversations, missed the point entirely by focusing on the whole obvious Lifesaver irony. The story had nothing to do with choking on a piece of candy and everything to do with the part of me that was able to watch myself living. That was the point. Grounding myself in the raw, realness of life, the ugly truth of inhabiting a physical being seems the only way to keep myself connected to conscious reality sometimes, to tie the tail of the kite that I am, to the bumper of a transport truck.

Marty waits for me at the door of the basement archives smiling a little, almost bashful. He bounds down the first few stairs, grabbing my hand and looking up at me. I stare into him, squeeze his hand and release. Maybe I could do this Marty thing. Maybe he's just what I need.

"Here we go, Serena, confidential." Waves a manila folder in my face. I snatch it. We stand so close, close enough that I could lick his face if I felt like it. The folder contains files of various clients and lists some proposed reasons for mental incapacity. IQ of eleven, IQ unable to assess, mother hypoglycemic, mother alcoholic, incorrect chromosomes, infantile hydrocephalous, profoundly autistic, cerebral hypoxia, hit on the head with a lead pipe. On and on, insane, simple, idiot, afflicted with idiocy, the labels are type written in black and white and backed by medical authorities in a vain attempt to categorize and isolate perceived defectives.

"How do they even come up with a number like IQ of eleven?" I say. Marty doesn't answer. Buries his face in my hair, inhales. The files spill from their folder, a hundred paper moths each stained with a life sentence flutter to the ground. When I bend to collect them, Marty stops me, arms looping round my middle. This decisiveness, like his high cheekbones, becomes him and I imagine him in ten years besuited and lawyerish. Where will I be, what will I be then? Brush my mouth across his thick lashes, their length and the way they gently trill along my lips trigger waves of goosebumps. He covers my mouth with his. I consider backing out, halting the proceedings. Order in the court, I object! But I don't. I clutch at his shoulders and draw him to me. He hoists me on top of the filing cabinet. My hands slide to his arms.

"I've wanted you for so long," he breathes into my ear. Words of devotion are aphrodisiac enough. Shorts and purple underwear slip down legs, to knees, to floor. He fumbles his button fly. Wrap my legs around his waist and lock my ankles at his back. We move together awhile until the thought of consequence gets the better of me.

"Pull out," I murmur. Then louder, "Pull out!"

"Jesus!" He extracts himself. "You didn't stop me, so I thought you were on the pill." We put ourselves back together. "That was irresponsible as hell." Scratches his head inadvertently fluffing his curly hair. Even though it's dim, I see patches of red rising up from his jaw line.

Stare off into nothing like Barney, my own rash of regret creeping up and through.

"Where are you?" he asks, giving me an affectionate squeeze. "Don't worry, I'm from a long line of infertile men. My father, for example, was infertile as well."

I'm not worried. I just hope he doesn't expect me to be his girlfriend.

Pedaling hard in high gear, I arrive at my Grandma's six-storey condo building half out of breath. Lock my bike to a handicapped parking sign and dash up the stairs to unit 408. Dunno, guess I had energy to spare. She doesn't answer the door, but I hear her calling so I let myself in. She's parked in her olive green velvet chair with a bag of Viva Puffs watching a previously recorded episode of *The Young and The Restless*. Lean over her back and kiss the soft powdered skin of her cheek. Ask her what Victor's been up to now. She touches my hand but doesn't speak. Eyes fixed on the screen, she holds out the bag of cookies. I sit on the pink satin chair inherited from her third husband, Barnaby, who died of Alzheimer's, munching their jammy, marshmellowy, waxy chocolate goodness, until the program's over.

"What a nice surprise, dear. I must tell you though—my friend Jean, you remember Jean, don't you?" I shake my head. "Oh sure, you remember Jean. She's an awful size and has a great, grey mop of hair?"

I nod. I *do remember* a woman matching this description.

"She's coming over in an hour or so to play Scrabble. You're welcome to join us."

"I wouldn't want to intrude..."

"Oh it's no intrusion." She examines herself in the bathroom mirror, coifs her grey perm with a metal Afro pick and scrunches up her face as she applies a fresh coat of melted peony lipstick. "Jean would be glad to have you."

"I'm not much of a Scrabble player." She's a cutthroat wordsmith, knows every adz and qat in the book.

She laughs. "There are a few things I need to do to get ready. You won't mind if I putter around."

We set up the card table and she places a thick mauve towel on the satin chair. "What's that for?"

"Jean likes to sit here."

"She likes to sit on a towel?"

"She stinks something terrible. I always set out a towel for her to sit on. She doesn't have proper hygiene. Raised way out in Missinaba County. Would you like a dish of ice cream?"

"She's your friend, Grandma."

"Oh yes, dear, we're great friends. We've traveled all over together. Down to Florida just last year. She's a little strange though, has to be told to cover herself up. Are you sure you won't have a dish of ice cream?"

"No thanks."

"Are you reducing?"

"What do you mean, *cover herself?*"

"When we were in Florida, she'd walk around the hotel room with her pussy hanging out. I'd have to tell her to go put something on, that sort of thing. I need to get out of this girdle. I only ever wear it to the bridge club. You know those old girls." She strides into the bedroom unbuttoning the brass buttons on her red dress. Loops a large, gold chain off of her neck and lets it collapse into her pink, velvet lined jewelry case. On her dresser is a book called *Dowsing Secrets.*

"What's this?" I flip through the book.

"Oh, that silly thing. Jean and I have been doing some dowsing."

"Dowsing?"

"Go ahead. Look under the bed. There are a couple of rods there." She plops down, the mattress sighs under her weight. She unlaces her girdle and as she does, relieved flesh squishes out of the constraints like bread dough rising up and poking out from under a kitchen towel.

I lift the pink floral bed skirt. Two copper rods bent at the ends to form handles lie crossed underneath her bed. "Are you looking for water?"

"Oh no, dear." She chuckles. "The rods are new but I've been using a dowsing pendulum for years to answer questions. Since we were girls. Daisy and I."

"Like what?"

"Will Sadie marry Ralph. Will Daisy have a healthy baby, will she have twins. Haven't you ever done something like that? Maybe your generation doesn't do that sort of thing."

"I've used a Ouija board."

She cocks her head to one side then shakes a finger at me. "Ouija is a little dangerous."

"Really?"

"Oh yes, when you use a board with several people it becomes a bit of a lark. Without proper respect, channels for unholy spirits can open." She chooses some black polyester slacks and a coral knitted sweater, which she pulls down past her waist emphasizing her abundant rump. Her hands float overtop her dresser searching for the next step in her getting ready sequence, the bottle of L'air du Temps from the mirrored perfume tray. Gives herself a generous squirt behind each ear followed by wrists rubs.

"We used to use a needle and a length of thread. Now I have this fancy brass weight." She lifts a bullet shaped object attached to a chain out of an old, hinged necklace box. "But you can use just about anything so long as it's suspended." She demonstrates pendulum dowsing by snapping her long, red lacquered nails together like crayfish pincers over the chain. "You have to remember," she continues, "this is not a game. You are making serious inquiries of the universe through a spirit guide."

My eyes are wide and must betray amused incredulity.

"We've all got one." We head to the living room and sit side by side on the pink satin sofa. Grandma holds the chain in the air about a ruler's length high. The pendulum swings. She steadies it. "This is called the waiting position. Once we ask the question, if it spins in a circle clockwise, the answer is yes, counterclockwise, the answer is no. Breathe deep. Concentrate. Invite our spirit guides to us and ask permission to use the pendulum for Good." She ends with an appeal. "May only Forces for Good respond. May I ask how long I have left on this earth?" We wait. The pendulum begins to sway and turn— counterclockwise. She laughs like she knew all along that the forces of the universe meant to put one over on her. "Drat! It never wants me to know. How about Scrabble. Will I beat Jean at Scrabble tonight?" Again, the pendulum begins to swing this time clockwise. She laughs again and smiles so wide I see where her bridge ends and the sides of her teeth begin to brown. "What do you know! Course, could have told you that myself. Now you go on."

I'm skeptical to say the least. Crazy old Grandma Dorothy surely influenced the swing of the pendulum. But I humour her. "Do I have a competent spirit guide?" The pendulum circles yes. I suppress a smirk.

"Good, dear!" After slowing to the waiting position, the pendulum revolves clockwise again. "So, there you go." She places the brass weight in my palm and sets about arranging for scrabble. Plunks a dictionary big as a phone book on the card table and pulls out the Deluxe Scrabble players game, the one with the little square plastic cribs for each letter. The doorbell rings. "Listen," she whispers, "You take that book. Jean'll never miss it."

"Thanks. What are the rods for?"

"Same kind of thing. Finding what you seek. I mostly use them to find what I've lost these days." She taps her temple and rolls her eyes.

October: Eleven Months Before

ALICE THE CAMEL

Just logged another eight highway hours. Suppose it's fair to say that I saw what I saw of Australia through the bug-splattered panes of Greyhound glass. The late afternoon sky of Alice Springs is a solid cerulean like a kid's painting, the air balmy and dry. Walking from the bus station to a downtown backpackers, I look up as clouds billow across the wide expanse, puffs of dragon's breath. A feeling in me bubbles up and through. Could this be the place?

Throw my pack onto a vacant bottom bunk when a girl in a green swirled bikini with pink-cropped hair introduces herself. Ute from Germany.

"When you get sorted, come and join me and my friends by the pool for watermelon."

Slip into my swimsuit and head downstairs. Ute passes me half a watermelon scraped out like a bowl filled with melon cut into chunks. It takes a minute or two before I realize the fruit is soaked with vodka.

"You like?" Ute asks.

Smile and nod, mouth full.

Ute flips a shock of pink hair out of her eyes and sucks a small piece of watermelon pressed between her thumb and fore-fingers before diving into the pool. She is small breasted and fit, a figure skater's butt like two pieces of popped corn side by side. A girl descends the wrought iron staircase on the side of the building from the third level shouting *Ute! Ute!* waving as she walks. Ute stands in the shallow end, calls Ursula and points to the watermelon on the patio table.

Another German girl with long brown dreads, small shells and beads woven into her nappy vines, puts on a reggae dance hall mix. Bikinied bodies writhe, dancing on the pool deck or draping themselves over lounge chairs while eating watermelon and drinking tall cans of beer. It appears all these women are German and familiar. Shove a few more boozy squares of watermelon in my mouth and float on my back in the pool, light and sunny.

On the way home from a nearby pub, we are loud and boisterous singing German songs as we walk. I teach them a song we used to sing at camp called *Alice the Camel*. You put your arms around each other's shoulders as you stand in a line and bump hips on the boom booms singing, *Alice the Camel has ten humps, Alice the Camel has ten humps, Alice the Camel has ten humps so go Alice go boom, boom, boom*. You count backwards down to no hump then everyone shouts *because Alice is a horse!* They love it, scream it all the way to their beds. I feel like Jerry Lewis must have when he went to France the first time.

Ursula and most of the others fall instantly asleep. I lie on my bed staring at the woven springs on the bunk above me thinking about nothing just a sort of happy drunkenness when Ute slides quick and smooth, feline-like, on top of me. Raises my hands above my head pinning me to the mattress, her hands on my hands, her lips on my lips, her body stretched out over the length of mine. I'm drunk shocked which means to say I don't react with any particular immediacy. *Uh oh*, I think, then, *Why not?* Why should I be so quick to say no? Shouldn't I just say *yes* to the experience? Shouldn't I just say *yes* to these soft fleshy lips, this boozy tongue that curls and flicks inside my mouth with just the right amount of tension, *yes* to this supple muscular body pressing into me? *Yes* to the silken skin of her cheek across my chest, or these fingers soft and knowing, skilled, not rough and demanding always prodding and shoving like a too hungry man's? When in Alice Springs, do as the German girls do. At least I won't get pregnant.

Early morning, Ute stirs. Slinks back into her bed. I lie awake while the rhythmic wheeze of slumber surrounds. Would

I have slept with her had I not been drunk? For sure I wouldn't have slept with small dicked Steve. Without intoxicants there are a lot of things I probably wouldn't have done, like leave the house. I'd just want to stay alone inside and read and paint. Being around people sometimes is sensory overload, leaves me raw and overwhelmed. I can be such a social subnormal.

Anyway, it felt good to be touched. Skin on skin, breath in breath. There was a guy on my ward, autistic I guess, who'd pace the halls wearing driving gloves because he found touching things with his bare fingers painful. Driving gloves guy would grab your hand sometimes when you least suspected and trail your fingertips along his arm, his mouth curved up in smile. A person doesn't get a lot of touch in a place like the MNC. Wish we could have hugged the guys just enough to let them know they're human.

Wake a couple of hours later to Ursula and Ute laughing and rolling up their sleeping bags. I pull on some shorts and climb out of bed.

"Good morning," says Ursula. "Sleep well?"

She knows. She pinches Ute's cheek, says, "Little rabbit." Grins at me. "We call her Ute the rabbit."

"My friend here studies 15th century history," says Ute, folding and stuffing garments into her pack. "There are stories of women, witches, who transform into familiars to perform deeds at night. Ursula says at night I become like a rabbit."

Ursula lets the screen door slam, and I am left alone with Ute who wraps her arms around my waist and kisses the back of my neck.

"Have fun last night?"

"Sure."

Ute ruffles her hair with her fingers, pats my hand and drops it. "Don't worry, I'm not looking for a girlfriend. I fly out today, back to Berlin. I study entomology at the university. You know, bugs, insects? Our holidays are over, that's why we made such a big party last night. Ursula and the others all will leave today. Come and have breakfast with us. You like muesli and yogurt?"

Drinking coffee and bottled water by the pool, the girls tell me everything I must do while in Alice Springs and fill my fist with leftover coupons and pamphlets. I nod off in a lounge chair under the shade of a thick-trunked palm. Wake to empty quiet, a shift in hostel clients. There's a folded piece of writing paper rolled into the collar of my T-shirt. Ute's address in Berlin, a standing invitation. I could spend my whole life traveling, flitting from one place to the next never laying down roots, always just meeting, connecting with strangers and moving on. That's pretend living though. Everyday can't be pineapple cheese sandwiches. That's like Steve. You can't just wake up in a new country and be someone else. You'll still be carrying around the same old suitcase full of garbage and by God the bears will sniff it out.

Stroll about town, buy some fruit and veggies for a stir-fry. The cashier from Coober Pedy was right; if you want to eat anything fresh you really have to cough up the bucks. Cook myself some lunch in the barren hostel kitchen leaning over the counter reading an old newspaper as I eat. The solitude is pedestrian and glorious.

Dangle my feet from the pool edge into the water, watching a guy in the shallow end unabashedly splashing about and singing aloud to himself. Hurtle myself into the water, a less than graceful dive. The guy pops up right beside my head like a surprise shark attack. He smooths his dark copper hair off his freckled forehead and looks straight at me.

"Do you like the Waterboys?"

"I know them," I say, treading water.

"But do you *like* them?"

"Yeah, sure I like them. Of course. How could I not like them?" He splashes his hand out from water to air, offering to shake.

"Congratulations. We can be friends. Where are you from? No, wait let me guess. Say *out and about*."

I do, he laughs.

"Toronto."

"Good guess. You?"

"Aubrey Santiago. Miami, F.L.A."

His eyes vary in hue from aqua to olive green depending on the angle of the sun. His lightly tanned skin is stained with rusty patches of freckles over his Ken-doll nose. His body is long and lean, nearly hairless in contrast to the shaggy heap of locks dripping down his back.

"Serena makes me think of sirens. Maybe I am Orpheus and I must subdue you with my songs. You've heard of an Oedipal complex? Well, I have an Orpheus complex: I think I'm the greatest musician that ever lived. I can charm beasts and fish. I can make trees sing and rocks dance." He submerges, then returns to the pool surface. "Not really," he says.

I'm drawn to his unselfconscious babble. It's light-hearted, seemingly genuine and kind of interesting. "You into mythology?"

"Hobby, not passion." He dolphin dives around the shallow end. I could be a kid at summer camp horsing around with my cabin mates. I take a running leap from the deck, cannonball into the pool.

"Three point seven," he says, climbing out of the pool and twisting himself into a hideous mockery of a swan dive, legs askew and face cockeyed. We continue with our fake diving competition until the deck begins to crowd with newcomers and we feel outnumbered. In the shallow end, we hold our breath and stand on our hands. Tell him how much I love swimming, especially in Lake Wissanotti where I grew up. He tells me about surfing in the ocean at a beach house in North Carolina where he spent his childhood.

"That's why I'm here, for the surfing. I started out on the west coast at Monkey Mia, few hours north of Perth. Amazing surfing, except for the sharks. I mean I didn't see any, but you always kind of know they're there and just knowing they could get you any minute scares the shit out of me. But you work through it, you know? Then I went to Brisbane, Bondi, also sharks. Can't let fear stop you."

"How do you do that? Just talk yourself into not being afraid? Sharks? That's some crazy shit. Dunno if I could do that."

"Surfing's such a head trip to begin with. I'm friends with this Native guy back home. He told me that rabbit used to be a brave warrior before a witch cursed him. She cursed him to become a fear caller. He'd hear an owl and call *Owl, owl I'm so scared of you* and the owl would know right where to find him and gobble him up. Same with wolves, bob-cats, fox. With his fear preceding him, he was always found. I just try to keep that in mind."

"So why here? Can't surf in Alice Springs."

"Met an Aussie dude surfing in Bondi, owns a restaurant way up in Darwin. Right at the tip of Northern Australia. Promised me a gig playing and singing at his place so I can get enough dough to head to Indonesia. There's this full moon rave in Bali that's supposed to be crazy transformational. He said I should stop in the Alice on my way up because it's a crime to come to Australia and not see Uluru."

We paddle around in the sunshine awhile then Aubrey grabs my hand and waltzes me around the shallow end singing the Waterboys.

"Come to dinner with me tonight, Serena."

Supposed to meet him out front at six-thirty. I'd be lying if I didn't admit that something keeps jumping inside me every time I think of his voice or the stare coming out of his blue-green eyes. Not stirring, actual jumping like one of those little larva filled Mexican jumping beans that pop and flip at random when exposed to heat. I decide to wear my only non-grubby article of clothing, a batik sundress I found at a market in Sydney with indigo dolphins diving over splotchy waves across the turquoise fabric. The halter-top of the dress creates an open v on my chest framing my Jimmy Birchbark necklace that sits in the dip of my clavicle.

Aubrey strolls out in front of the hostel in a red and orange Hawaiian type shirt covered in black-silhouetted palm trees. His white coral necklace seems strung together of shark teeth. Slips his hand in mine. Walk together toward the main street.

"My buddy from Darwin told me about this place called the Coolabah where you can eat crocodile, emu and kangaroo. You *game?*" He laughs at his pun with a raucous pretend laugh. "Guy at the desk said eight blocks that way. Did you know Alice Springs is the lesbian capital of Australia?"

"C'mon."

"Seriously! That's what my friend from Darwin said."

"How could anyone know that?"

"I don't know if there's been an actual census or anything but that's the Australian gossip. Lesbians are old news in the rest of the world."

The restaurant is a set for a *Foster's Lager* commercial. Horns, various skulls and taxidermied heads of bison and roo hang from wood-paneled walls. Our server's massive arms plunk down a pitcher of beer on the thick wood table along with two gigantic menus advertising the Drover's special that promises a sampling of camel, emu, crocodile, barramundi fish, snake and bison. We order one to split. Hank luvs Linda is gouged into the table.

"You an only child?" Aubrey asks. "I am."

"Older brother by six years. Stanley."

"You two close?"

"Not especially."

"That's so crazy. If I had a brother or sister we'd be tight."

I want to know everything about him. I want to attach my brain to his with some kind of a plug and transfer in all the pre-liminary information so we can skip all this and get to the good stuff. I ask him to tell me about Miami. He says his mom's parents, who are both doctors, moved to Florida from Spain just before WWII. He says he loves it there because he stayed with his grandparents to finish school after his parents got divorced. I ask why he didn't live with either his dad or mom.

He says, "That's where things get complicated. But here we are and we've got a whole tray of meat to be delivered, so."

I listen and nod all the while wondering what he tastes like, what it would be like to lie on top of him melding the entire surface of my body with his. He tells me about his dad, a Scottish philosophy professor, who announced being gay when Aubrey was fourteen. I replay the afternoon, him wearing his swimsuit, diving into the pool. The little path of auburn hair trailing down from his belly button. Oh God. What if he has a shrinky dink? That would be luck most foul.

"I wasn't surprised. I'd been finding gay porn hidden around the house for years. My mom took it hard. How could she not have known? She must have known. I was a kid so all I was thinking about was myself, like, what are my friends gonna say? Charlotte isn't exactly New York City. I was pissed off at the world. Then my mom's all, 'Your father has decided to live his dreams as a gay man, so I've decided to live my dreams as well. I'm moving to Granada to study flamenco and open my own dance studio.' She did invite me along but didn't lose sleep when I declined. I tried staying with my dad, but he was exploring his new, shall we say, lifestyle? It was too much for my teenage brain to handle."

I pause resting my chin on my hand as though I've been listening, which I have been, but I'm also thinking about casually brushing the top of my foot and ankle along the backside of his calf. When I do, he raises his right eyebrow and extends his leg a little more.

"One night, a guy named Lance came to the door to take my dad clubbing. I packed whatever I could carry and hopped on a bus to Miami. Best move I ever made. Spent most of my life being in the way of my parents' social calendar. My grandparents made me the centre of theirs. Even changed my last name to my Grandpa's. Santiago. That wasn't the only reason. It's hard to get a gig playing a Latin club with a name like Aubrey Stewart."

"What did you study in Miami?"

"Classical guitar. You?"

"Art."

"Did you parents ever give you a hard time about going into music?"

"My dad said I should work at a mattress store so I'd have something to fall back on. They were good about it. They were just glad I wasn't a total fuck up."

The burly-armed server arrives. "Gonna 'ave to move them beers so as I'll 'ave room for the Drover's plate."

On an enormous platter sit hunks of white, pink, grey, brown and red flesh each stuck with a plastic version of the whole animal along with three wizened pieces of pale-green, curly endive.

"Are we meant to be eating camel?"

"Hmmm. More like one of those things to be done once in life. Though I do recall seeing a charming recipe once for roast hump. Shall we start with snake or crocodile?" he asks, knife poised.

"Why don't we start with something recognizable like fish and work our way along the food chain."

Aubrey carves the piece of barramundi in two and slides it onto the square white side plates. Stabs a chunk with his fork and holds it up for me, staring at my mouth and the way my lips curl around it.

"You ever see your mom?"

"Oh sure. Everything's fine between us all now. I've been to Granada a bunch of times. She's doing well, lives with an old Spanish guy who paints water colours. You'd love Granada. Everybody loves Granada. I'd love to take you there."

I'd go anywhere with him.

"Emu?" I hold a piece of dead bird toward him. Surprisingly beefy. The crocodile is a cross between chicken and beef with a kiss of lobster.

"Tell me about you. What do you do when you're not swimming in pools in Australia? Boyfriend?"

Fill him in on all the boring details, eventually telling him in the best way I know how about MNC. I start out with *developmentally delayed* move on down to *clients* and finish up with the local vernacular.

As we walk toward the hostel, Aubrey loops his arm over my shoulders. Like a wing, it's familiar and comforting. Grazes my collarbone with soft fingertips and touches my necklace. It's my albatross, I say. Then I tell him all about Jimmy Birchbark, how he choked on a hard-boiled egg and how I quit.

"Shit happens. What could you have done?"

"Something. The meatheads that work there always look to someone else, always say it's not *my* responsibility. Sorry, but yes it fucking is *your* responsibility, we are all each *other's* responsibility. I let it happen by not changing circumstances I knew intuitively would contribute to his demise."

"You were doing the best you could in a place ensconced in layers of bureaucracy like every institution. What more can you ask of yourself?"

"Yeah. Maybe he's better off. Better than rotting away for the rest of his life in that hell hole."

Aubrey stops walking. Puts his hands on my shoulders and looks right into me.

Waves roll and crack in my ears. External life carries on around me but all I hear is mechanical buzzing, the sound of a motorboat driving by when you're underwater. *How can I ever give him enough? He's going to keep wanting more and more and more of me. Is there even anything in there to give?* He holds my eyes with so much intensity, I chicken out. Yank away from the gaze, kiss his mouth almost roughly. Too rough for the mood, he softens it with lazy lips, a kiss that takes its time, warm and sweet on my mouth like a sip of ice wine. A knuckle of anxiety works its way up from my stomach and lodges itself in my throat, shortening my breath.

At the door to my room, a second kiss and the promise of tomorrow is all I can offer. Brush my teeth, wash my face. Tell the mirror not to fuck this up. The thin sleeping bag on the narrow plastic mattress feels positively luxurious and I'm grateful for a good night's sleep. Grateful I haven't jumped into anything. Can still get away scot-free. Can't stop smiling, not that I try. Is he why I've come all this way? *Oh, man, this could really hurt.* I cross my forearms over my chest hugging myself and knowing for certain that now is all there is, and that I'm happy here, am happy now.

March: Three Months Before

ANIMAL MEDICINE

Byron reads the paper at the bar while he drinks his pint. Lisa and I fill up ketchups and vinegars for the tables from two large jugs.

"I like your necklace."

"It's otter medicine," she says.

"What's that mean?"

"Otter is my animal. Otter is women's medicine, feminine earth and water balanced in strength and softness." She points to my necklace. "What's that all about?"

I explain how I got the opal in Australia and sent it to my ailing Grandma who subsequently died.

"I meant this one." She prods the wooden circular Jimmy Birchbark amulet with the tip of her finger.

"Oh, I guess you could say I've got Winkie medicine. It represents all that is good about being born imperfect—you live without striving, you're unconcerned with permanence, content in the moment with just being."

She laughs. "You don't got no Winkie medicine, you got bear medicine."

I set the vinegar jug down. It's full, sloshes back on my hand burning my skin but I don't move to wipe it for fear of missing what Lisa's saying.

"Bear is the sun and the moon. Power of the sun, intuition of the moon. Sometimes, you gotta fight to the death and scavenge for survival. And sometimes you gotta pause to collect yourself, hibernate and lay low, dig within. But always yer looking for the honey inside an old tree."

Byron looks up from the *New York Times Book Review*. "Seeking the sweetness of truth. Genius. If Serena has bear medicine, Lisa, what about me?"

"You?" says Lisa, turning her back to Byron and wiping the spots from a wine glass with the tail of her apron, "You got ass medicine."

Must have fallen asleep thinking about what Lisa said that night, because I wake in the middle of one of those dreams where I'm falling, jolted into consciousness by a plummeting body that turns out to be my own. I'd been climbing the stairs of the CN tower lifting my heavy, exhausted legs slowly up each step when, just as I neared the top, I began to feel pursued. No, hunted. Even though my legs were weak and burned with lactic acid, I forced myself to go faster, and faster refusing to look behind and then I pull an Orpheus. I turn around to a giant, snarling King Kong-sized black bear, woolly and fierce, and swiping at my ankles. Then, just as I can't go any faster, just as I can't lift my tired legs up one more step, the entire staircase crumbles beneath my feet and disintegrates into cement fragments tumbling through the bottomless sky.

All morning I'm in bed thinking about the seventh time I almost died. It was the middle of March, with Matt, my boyfriend after Tim and before Jinglenuts. It'd been a really cold spring, and even though the inevitable melt had begun, greasing the fresh snow along the surface of the lake, there wasn't a sledder around who wouldn't have traversed it just the same as we did on our way back to his parents' cottage from the hotel tavern in the centre of town. Matt gripped the snowmobile handlebars with one hand, using the other to swipe the wet snow away from his plastic face shield. He was driving slower than usual because he couldn't see. Had he been going full throttle, the machine would have leapt the puddle and skimmed over the sinkhole in the ice instead of catching in slush and sucking us down into blackness. Sinking under the weight of our sodden suits, we clawed for our lives at the icy edge that melted and snapped in bobbing chunks. Matt grabbed the rear of my suit and tossed me up on the ice. I spread out like a starfish in the wet snow intuitively distributing my weight, inching back from the edge and digging in the toes of my boots to help anchor him as he dragged himself out. Soaked through, we trudged in shock towards the cottage about a kilometre away. We were so much younger than we'd thought.

So many times now I've very nearly transcended my physical being. Makes me wonder if my spirit or soul or whatever you want to call it has been trying to get out of my body and back into the infinite since conception. The next time could really be the death of me.

Or, maybe, the life of me. After all, eight is the atomic number of oxygen. Eight on its side is infinity. Eight spokes on the Buddhist wheel are the steering wheel that guides the ship of life and the Noble Eightfold path. One more chance for me to evade the ghosts of karma past and slowly choose the most desirable womb cave in which to grow. Maybe then I'll be happy, satisfied and at peace. As if.

I climb out of bed after all this thought, knowing just how to salvage the painting behind the dresser. I set about squeezing tubes of paint on my palette hollowing out the eyes of the split face using black and some tricks of perspective. Re-create the background by globbing white, blue and silver bubbles around and over the face so it looks like this half-animal half-human is underwater and tilted looking up toward the surface, its empty eyes searching for the sun. Lace strips of white, gold, yellow paint along the top. Transform streaks of bloody red into sea plants with flowing tendrils. I've been at it all day, not done, but closer. Clean my brushes and head upstairs.

Dad has the paper in his lap. "An article here says the casino is nearing completion. Apparently they'll have hotel rooms by the thousands."

Mom and I nod, otherwise occupied by the television, shouting out guesses for final *Jeopardy*.

"Says here Dolly Parton is set to open the casino on the first night. Can you imagine? Thousands of people streaming into

Mariposa to listen to Dolly Parton. I thought they'd try to get Ace Fitzgerald."

Next commercial break, mom says she heard that MNC is closing sooner than expected. "What a shame," she says, "they just sunk hundreds of thousands of dollars into renovations a few years ago."

"Where are they going to put everyone?" dad asks.

"Group homes."

"Certainly cheaper to run a handful of group homes than it is to run an institution. The cost of MNC's infrastructure alone must be staggering," he says. Dad shifts the couch pillow behind his back, stretches his legs and leans forward. "Hope McLaughlin doesn't try to use the job losses as a way to boost support for the incinerator plant."

Mom lowers the volume on the remote before chiming in. "It may be cheaper but is the care any better? Privatized homes have been known to scrimp on meals and other essentials to save a buck, feeding clients Kraft Dinner every night. There's a case before the courts right now of a staff member in a group home in Beaverton who left a non-ambulatory client on the toilet for nearly three hours. There's got to be some kind of happy medium that will allow for some decent standard of care."

The casino is finally built but won't be open for another few months because Willy Simcoe's having trouble getting the license in order. Even though the government doesn't have authority to regulate activities on the Missinaba Reservation, he still has hoops to jump through. So said Lisa, anyway. She also said Simcoe is having problems with a shortage of Native security. Said he's sent a bunch of young people from Missinaba down to Quinte to be trained at the security institute.

Lisa invites Byron and me to take a look at the casino. So early one Tuesday morning we drive out to Missinaba in his ancient green Subaru. On either side of the road leading up to the casino are disheveled houses patched together with tarpaper and aluminum flashing. Where eavestroughs should be,

Christmas lights hang down and yellow electric cord is stapled to fascia. Toboggans and other kids' winter paraphernalia lean up against houses and litter the snow-covered yards. Not all the houses on the reserve are run down; some are perfect bungalows that would easily fit in on my parents' street, but it's the ones that aren't that stick in your brain. Then we see it, a behemoth post and beam entrance to a building of glass and stone that fronts a tall hotel rising from the earth like some kind of crystal stalagmite towering over Lake Wissanotti.

Front doors on sensors retract as we approach the artificial rock waterfall that graces the foyer, the crashing water and burbling fountain muffling the unnatural, digital bings of slot machines that erupt every few seconds in robotic seizures. Every surface surrounding us seems plastered with fake granite boulders and fake leafy trees. And with dark carpets, no windows to speak of and energy saving lights, the place would feel positively cave-like were it not for the neon dream catcher suspended thirty metres in diameter above the blackjack tables, the poker rooms, the roulette wheels, and row upon row of slot machines. Then I see the pattern on the carpet. In jewel tones of red, teal and purple on black are silhouettes of animals styled like cave drawings loping across the floor, surreal, but somehow making perfect sense. Nested atop each wall are alcoves housing papier mâché animal vignettes. To the east a pack of wolves, to the west a family of deer, to the north a moose, and to the south a family of beavers hard at work on its pretend dam. The artifice, this mockery of all that is right and just in the natural world, suits this house of avarice to the proverbial tee. It is stunning, just not in the way you expect.

"Isn't it fantastic?" Lisa says.

"Yeah," says Byron. We look at each other and then at the joy on Lisa's face which neither of us would ever dare to flatten.

"Fantastic," I say.

Byron puts his arm around her. "It's lovely, dear."

Taking the stairs two at a time down toward my lair, I pounce on the ringing phone before Margaret can dry her dishpan hands on the checkered kitchen towel and trill surprised hellos into the receiver. Heart thumps loud against my ribs. The receiver's perforations connect me somehow to mystical airwaves in Australia, to the one I left behind.

"Tell me again why you don't have a ticket?"

I don't know the right thing to say, what he wants me to say. Silence. Dead air.

"Hello? You there?"

"Sorry, sorry, yeah, I'm here."

"So?"

"Remember? My dad asked me to stick around and help my mom. But I can get a ticket and be out of here in two weeks. I've totally been planning that all along. By the end of March, I've been saying to myself. I just haven't booked it yet."

"It'll be April in two days. Don't you want to be here?"

"Of course! It's all I think about. Guess I feel a little guilty, like I'm abandoning my parents. And I want to come back with some money too."

"Parents are supposed to let you live. Roots and wings, baby. You can spend your whole life doubting, but then you're going to end up eating your own heart. Sure, you're not using them as an excuse to avoid committing to me?"

Why good heavens no!

But of course, there it is. Classic Bardo. Fear has sustained my limbo, the twin tails of shame and guilt writhe and tangle together infinitely vying for victory over my gut.

While searching my dresser drawers for a clean shirt for work, I uncover a lavender sachet my mom made years ago and press the flower filled bag to my nose. In spite of the dust, it still has some scent. Scoop my hand at the back of the drawer and pull out a piece of paper I made with dried petals from the first bouquet of flowers Jason ever gave me. I blended and formed the flowers and other natural fibers, like bits of grass from the park we always walked through, into paper. Smoothed the wet paste onto screens and left it to dry in the sun. He used to make such a big deal about the written word, about receiving a handwritten note on paper. Our first Christmas, I gave him a stack of these handmade note cards. It was so like him to use something senti-mental for a break-up note. Here's metaphor in an envelope, aren't I clever. A note, for God's sake. We fucking lived togeth-er, and he gives me a break-up note. I unfold the card, black felt pen shines garish and human against the pale, fibrous paper. Couldn't even use his own words. *Schopenhauer writes, all that is, is the way it must be. For my journey and yours, Serena, our paths must diverge.* Suppose he'd already started seeing that Sarah girl by then. Salty water droplets slide down cheeks and onto paper, blurring ink, not meaning. Felt relieved when I first read it, yes, I thought, no more pretending.

What if, after Aubrey *really* gets to know me, and all the bull-shit that goes along with my subnormal self, he decides I'm rotten to the core and hardly worth the effort? What if I get there and he's been fooling around with Gina? What if I'm unable to appear happy and pleasant and likable at all times as is expected of me as a girl child?

Mom interrupts her thorough kitchen cleaning to knock on my door, says, referring to the phone call, "Was that Aubrey?" As if she didn't know. The futon is lower and harder than she expected, and this jostles her as she sits. Then her lip corners tighten, penciled brows furrow, revealing concern. Deep sighs, she stalls. "Is everything okay? It's been two months. Tim's been calling. Do you still want that money for a flight to Australia?"

The warmth of impending spring creeps through the win-dows of the Queen and clings to the worn wood cutouts of hearts, spades, clubs and diamonds highlighting dust on the edge of every lame-ass black and white photograph of Marilyn Monroe and James Dean. On the scratched and cigarette burned bar, on the peeling burgundy paint seams between wall and ceil-ing, dust. It's as though in the glare I see the Queen, naked and undignified, caught between trying to appeal to everyone and the potential to be something truly special. I dampen a white terry bar towel and set to work wiping the film of dust from every-thing you can't set a drink on while the illumination lasts.

Byron enters, stomping snow off boots. He says I look like I just lost my best friend. Tears drip from cheek to mouth. On the way to pull his pint, I mean to sniffle, but it comes out a snort. He catches me there, wraps his warm fisherman's knit sweater arms around me.

"What is it darlin', the Spaniard?"

"Florida. He's from Florida." And it isn't him, it's me. Something is seriously fucking wrong with me.

"What happened?"

"Nothing happened. I just don't know what I'm doing here."

"Is this a why am I here on the planet kind of question or why am I here in this bar in Mariposa question? Because if it is the former, I can tell you, sweetheart, I got the same question and it ain't gonna be resolved tonight."

I ditch my rag in the hamper and slide his ale along the bar.

"It's more like, I meet this great guy, then due to circumstance we're apart and I'm doing nothing to try and get back to him."

He swings his leg over a stool. Puts his cap and scarf on the bar and hmmms thoughtfully to himself. "Love at a distance is safer. Look at it this way: someone presents you with the gift of a beautiful cake. Should you eat it? Untouched it's divine perfection. What if upon eating it, you learn that it is too heavy, or too dry, maybe the icing's a little sweet for your taste, or maybe it is exactly as you wanted, as you expected. Still, in eating it's destroyed. That is to say it's no longer in the form of a cake but part of you and part of your mind's memory. It's not the cake but the experience, as you perceive it. And perception, as they say, is everything. But that's neither here nor there. Who wants to go through life never having tasted cake?"

He sips his beer a few times. "Fear of success is a powerful deterrent. Of course, it does leave the perpetrator perpetually unsatisfied." Raises his glass to me. "Courage, my love."

CLASH OF THE EARTHWORMS

Candice and I treat the guys to some TV time and popcorn after dinner. She's always bringing in little treats for everybody. She even thought to bring Freezie pops for the *grounds*. Like Tom, she was probably attractive in her prime. Her auburn hair seems a little too orange and dulls her skin in spite of the pink rouge, heavy black eyeliner and mascara.

We laugh together about the guys and their idiosyncratic habits as we dole out small brown sacks of popcorn or Freezie pops so each one can have his own ration and settle in to watch a little *Jeopardy*. Only two are not content. There's Popeye, who looks as his name suggests, particularly in the mouth area, and Bruce, otherwise known as Shaw's most dangerous man. Popeye's agitated, grumbling, keeps invading others personal space. Bruce, one of the youngest guys, maybe twenty-five, lives to shred bed sheets. We have a stack of stained and ripped sheets in the storage closet for him. He must go through one a night. He has black hair cut in a mullet so that if you saw him on the street or in a bar or something and didn't look too close at his eyes, which stare in different directions, or at his Velcro shoes, he might look like your average hockey player who's been hit in the head one too many times. Dark crescents swell under his eyes. I wonder if he sleeps or just tears sheets in the hush of night, playing with the threads as he sits on his knees in the centre of the floor as he is right now. He pulls the long sheet thread over his tongue and through his mouth as he hums *When the Saints Go Marching In*. You might be thinking that he looks all apple juice and cookies playing on the floor, but you'd be a fool. If provoked, not even provoked, if interrupted, he morphs into an angry pit-bull with a meat Frisbee. The others give him a wide berth. It's as though they've drawn an invisible circle around him. Forget *Jeopardy*. I'm watching *Wild Kingdom*. Candice leaves to change a diaper and I notice her waving wildly to me from the other side of the Plexiglass just as Natalie enters and catches me in the craven act of popcorn and *Jeopardy* consumption.

"Serena. May I speak to you a moment please." If Natalie played a sport in high school, I'd wager field hockey. She holds the door, ushers me out of the common room and plants her sturdy legs in her no-nonsense black sneakers. Through the window I see Bobbie using a mittened hand to dip a piece of popcorn in dirt from the corner of the floor and pop it in his mouth. Ronald sticks bits of floor lint in the cleft of his chin and pushes out his bottom lip to hold it there.

"Can you explain how watching *Jeopardy* will assist with client's social and/or intellectual rehabilitation?"

Maurice has spilled his popcorn and is walking over it crushing it to powder. Sorry, Natalie, rehabilitation? Bruce slings and flings his wet thread from one end of his invisible circle to the other. Bad shit is going to happen if I don't get back in there. Natalie should know that.

"Only play the music station then?"

"I believe that is the protocol we agreed upon."

As Natalie finishes speaking, I see in my periphery, as if in a televised replay, Popeye grabbing Lenny's popcorn. Kernels fly slow motion through the air. Lenny sits empty and blinking, as responsive as a tire. Popeye, in his fevered snatching, unwittingly steps into Bruce's ring. Bruce grabs his ankles and hoists his feet up so that Popeye's head smashes to the cement floor and blood seeps out of his left nostril. Growling and screeching like a berserker, Bruce pounces on Lenny, who doesn't have sense enough to squeal. Natalie and I burst in shouting, each of us grabs one of Bruce's arms. Lenny lies inert, his eyes darting back and forth like one of those kitchen cat clocks from the fifties. Candice tends to Popeye, Ken grabs one of Bruce's legs. He thrashes, a marlin on a boat deck, so that the three of us can hardly restrain him. Natalie barks at Ken to take care of Popeye and Robbie, to call the doctor and emergency services.

"Serena," she huffs from the exertion, "we'll drag him to the room at the end of the hall—four-point restraints there. Pressure points if he gives you trouble."

I'm glad it's her and not Ken or Lillian because this feels really wrong.

"The first door," she pants.

I kick open the door and we wrestle Bruce through flailing arms and wordless screams onto the bed, onto his back. Natalie kneels on his chest holding his arms stretched out, the rest of her bodyweight on his forearms. I scurry around and buckle his wrists and ankles in the leather restraints, heaving on the excess strap length to tighten as much as possible. As we turn to leave, through the window I see his torso buck the air.

In the TV room, Candice sits on the floor cradling Popeye, whose eyes are now open. Ken holds Lenny in his lap with a towel pressed to the left side of his head.

"Fucker bit his ear off," Ken says.

"Did you call medical services?" asks Natalie. Ken nods. "Do you have the ear?" He shrugs. "Let me look." She removes the towel. "Not too bad. The piece of lobe must be around here somewhere."

All of the other clients are backed into the corner opposite the TV, farthest from the action. Some are giddy with excitement, clapping and chirping. Others have wilted down to knee hugging knots, rocking themselves like human balls. Pat Sejak spins the Wheel of Fortune. I don't know who Natalie thinks she's dealing with, but I have no intention of being the hero by rescuing some piece of chewed ear from oblivion. I pretend to scan the room, squinting, checking corners.

"I've got it," Natalie says, raising the lobe high. "I'll wrap this in ice until the paramedics arrive.

"Aren't you supposed to put it in milk?"

"That's teeth, Candice. Serena, come with me. We need to complete an incident report."

We fill out paperwork in the staff office using phrases like *the client appeared agitated, the client reacted to provocation with violence, four-point restraining device employed to ensure safety of disturbed client as well as others on ward.* I'd like to mention that if I'd been in the room instead of being scolded for incorrect television programming this probably would not have happened. Natalie would never admit to it. I sign my name. My complicity forever recorded in the files of the damned.

It's early enough in the evening that the sun hasn't quite set, though bands of amber wash the sky above the trees. I hop on my bike and consider seeing Tim. Probably a bad idea, but I don't stop myself. My spirit guide needs firing. Bang on the door to his basement apartment with the soft side of my fist and shout for him. It doesn't occur to me that he might be indisposed until I'm at the bottom of the stairs facing the stolen red and white sign that reads, *No Alcoholic Beverages Beyond this Point.* Music throbs through thin walls.

"Hey Tim! Tim, hello? You here?" I kick a few cases of empties and rattle the recycling bin to create a disturbance. Finally he emerges from under the sloped ceiling, like Alice, popping out through the little door, though with his long, unruly black hair, widow's peak and stubble he looks more like Alice Cooper than Alice in Wonderland. His jeans and Jim Morrison T-shirt are standard. The TV's on, he's been playing his guitar to an old videotape of Stevie Ray Vaughan. The last of the day's light peaks in through broken Venetian blind slats. He throws arms around me, invites me into his lair. We sit together on the dingy couch awhile.

From the coffee table, he opens a little black box with a skull carved on the lid and takes out some weed. He packs the bowl of his alien head bong, offering it to me. "We leave in a few days," he says. Then he's in the kitchen whizzing and crashing, the fridge and cupboard doors creaking and banging, glasses tinkling. Returns with two frothy pale orange drinks in glass beer mugs. Mango Tango Surprise, he calls it. I recoil at first sip. It's stiff with vodka, gin and dark rum—the tail end of all his liquor bottles and some frozen mango tangerine punch from concentrate.

"You gonna miss me, Serena?"

And here I thought he had no feelings. He waits 'til now to start this? "Yes," I say. I'll miss this. But I'll be relieved he'll be physically out of my life because no matter how hard I try, I can't seem to stay away from him. He's like quicksand. "You worried about the tour?"

"No. Yes. No and yes. I can't believe it's finally happening. This is just the beginning. Will the Royal Frenzy make it? Are we good enough? Is it even going to be worth it? Or should I just sign on at Honda like Jay's old man. He said he'd put in a good word for me."

"You've gotta go! You've got to! All those times we talked about this in high school, you are the Royal Frenzy—if not now, when? What else are you going to do? Sit around Mariposa, fucking the dog at the Queen?"

"It's what I know, man. I'm gonna miss people. It's a long time to be away."

"Oh for God's sake."

"I'm gonna miss *you*." He strokes my thigh.

"I'm going to be on a plane to Australia in a few weeks. I'm not even going to be around. I'm not your excuse."

"What about us?" He hugs me with one arm, the other still draped over his guitar. "Hanging out with you, it's been cool this summer having you around."

He sets his guitar down and kisses me slowly on the lips. The kind of kiss that grows bigger the longer you've known a person so you keep your mouth open, ready for whatever he's willing to give. We're standing now, his hands in my hands pinning me against the wall between the living room and bathroom. Life with Tim might not be so bad. Hands entwined he leads me to the shower. We peel clothes from each other, melding damp skin. The scented soap I gave him when I first started spending time here this summer fills my nose with citrus and ginger as we gently wash each other's bodies. He slides behind spooning my back, reaching up to cup my breasts in his hands. Fits himself into me. It's dangerous here with him. I could fall in.

We lie on his bed our towels tangled and clammy on the floor. His red striped sheets are in desperate need of a wash, I don't mention this.

"You could come with us?"

I laugh, give him a look.

"Why not?" He bolts upright, eyes glazed with indignation. "You said you wanted an adventure."

I soften my voice. "Because, you know, it's Tim and Serena. We're just hanging out, having fun."

"You know what your problem is? You have no faith." He wraps a soggy towel around his waist and sits on the couch. I hear him from the bedroom playing his guitar. Fuck. Put my clothes on, sober now, and walk to the living room. He turns away and plugs the guitar into the amplifier, increasing the volume dramatically.

I ride uphill all the way home, pumping my legs. The muscles in my thighs strain but I pedal on, suddenly elated, elevated. My bike takes flight. I am Elliot in *ET* lifting off into the night sky, girl on bike silhouetted by the moon.

Then, unable to sleep once again, I crack the dowsing book from Grandma Dorothy. Who knew she was into such weird shit. The first page is all about Einstein's theory of relativity, the equation between energy and matter and that gravity holds matter together. The dowsing book argues that there is a similar force that binds energies together and pervades the whole universe and that dowsing pendulums and rods are tools for those seeking such universal knowledge, a conduit for accessing and interpreting intuition. And spirit guides are not necessarily humans or animals, though they could be either. Some people think of them as angels, but a spirit guide could be anything in creation that speaks to a person through symbols, through vibrations. Grandma and I talked once about whether or not she believed in life after death. She promised to give me a sign from the afterlife.

I just about fall asleep thinking about the fourth time I almost died. I'd been wearing Stanley's old, powder blue argyle cardigan and walking in the woods outside of the cottage we rented when

I bumped into a branch and the tip poked me in the eye. I went inside to whine about it and to lie down a short time later becoming violently ill—not that the two things are related, that's just how I remember it. Next thing I know, Margaret finds me screaming and flailing on the yellow and green floral couch. I'd been hallucinating that a giant man made of toothpicks and plasticine balls was chasing me. She knelt down and squeezed me tight around the middle, immobilizing my arms. Woke up later at Sick Kids hospital with a fever of one hundred and five and a declared case of meningitis. I was seven. On the third day I was there, Margaret and Dave arrived worried and distraught, trying to comfort and cheer me with a plush Smurf wearing a jersey, a small brown football Velcroed to his blue hand. Margaret held it out to me, and I could see their hovering faces full of fear and doubt explaining that I needed to have a needle in my spine and acting like this time I would surely be the death of them.

October: Eight Months Before

THE RED CENTRE

Next day, we lounge on towels in deck chairs, write post-cards, share intimate details of past lives. I tell him about Tim and Jinglenuts, he tells me about Holly and Christine and the dolled-up older Latin women who follow him around to clubs. Rub sunscreen over each other's bodies as much for sensuality's sake as for sun block. Plot adventures together starting with Uluru going as far as discussing the possibility of making that full moon rave together in Bali. Give each other little bird kisses on our faces and necks so far as the decorum of public pool decks will allow. I show him my piece of opal wrapped in thin wire and threaded onto jewelry cord. He rummages in his pack and finds an empty tin lozenge box left over from a long healed sore throat. Gives it to me for mailing the opal flake necklace to my grandma. He sits crossed-legged on the pool deck in front of my chair while I comb my fingers through his long, damp hair, weaving strands into a French braid down the back of his head. That night we press up against each other in front of the door to my room. We're both in dorms, so that's the extent of it.

During the early morning bus ride from Alice Springs into the red heart of the country, Aubrey falls asleep with his head on my shoulder. I stroke his hair as he sleeps.

We store our gear at the Yulara campground, where we've rented swags for the night. It's nothing more than a field of scattered eucalyptus trees, a single fire pit and two huts of sinks and toilets then make our way to the Aboriginal Culture Centre on our way to Uluru. An Aborigine man demonstrates the playing of a didgeridoo. Women are not allowed to play the giant phallus, oh no, our lips are far too filthy. And, by the time we get close enough to Uluru to actually see it, it feels like deja vu. Signs abound proclaiming Uluru a sacred male space, a sacred route taken by ancestral Mala man during creation.

"I don't know if I want to climb it. I feel kind of culturally insensitive," says Aubrey.

"Yeah, I got some white guilt."

"I'm a Spanish, Scottish, American white man. I got guilt like crazy."

"You believe all this sacred stuff?"

"I don't think it matters if I believe it," he says, "there's a lot of stuff I don't believe but have to respect."

"Yeah, but isn't it a little contrary to the whole idea of everyone being part of the *oneness* when certain people i.e. men start deciding for others i.e. women who can do what, who can go where, who can wear whatever?"

I walk toward the monolith grabbing the chain rope to take my first step. Now, I've really blown it. I look back tentatively at Aubrey. See him stroke his chin, says, "You might have a point. It doesn't say not to climb it."

I let go of the chain and turn back. He takes my hand, and we walk around the rock instead. At the far side, the desert wind blows our clothes tight against our bodies. We raise our faces to the sun, guzzle the last of our water. There is something sublime, sacred, about having our feet planted on the base of this smooth rock and staring off into the distance together for miles and miles at a few bumpy red ranges in an otherwise completely flat terrain. Except for the murmur of other voices swept along by the wind, we could be the first people on earth.

He grabs me, pulls me into him. Whispers in my ear, "I saw the crescent, you saw the whole of the moon. I can't believe I've only known you for a couple of days."

We're back at the Yulara campground by nightfall laying out rented canvas swags in a flat spot under a eucalyptus in the dry open air.

"Every time I try to relax, I imagine one of those things with the Elizabethan collars sneaking up and licking my cheek," I say, lying on my side, propped up on an elbow in the sand.

"Frilled lizards ain't no teddy bears. Come share my swag. Safety in numbers."

There is only room enough in his swag for me on top. A current flows between us, shoots down the length of my spine, reaches into the earth. Runs his hand beneath my shirt from the small of my back to the nape of my neck. I can hardly breathe. *He could do so much damage.* Stale sweat on heated bodies. Rough bumps of tongue on top of tongue. Salty earlobes, nose into hair that smells of scalp, slide my ear along the smooth skin of his chest. Listen for the throbbing of his heart. Our naked ribs rise and fall and breathe as we fuse together. *Sure, he loves me now, he hardly knows me. Wait. Just wait and see.* I draw his breath into me then we become the perfect complement to each other, male and female form rocking into the darkness, rocking under the blue green leaves of the gum tree.

Pink sun bleeds up from the earth into a silver white sky. The gum tree fills with what seems like a hundred pink and grey galah birds singing and tweeting their little feathered heads off. We hike King's Canyon, a giant gorge, the sides of which, with its irregular stripes of tan and brown, resemble a sand-layered vase from the seventies. We sit silent on the edge and dangle our legs down into the vastness. Imagine myself walking too close to the edge, sand eroding, my legs slipping out from under me. I am falling. Falling and twisting and tumbling through space like an astronaut in zero gravity. My mouth breaks into an ever-widening smile, my arms shift into wings in flight. A rush of relief. A rush of freedom. Put my hand on Aubrey's knee.

We descend a lumpy trail walking along the canyon's base looking for some place called the Garden of Eden, so called because it's a waterhole with green shrubs and plants on these plains of rusty dust. Aubrey chooses a tree for us to sit under. I ambush him and kiss him like he's about to disappear. I'm so fucking hungry I could gobble him. But then I'd choke like Jimmy Birchbark with his throat full of egg. Mustn't rush. Mustn't be so greedy. Aubrey's fingers trail the length of my torso and stop at my pocket.

"What do you always have in here? What is this weird bulge."

"My knife."

He reaches down inside my pocket and retrieves the knife. "Is that a knife in your pocket or are you happy to see me?" He flips me onto my back, his hands cover my hands, knife between them.

"Be prepared," I manage to fit in between kisses.

Aubrey stops, slides off and carves the brie and pear we brought for lunch. I try not to think of Fugima's corns as the blade presses into the soft rind of cheese.

"I hope you don't think I'm some kind of player 'cause I brought a condom last night."

"You were exceedingly responsible. Organized."

"I'm not really the kind of guy who goes around screwing just whoever."

"Me either." *Umm, sort of.* "I'm glad you brought one, it's smart."

"I got a girl pregnant once."

Oh boy. Holy fuck. Here we go. Now things are getting serious.

"It was horrible. So fucked up. I never want to go through that again. I don't want you to have to go thorough it either."

The stars in the clear dark night look as though they might have been configured just for us, flown up by the hundred pink galah birds from the gum tree this morning for our temporary viewing pleasure this evening. The Southern Cross disorients. Our world is upside down. Pull on my T-shirt while the rest of our clothes remain happily crumpled underfoot at the bottom of our swag. Aubrey twists off the cap from the last bottle of VB and hands it to me for first sip. I drink a bit, pass it back and nestle my head in the curve of his arm. His voice is steady and measured.

"I never meant to stay so long in Alice Springs. I gotta get to Darwin, like I said."

Heat prickles up my body swelling behind my eyes.

"But I need to be with you. Pathetic, I'm never normally like this. I don't want to leave you. You could come with me. We could go together to Darwin."

"I don't know. I think I'm a lesbian."

"Aw c'mon. We both could work in Darwin, save a little. Maybe we could aim for Indonesia? Have that full moon experience together?"

"Whatever would I tell my dear sweet parents? That I've shacked up with an American musician?"

"Everyone's always down on musicians. What's wrong with musicians, it's not like I'm a drummer."

"They're big fans of plan B. This is too plan A. I know, I'll tell them you're Scottish. That'll make up for the American thing. And that your dad is a professor. That'll make up for the musician thing."

What the hell? Don't get attached. Just have fun, be fun. Everyone loves a fun party girl. It doesn't have to mean anything. I tell Aubrey about my grandma and about her dowsing pendulum, that I hope he can meet her someday. Take off my Jimmy Birchbark necklace, let it hang in a neutral position. Circle, circle yes.

The coach carries us north through the dusty land, through the fading light. You think when you're driving along through the outback it will be desolate and flat but it's not entirely. Something always surprises. Strange shapes like sandcastle spires dripped from wet orange clay become, as the bus pulls closer, termite hills. Then dust devils whip sandy tornados across the road causing temporary blindness. Reminds me of the opening of that documentary I saw on the pyramids.

Aubrey, sitting beside me kisses my cheek, interlaces his fingers with mine and squeezes. Maybe *this* is transcendence. Once blackness envelops the bus, a blanket over a birdcage, there's not much to see or do but stare at each other and at ourselves, reflected in the darkened window.

We move to the empty triple seat at the back. I wonder who he knocked up. Together they decided to kill it.

"What's up?" asks Aubrey.

"Nothing. Just thinking."

"About?"

"Home."

"Homesick?"

I laugh. "No, God no. The opposite. It's like this place called 'home' I'm supposed to feel 'from' is the place where I feel least 'at home.' As though I'm an interloper in the lives of my friends and family like I was dropped by a reckless stork and just landed randomly in a place called Mariposa. I don't know. I must belong somewhere because here I am. And no matter how many times or how many things conspire to potentially end my life, I'm still here."

"It's pretty normal to want to belong. Fitting in is one thing. Belonging another. I know this Seminole guy, Jeremy, the guy with the rabbit story. We were roommates in college. Hell of a guitar player. Jeremy knows a lot of interesting stuff, but I wouldn't exactly say he's a spiritual guy. His dad's a traditional shaman and told him a cool story about how the Seminole had changed over a period of a hundred years because of invasions from the Spanish, from escaped slaves, white southerners and different 'Indian' tribes. Instead of having the traditional clans like eagle, panther, bear they suddenly had all these jumbled up people. Then they'd go and have clanless kids and the next thing you know, the whole community begins to weaken because no one knows where or to whom he belongs. The elders tell the clanless women to wander the land, to pray with sincerity and hearts full of love for the answer to which clan they belong. They're starving, exhausted, about to lose faith, then a plant starts talking to them. Tells them to dig it up, cut the dots off the tuber, bury them and more plants will grow and feed the people forever. The clanless people become the White Potato Clan. Not everyone is born into a ready-made clan, sometimes you have to get out there and create your own."

He balls his sweatshirt up and props his head against the window. I lay my head on his lap and curl the rest of myself onto the seats. Maybe he's right.

November: Seven Months Before

The Flash In the Pan

Before settling down to work for Aubrey's friend Chris at his restaurant, we spend a couple days sightseeing in Kakadu National Park just outside of Darwin where I hope to finally unlock the secrets of the Aborigine. Sergio would be so proud. I am water over pebbles, being.

We follow the self-guided tour map and hike along a narrow grassy trail until we reach cave drawings. It's so cool the way these drawings show animal spirit through the flow of line. It's like the artists spoke animal. Or they just knew how to listen. Under the overhang of rock ledge, in crushed minerals and animal fat, kangaroos and dingos lope across the plains. They're childlike, but not childish. It's life in action. Picasso said it took him a lifetime to learn to paint like a child.

Aubrey wraps an arm around my waist, points to a red, large-dicked kangaroo man. "What do you think that's all about?"

"Therimorphs. Every culture has a version. Half human, half animal," I say.

"Why?"

"Maybe it's a Chief Seattle kind of thing, humans depend on animals for survival so what we do to them we do to ourselves. At our worst we are still just animals, at our best we are still just animals. That they drew them at all shows reverence. Maybe it's something about humans and beasts being one, like we share spirits. You know, like spirit guides?"

"Jeremy told me about his dad helping people take shamanistic journeys as their animal selves. You know, like they drink a potion and morph into the animal that represents their spirit. Wonder if the Aborigines were into that."

We paddle our rented canoe along the Katherine Gorge, stare up at ragged sandy cliffs fringed with trees. The water carries us along with minimal exertion and as we float I think about all of us being born in the dreamtime. If that's true, then all of us have always been here, crocodile, kangaroo, Serena, Aubrey, Jimmy Birchbark. Aborigines say the spirits of children enter into the fetus in the fifth month when the mother feels the quickening.

"You told me you got a girl pregnant once. How old were you?"

"I hate talking about this shit."

An apology begins to squirm out from between my lips.

"No, it's okay. I brought it up. I just hate reliving every detail." Sets his paddle across the gunwales and faces me.

"I was fourteen. We both were. Emily. We were stupid kids who fooled around a couple of times and all of a sudden she was like, *I missed my period, I took a test at the doctor's, I'm pregnant. I told my mom and dad and they talked to your mom and dad and we're coming to your house tonight to discuss what to do.*

"Yeah," he says nodding, acknowledging the increasing size of the whites of my eyes. "So, there we all were, it was just before my dad came out, sitting in the *parlor* with me, my mom and dad on one couch and her and her mom and dad on the three chairs opposite. And her dad is just staring lasers at my nuts the whole time and my dad's asking me how I could be so stupid. And then they all decide an abortion's the only decision. *Their* decision, like we were simple minded. Can you imagine me having a ten-year-old kid right now?"

"I can barely take care of myself."

"Exactly."

"Did you keep going out with her after that?"

"Not really. But for the next few years she'd call me up every June and say something weird like, *It's June 15th. Our baby would have been born today.* Or *It's June 15th, our baby would be one year old.*"

"No wonder you moved to Miami."

"I don't want to seem callous; she was only six weeks and we were fourteen."

It's a miracle any of us managed to get here.

In Darwin we find a rental house on a side street in walking distance from downtown and not far from Chris' restaurant, the Flash in the Pan. It's a wartime bungalow hiding lemon cream paint under a thin layer of grime in a neighbourhood of other small houses. We don't furnish it much, a hand-me-down mattress, a picture of dogs playing poker, a thrift store rotary phone. Shacking-up with Aubrey is nothing like it was with Jinglenuts, who was so concerned with getting our apartment just right. He was always circling things in the Ikea catalogue. Trying to organize dinner parties, showing off. Making sure we had the *Grüntal* shoe rack for the front hall while our love crumbled all around us.

Here in the far, far north of Australia humidity stifles. The delicate skin beneath my eyes beads with moisture and feels perpetually damp. Aubrey says the mugginess reminds him of home. I have no frame of reference for oppressive, wet heat. Sometimes it's hard for me to fall asleep. I like to watch him as he does, though. Open the screen door hoping to coax a breeze in from the front of the house through to the back to no avail.

Aubrey sleeps diagonally on the mattress. I pet the hair away from his forehead. Just looking at him lying so still in bed makes me ache with the fear that I might lose him. Careful not to wake him, I slip away and lie in my underwear, in the dark, on the tiled floor of the kitchen and call my Grandma. Let it ring ten times almost giving up when she answers. Tell her about falling for Aubrey, that I think he's the cat's ass. She seems distracted. When I ask how she is, she goes straight to the heart of the matter.

"Your parents have got me rigged up with that old Dr. Stephenson. He has a pill for this, a capsule for that. A real quack."

"What's Mom think?"

"Margaret? Oh, Christ, she knows as much about medicine as a dog does about its father."

She hears me laughing and she laughs too.

"There's no cure for when a person's time has come."

"I'm sure you have a few years left in you yet, Grandma."

"Well, we'll see. Remember Barnaby?"

Of course I remember Barnaby. Visiting him in the nursing home goes on record as one of my great childhood traumas. I'd cling to the strap of Grandma's red patent leather purse as she'd walk me through a narrow hallway of decrepitude, wheelchairs and recliners stuffed with the gnarly old folks, long fallen off their rockers. It was a sick gauntlet of the future, peas rolling out from paralyzed drooling mouths onto trays. Straps and buckles keeping withered torsos upright and arthritic claws sticking out the ends of robe sleeves as they grasped for me, yeah, I remember Barnaby.

"When he was just getting sick with the Alzheimer's, we took a trip to a cottage. We hadn't even taken out the luggage, when he strips down just as naked as the day he was born, and dives into the water. I watched him from the kitchen window. He took off like a shot around the back of the place, right past the neighbours, who were sitting in lawn chairs on their back deck. Course I went running after him with a towel. One of the neighbours, an older couple, looked at his wife, said, 'Sometimes...'"—her voice falters, she's laughing so hard—"'Sometimes, it's hard to believe whatcha just seen.'" I imagine her wiping her eyes. She collects herself affects a more serious tone. "Rest his soul. I can guarantee you, Serena darling, that will not happen to me."

After the story, which takes about as long as a commercial, Grandma returns to a state of distraction. "Are you watching *The Young and the Restless*?" I ask.

"Sorry, dear, it's that Victor. He's up to his old tricks."

I promise to call again in a couple of weeks.

Work at the Flash in the Pan is mindless, but allows me to live here with Aubrey and I'll take in love and mindless over depressed and ass-wiping any day of the week. Focusing on daily minutiae frees my brain, allows me time to think, the wherewith-al to sketch and write my thoughts down at the end of my shift. I'm still mostly drawing scenes of Mariposa. It's like it oozes from my pores. Separately, none of the images is anything special, but collectively, they begin to resemble a kind of Mariposa puzzle, the pieces of which I shift around wondering where they fit into me and I into them.

Last time I talked to my parents, they said the final decision on the incinerator had stalled and wasn't likely to happen until spring. Mom said Grandma was acting crazier than usual, she tried to read her tea leaves by exploding a Red Rose sachet in a mug. It's hard to know at this point if she's going crazy, developing Alzheimer's like Barnaby, or if she's always kind of been that way and is just saying to hell with the pretense of normalcy.

Santa Claus is popping his furry face up all over Darwin. Posters, billboards, giant cardboard cut outs of his likeness dressed in Hawaiian shirts and sunglasses selling toys, Coca-Cola, chocolate, pet food, stocking stuffers. Makes me think of Tracy's dad. Mom's excited that Stanley and Hazel are flying back for Christmas. She gave me a bit of a guilt trip saying how lovely it would be to have them, and how much they'd miss me, and how wouldn't it be wonderful if I could be there too. I'm more excited to spend Christmas with Aubrey than I am nostalgic for home. Besides, with Aubrey as my partner, this dirty little lemon drop house is starting to feel kind of like my home. Dare I say I may feel a twinge of belonging? I paint a sign on a strong piece of cardboard and hang it inside the front door. White Potato Clan. New members welcome.

On the twenty-third of December, I call my Grandma again. Talk about Christmas and dowsing. I've been doing a little here and there, I say. She says she's been doing some too.

"It doesn't always tell me what I want to know," she says with a giggle.

"You're not asking weird stuff like when you're going to die or anything are you?"

"Not when I'll die, when I'll move forward into the next world. There is no death really, dear."

"Uh huh."

When I hang up the phone, I start thinking about a field trip we took with some of the clients. We stood around the edge of a fenced pond watching a handful of swans skim along the surface. One of them fluttered his wings. One guy groaned loudly, causing the fluttering swan to spread his wings wide, a six-foot span with black beak thrust up as if to pierce the sun. It couldn't go anywhere due to injury, just paddled away from us with its big orange feet and I thought of Odette from *Swan Lake* bashing herself against the window of the ballroom while the love of her life danced the night away with a bewitched impostor. Powerless and broken, her heart collapsed from disappointment. I wondered then, if that's what it was like to be a client, to have this intelligent part of yourself disassociated from your body watching helplessly as the rest of you fumbles around in the world. Wonder if that's what it's like to watch yourself grow old too.

On Christmas Eve, Aubrey and I chop the branch off a dead gum tree from a vacant lot, lugging it home to a stone filled clay pot left by previous tenants. String a small set of lights around its stick branches until it twinkles in the dark like a jar full of fireflies. For ornaments we stir salt, water, and flour into the same kind of playdough mix my mom used to make when Stanley and I were little. Begin with stars, balls, hearts, and other festive shapes until this deteriorates, with the help of some sparkling wine, into shapes of increasing vulgarity. After having cooked and painted them silver, gold and red, we string them up with fishing line around the tree. Aubrey drags it into our bedroom so we can stare at it from damp sheets while basking in its Charlie Brownness.

Christmas morning stumbles awake helped along by various bird squawks and a staggering heat hanging in the air like an extra layer of gauze. Hard to wrap my brain around the absence of snow and mistletoe. The news says Ontario's been having a record cold snap so I'm looking forward to calling my family to complain about no air-conditioning. Then we're hosting a potluck Christmas supper for all the displaced persons from the Flash. The chef is cooking a turkey at the restaurant, then bringing it over so thankfully that won't be roasting in our oven all day. Chris, and his wife, Martina, are bringing bread, wine and a crate of dishes and cutlery. Gina and Melissa, my fellow servers, are bringing salads. The kitchen guys scrounged up some used chairs and a Formica table. And Aubrey's making some southern US traditional dish with sweet potatoes and marshmallows, which sounds revolting in a *Good Housekeeping* 1957 extra Miracle Whip kind of way. I'm just going to mash some white potatoes and open a couple cans of corn.

Eventually everyone arrives as rum soaked as any fruitcake I've ever tasted and by the time dinner is actually on the table, so much booze has flowed, the music blares and we dance and shout-sing spontaneously like it's Christmas time with Sid and Nancy. Gina is sloppy flirtatious with everyone which is no big deal except she can't keep her hands off Aubrey. Many slobbery toasts later, the kitchen guys crash, Gina on top of one of them. Everybody else gradually disperses to their respective homes.

Early in the New Year, (I can hardly believe it's 1995!) I bump into a woman outside an art gallery. She's struggling to bring pieces in for her first exhibit, an installation of works made from garbage and recycled materials, huge canvases covered in paper snipped from magazines. I help her carry the pieces in from her car, explaining that I'm an artist too. She says she's part of a collective and offers me cheap studio space if I want to join. At long last, the gods have begun to smile on me and I'm starting to actually feel like I can make a place for myself here.

On January twenty-first at four o'clock in the afternoon, sun streams through the windows leaving golden streaks along the dark wood bar where I'm chopping lemons and limes into wedges. In the quiet, the trill of the phone rings out, reverberating sound throughout the empty room. Chris lunges toward it, speaks, his face changes, then he hands it to me. It's my dad. I must look shocked because the people around me freeze. Aubrey stops tuning his guitar, leans it against his stool and stands with me behind the bar. My Grandma is dead and they want me to come home. I knew all along this Australia affair was going to be one big hot air balloon ride. My basket hitting the ground with a thud, a deflated rainbow falling down all around me.

On the way to the airport, Aubrey reminds me of Orpheus and his lover Eurydice. "She's killed by a snakebite. Orpheus is so bummed he keeps singing all these mournful songs until the gods weep and feel so sorry for him they give him a chance to see her again. He makes a deal with Hades that if he performs in the underworld, he can travel back with Eurydice so long as he walks in front of her and never looks back. So, he does, but on the way back up he keeps second-guessing himself, keeps second-guessing his trust in Hades' word. He forgets himself, looks back to check that Eurydice is there and watches her disappear forever. This can't happen to us. After we say good-bye at the airport, we're going to walk away and not look back. I'll see you here in a month and we'll start getting ready for Indonesia. If we both hold the vision in our minds, we can make it real."

Keep my head down, knapsack clutched to my chest, eyes stinging. Try to keep my face from scrunching up with hideous grief as I walk the long hallway tube to the plane restraining myself from full out blubbering. I won't look back. No, I won't look back.

August: Ten Months Before

The Unknown Winkie

As I crest the hill and ride past the waving clients down into Shaw, the tops of former clients' graves become visible. Up 'til the fifties, graves here were identified by registration number on cement brick. Ashamed of their flawed family members, people wanted to keep quiet about their deaths too, hoping their imperfect relations would simply be spirited away, family name intact, good society unsuspecting. Imagine even in death not being forgiven your defects.

Was out of my tree at the Queen again last night. Tim took the stage, one more last hurrah. Marty was there. Can't remember much. Tracy, dear friend that she is, sent me home in a cab as per request so I didn't end up at Tim's. She was cranky all night because she found out her dad is going to star as Santa Claus in the annual Thanksgiving flotilla at the waterfront. Don't know why she's so bothered, it's not like he's hurting anyone. Maybe she's frustrated that her dad doesn't need the looking after she thought he would since her mom died and she's been trying to use that as an excuse not to make a decision about whether to go back to school or to stay on in Mariposa and work awhile. This place can do that to a person, hold you down, strap you in. Just as well she isn't interested in traveling because if she came with me I'd feel like I was dragging a piece of here around my ankle. Time to untie the kite string and disappear into the world unattached, invisible and anonymous, to end the Bardo and be reborn.

Ken and Candice are on our ward again. There's a different vibe around the place; some of the routines are a little off because of inconsistent staffing. We've had a rotating group of people filling in while the usual staff is away on holiday. That, and there's a full moon. People here joke, or act as though they are joking, about the full moon. One of the guys will freak out and they'll say *so and so went on the rip, must be a full moon.* And usually, there is.

Bruce kneels on the floor of his bedroom with his ankles splayed out to the sides like a kindergarten kid at story time. He must have just had a shot. He hums *When the Saints* and trawls the sheet thread through his mouth. Thorazine aside, how can he be mellow one minute and rabid the next? He really is like a berserker. Puts on his bear cape and charges into battle, balls forward, prepared to lose it all. Wonder if he was a Viking warrior in his former life and missed his opportunity to transcend and liberate himself, touching down from his own Bardo into life as a Wink. Talk about losing the womb lottery. *Be not fond of the smoke coloured light from hell.*

Today is beach day. You might think it's easy at the beach; truth is, it's like having a bunch of toddlers on the loose in a total danger zone. There's so much more for them to get into, not to mention as soon as we turn our backs at least half of them start humping the sand. The waterfront looks like a seal colony of guys humping and flopping their way across the sand, leaving only penile divots in their wake. Then of course we have to bathe them all again before lunch making sure to rinse the sand off their privates.

As I pass the admin building on the way to the water, Marty darts out from nowhere. He shoves his hands down the pockets of his baggy green shorts, saying with all kinds of hostility, "What's up? Saw you at the Queen last night."

"I know, I was there."

"Oh ya? Do you remember sticking your tongue in my ear and falling all over me?"

My face burns all the way down my neck, turning into a serious throbbing port-wine stain situation.

"Tim was staring at me from the stage the whole time like he couldn't wait to pummel my face. So what the fuck, Serena? Are you with him or what?"

"No. I'm not with him."

"What are you *doing to me?*"

"I'm not *doing* anything. I don't know. They're waiting for me at the beach."

"You're just going to walk away from me?"

"I'm not *walking away from you*, I'm working. Sorry, Marty, I gotta go."

He squints his green eyes at me and shakes his head. His lips curl into a snarl and he mumbles something, still standing there, watching me as I scurry away like Ratso Rizzo.

Sunshine, lollipops and rainbows, it's gonna be a great day. God, it's not like I signed a commitment form contractually pledging my loins to him and him alone. To either of them, for fucksakes.

At lunch we have the guys all cleaned up from the beach and we're awaiting the arrival of food trolleys. There's uneasiness in the air today. Lunch is late, guys famished. It's a cold meal of bean salad, tuna sandwiches and hard-boiled eggs. Ken sings *She'll be Coming Round the Mountain* as he pushes the food into the dining room. Out of nowhere Jimmy Birchbark dances around all agitated on his tiptoes holding his wrists high. Next thing we know, he's got one egg in his fist and one egg in his mouth, and I see his eyes bulging as he gasps for air. He continues to try to swallow, looking vaguely snake-with-a-rodent-like and snorting through his nostrils.

I don't know what else to do so I yell at him as though he's a disobedient dog. "Spit it out! Drop it! Drop it!" He spins around gulping, silently gasping. The egg has lodged itself in his throat. Ken whacks him on the back. I grab Jimmy from behind around the waist and start ramming my right fist clasped by my left palm up and under his ribs. "Call medical services!" I scream to Ken, to Candice. Somebody just fucking do something because this Heimlich maneuver isn't cutting it. Candice makes the call and Julie leads the remaining guys into another room. I keep thrusting under Jimmy's solar plexus to no avail. I expect the egg at any moment to jettison across the room like a Lifesaver, like a golf ball across the green. Then we'll all sigh with relief and get back to scraping plates into the slop bucket.

"Spit it out you stupid fucker," yells Ken.

"C'mon Jimmy," I plead, "cough it out." It's no use. He flops over my arms though I continue to dig in his gut with my fist. I can't support his heavy body and he slumps to the speckled concrete as the medics arrive.

Jimmy's eyes are wide with white, the second egg still clutched inside his left hand as the medics work on him. An ambulance arrives and the paramedics confer rapid-fire with those on site. I can't stop myself from thinking that his esophagus is blocked by an embryo, something that if circumstances had been different could have sparked a life just as easily as ended one. Jimmy is lifted onto a stretcher and whisked away attached to oxygen masks and tubes and all sorts of lifesaving devices. But we all know that this process is perfunctory, futile, that he's already dead.

After completing the paperwork, I dash off ward, leaving Ken, Candice and Julie to sort out the pieces. Pause on my bike at the graveyard and think, maybe the only life I can save is my own. A squirrel catches my eye, hops on top of a gravestone with a nut. He stares at me, nibbling slowly, so I too slow down, and sit under the big white pine and watch him do his squirrel thing. Our eyes meet and we blink a couple of times in unison until he breaks the bond and darts off leaving me alone with the trees and the stones and the dusty trail that winds its way through the parched earth between cement blocks. What would Jimmy Birchbark's epitaph be? And the worms crawl in and the worms crawl out and they eat your brains, and they spit them out. I park my bike and walk up to Natalie's office.

When I tell her I simply cannot spend another day of my life here, or that I "quit," she informs me that "the proper procedure for resignation is through a letter two weeks in advance to allow your employer adequate time to replace you. It is what is required for you to receive your vacation pay. Considering you've worked here for several months, that could be substantial." I start walking away. "If you leave," she says, "don't bother using me as a reference."

A human being has died. His name was Jimmy Birchbark and his life rose up and evaporated into the heavens, morphing into whatever energy does when the gravitational pull of its matter no longer exists. Free at last. Free at last. Thank God Almighty, Jimmy, you're free at last. I fling my keys at Natalie's office window. They crash and descend before her pursed face, obscured by the glass, by the distance, and without looking back I run great loping strides toward my bike. No web can contain me. No one restrain me.

January: Five Months Before

CLICKING RUBY SLIPPERS

Giant airport windows in Toronto. Snow falling in slow inconsistent flakes. In the sky and on the ground, lost in transition for more than twenty-four hours. I shuffle along grey polished concrete to meet my dad and then toward grey skies and concrete sidewalks to the car. A sweatshirt and windbreaker hardly protect against the marrow chill coming up from the soles of my sneakers to the top of my skull. The deep cold persists even as I confound my father by pointing heating vents at my face. A smell of plastic so intense it could make your nose bleed from all the hot, dry air. Dad clicks the radio on, the dial already tuned to his usual easy listening station playing bastardized versions of yesterday's favourites.

Five-thirty in the afternoon and the sun already has its mind on disappearing. Sick of winter too, I suppose. Miss it already. The sun, Aubrey, the little yellow house. So much for my near-life experience in Oz. Snow falls harder on the windshield of the Camry, connects with hot glass and spreads like a spill, like a sore as we drive north past the ever-increasing Toronto sprawl, mounds of accumulated snow creating a dune-like landscape of dirty lumps and naked trees along the sides of the 400. Maybe dad will get so caught up in the Muzaked version of the *Sounds of Silence* he'll crash the passenger side into a lamppost and put me out of my misery.

He throws his brown wool cap on the dashboard, wipes his sweaty brow with the back of his hand, and fumbles around with the heating vents.

"Wonder how you mother is getting along with Aunt Kathy."

"She's there?"

"Uncle George too."

In the back of the wood-paneled station wagon we pass, a kid holding an inflated corncob on a string stares out the window and rests his sad, small face on a Cookie Monster doll. I nod in his direction.

"So, what happened?"

He rubs a hand through thinning hair, fills his mouth with the dry plastic air of the car and blows it out.

"How did you find her?"

"Your mother doesn't think I should tell you."

"Tell me what? Why does she always treat me like I'm a moron?"

"It's not that, she wants to protect you."

He doesn't speak for a minute, adjusts his hands from ten and two to four and seven, in accordance with the Dave Palmer school of driver training.

"She was supposed to pick your grandma up for her weekly appointment at the Best Little Hair House. Your grandmother had hit a cat the day before and was apprehensive to get behind the wheel so soon. When your mom went inside the building she knocked and knocked and finally ended up using her key to get into the condo. And, there was Dorothy, lying on the bed, still as could be."

"Heart attack?"

"Well." Big pause. "There was some evidence to suggest the death was not entirely of natural causes."

Heat radiates up from my solar plexus to my neck and burns purple shame across my face. I should have been here.

"It's tempting to think it was dementia or Alzheimer's, but you have to realize that your grandma's had a rather checkered history." He scratches behind his left ear, turns the radio down. "Her behaviour's always been erratic. She's had all those marriages."

"So, she was eccentric. And three marriages doesn't equal craziness."

"You're right. Dowsing?"

"Lots of people are involved with hokey 'spiritual' things, that doesn't make them mentally ill."

"Debatable, but point taken. When your mother was small, she remembers Dorothy being hospitalized and medicated for some kind of nervous breakdown. Apparently, she would just sit at the kitchen table drinking coffee and repeating, 'All the boys are gone, all the boys are gone.'"

"Because of the war? She used to tell me about nursing injured soldiers. Maggots inside casts to keep away the gangrene."

"Imagine. Kids your age. Whole towns emptied. Anyway, who knows if it was some kind of post-traumatic stress from nursing overseas or post-partum depression after George was born, but that's when Mrs. O'Leary came into the picture as a housekeeper. Remember your mom telling stories about Mrs. O'Leary? Of course, in those days, no one said anything about it to the children."

He looks over his left shoulder, checking his blind spot before changing lanes. Damn his careful driving. There'll be no chance of my accidental death and dismemberment.

"Doc Stephenson gave her pills for her memory, pills for depression, pills for paranoia, they helped—when she took them."

"How do you know it wasn't just a heart attack?"

"There was a pile of vomit beside the bed, empty pill bottles in the kitchen and an empty bottle of rye beside the stove. Can you even believe?"

"Did you call the police?"

"No. Your mother called me. You know your mother. Always trying to Scotch-tape things back together. Look, I know you were making your way in Australia and you're probably eager to return. And Stanley's got to head back to Lethbridge in a couple of days. But it would sure mean a lot to your mother and me if you stuck around and helped out for a little while."

By the time we get to town, snow chunks pelt the windshield. Mariposa feels less of a puzzle and more of a pillow. Over my face. Dave has the wipers going full tilt, back and forth, back and forth, the relentless marching of the blades marking incrementally with a click each second Aubrey and I are apart. Outside is black as midnight though a green 7:43 glows from inside the Camry console. I imagine Aubrey fourteen hours ahead, his auburn curls spilling over the plaid pillowcase and him, still nestled like a cat on the right side of our half-empty bed underneath the picture of dogs playing poker.

Behind the blue and white population road sign, there are three other signposts welcoming visitors to Mariposa. One says *Home of Ace Fitzgerald* next to a picture of an acoustic guitar. Another suggests visiting the newly restored summer residence of Stephen Leacock. The third lists service clubs and events by symbols: Rotary, Masons, Eastern Star, Lions Club, Kiwanis, the Perch Festival, the Scottish festival, the Elvis Festival. It's a lot to take in at fifty k, but I suppose the place needs to flash its assets from the start.

The slow-rising electric garage door at our house foreshadows the deliberate unveiling of the unpleasant. Melissa and Mathew greet me at the door into the foyer from the garage; they look about ten. Grade five, my dad said. Unmistakably brother and sister with matching mops of ginger hair, his short, hers bobbed, blue eyes, their mother's ski-jump nose. They smile at me, wave, run back to their interrupted program like I'm any other grown up. But I don't feel grown up. Aunt Kathy considers me, removes her green striped Paderno apron and hangs it on the hook inside the pantry door. Uncle George squeezes me tight and thumps my back.

"Good flight?" he asks, cautiously jovial.

"Long," I say.

"Saved you a plate of leftovers," Aunt Kathy says. "Stanley's in the attic looking through boxes for his old hockey cards. I'm sure he'll be down shortly."

When I hug mom and tell her I'm sorry, the blubbering snot fest begins. Right in front of Uncle George and Aunt Kathy and everything.

Saw a movie once where a kid drowned and when his brother returned from the funeral, he sat on the dead kid's bed thinking about how everything was still in the same place as it was when the kid was alive. Pennants and posters still on walls, photographs taped to his mirror. That's how I feel right now, like I'm looking through a dead kid's room. My parents have returned my huge piece of crap painting to my room. I see it poking out from between the wall and my dresser. More unfinished business rising to the surface. Flop face down on my futon and bawl. Not dainty little hanky dabbing tears but great heaving sobs, some for grandma, some for me. When I finish blowing my nose, I hear three curt knocks.

"Hey loser," Stanley hisses breathily through the crack in the shut door. And again, "Hey loser. Can I come in?" He opens the door before I can answer. I sit up and wipe my eyes discreetly, can't show any weakness.

"So, you're back from your *big trip*."

"What do you want?"

"I'm looking for my hockey cards. I used to have all these old cards from the sixties this stupid kid at school traded me for brand new ones. Gave me Gordie Howe's rookie card for a Guy Lafleur. Can you imagine how mad his dad would have been, him giving away all his old hockey cards. They must be worth a shitload today." Stanley shakes his head, walks over to the wooden box on my dresser and pokes around with his finger. He picks up the Buddha necklace, smirks and tosses it back. "You know where mom or dad woulda put them? Have you seen 'em?"

"No. I don't give a shit about your stupid hockey cards."

"What're you gonna do now that you're home? Sit around the house and mooch off mom and dad like you did all summer?"

"You're one to talk, dinosaur boy."

"Yeah, well, the university pays me for it now." He licks his index finger smoothing his barely-there brows in my mirror. People say we look alike. That's insulting as hell.

"Congratulations," I say and point to the door.

"Your loser boyfriend couldn't come with you? Or wouldn't mom and dad pay for a ticket for his broke ass too?"

"They didn't pay for my flight. I had a round trip ticket. They told me they'd pay for a return flight since I ended my trip short. So fuck off!"

"Okay. I'll leave you to your weeping."

"Shut the door!" I yell, leaping up and kicking it shut with my foot. Fuck. I hate that I let him get to me like that. I picture his triumphant grin as he walks down the hall. I'm twelve again.

Last funeral I went to was for Tracy's mom two years ago. Open casket. Her mom wore a fitted black dress and black pumps. A peach satin lined coffin. Eyelids frosted with silver shadow, eyelashes caked in black mascara, red circles of rouge on ghastly rubber skin, earrings dangling down her dead freckled neck, all hooched up for that grand cocktail soiree in the sky. I kept trying to think about Tracy and her dad and how sad and sudden her mother's death from ovarian cancer had been but all I really thought about was who put all that make-up on Tracy's mom and what it would feel like to powder some dead woman's skin. Grandma's funeral had better be closed casket. Though, if Barnaby's funeral was any indication, that was just the sort of ritual morbidity she enjoyed.

There's another knock on my door.

"Honey?" Mom sits on the edge of my bed. "Thank you for coming home. Your grandmother loved you so much."

I nod. Wonder if she knows what dad's told me.

"Have you thought about speaking at the funeral?"

"What would I say?"

"It's up to you."

"Do you want me to?"

"If you feel you can."

"Are you?"

"I don't think I'm up to it." She puts her hand on my knee.

"Sorry I wasn't here," I say.

"Your grandmother was a challenging person. We all loved her very much. And she always did just as she pleased."

She hugs me, lingers in the doorway.

"We've invited everyone to the house after the funeral for a bite to eat and to share happy memories."

Even if I thought I could stand up in front of everyone and speak, what would I say? I peer out between the beige woven curtains of the tiny basement window, lights from the kitchen shine on the snowy backyard casting a glow along the shadows of the treed perimeter. A high bush cranberry branch pokes out from the others, its wizened fruit still attached and bowing gracefully over a mound of snow. Totally wabi sabi: a dip in the edge of an otherwise perfect bowl, a patch of cherry blossoms scattered under a tree in a spotless garden. That's what I'd say, if I had any guts. I'd say my grandma was perfectly imperfect like flecks of red in a snow-sheltered yard.

Morning. The kitchen is a hive of olfactory activity: bread toasting, bacon sizzling, coffee percolating. Between school and work and travel it's been ages since I've participated in this suburban breakfast ritual. The twins are chomping toast and orange juice, showing each other chewed boluses when their mother's back is turned. Aunt Kathy's at the stove pushing greasy bacon around a non-stick frying pan with a black plastic spatula. Dave's face is obscured by the *Times Herald* he holds while the *News Packet* lies in wait on his lap. George folds and unfolds the *Toronto Star*. It's as though the pair of them are performing some weird middle-aged man camouflage.

Stanley's on the phone with Hazel. Has taken it around the corner into the hallway, stretching the cord to its zenith, though we can all still hear his sly whispers. Mom fills the coffee pot for the next round, her velour housecoat wrapped and tied around her skinny waist. Has she always been this thin? Her hair is rumpled and fine. Without make-up she looks older than I remember. Maybe it's just that I haven't really seen her in a while. Hands me a plate with piece of whole grain toast lightly smeared with heart healthy margarine.

Stanley hangs up the phone. He's wearing the plaid robe that's been in his closet since high school. "Mom, can you think of anywhere else you might have put my hockey cards?" She doesn't answer.

Dad shakes his head, sips coffee out of his favourite mug with the picture of the parliament buildings on it, and buries his head in the paper. I catch Mathew and Melissa's eyes and stick my tongue out with chewed toast on it. They laugh like hell to the bemusement of the fogies.

"Look at this, Serena," Dad says to me, though everyone is listening. "There's an article here about MNC shutting down."

"About time," I say.

"Maybe." He nods, folds the paper back into itself the way my mother hates. "Those lost jobs will be a big hit to Mariposa."

I meet mom later in their bedroom walk-in closet. "What are you wearing to the thing?"

"I don't know. What do you think of this? She holds out a navy dress with thin white stripes. Would you like to borrow something?"

"Yeah, maybe."

"I hate to think of us all looking so morose. Your grandmother was the first to arrive at a funeral wearing her red blazer with the big, black buttons. All this somberness doesn't seem right. She'd want us to be joyful, to wear something fun." She moves the hangers around between navy suits, grey skirts, black pants, bone shirts, camel-coloured dresses.

"You should wear something a little different. You have her adventurous spirit. At your age, you can get away with it." She holds out a frock of large pastel pink flowers, presses the hanger against my collarbone and stands back as the fabric falls below my knees. "You know, she bought this for me at Laura Ashley years ago and I've never worn it. Probably cost a fortune."

I recoil from my mother's offerings, scouring my own closet of limited choices eventually settling for a wine-coloured crushed velvet shift dress with three quarter sleeves and a scooped neckline. Layer on a few necklaces. Think both Margaret and Dorothy will approve.

As per her wishes, Grandma was cremated. Her ashes sit in a wooden box on a funeral parlor table at the front of the reception room. Hard to imagine that's all that's left of her. I keep expecting her ghost to show up and rattle the plates at night just to keep us guessing. The table also houses a swatch of brown fabric and framed photos of Dorothy's life. As a child in ringlets and bows, as a teen red lipped and slight, as a proud, young nurse in uniform, as a bride, only the first time for the sake of decency, of course. As a mother holding a small George with Margaret kneeling, as a handsome woman in her middle years traveling the globe, and as a smiling grandmother in front of our Christmas tree the year I left for university. I know if I were to stand up and tell everyone how much I loved this crazy old woman, I would dissolve into a puddle. So I don't say a word. Whimper instead into a Kleenex on the wooden pew at all that is unsaid.

At home, Tracy and her dad pay their respects during the post-funeral reception. Must be weird for her. Must be thinking of her own mom every time she's at one of these things. As she's hugging me, I see Tim shuffle awkwardly between the kitchen and the dining room. He slinks over. Tracy wiggles her eyebrows at me. Tim leans in holding on tight, kissing the top of my cheekbone and letting his lips graze my neck. "Sorry," he whispers. Asks me if I'd fancy a drink later. I tell him I can't.

After they leave, I sneak away from the other visitors, Grandma's decrepit, weird friends, who eat their fill, offer their teary-eyed condolences and leave, and play Monopoly with Melissa and Mathew, asking them about their ten-year old lives. Science fair projects, karate lessons, power skating. Stanley isolates himself by watching television downstairs. *Doctor Who* or *Star Trek* probably. Is this what it all comes to in the end? People you've known eating egg salad and gherkins and saying what a shame it is you're dead while inadvertently spitting food at your granddaughter? Decide that maybe I do need a drink after all.

Around the kitchen table are several bottles and glasses of wine in various states of emptiness. George, Kathy, Dave and Margaret, along with some others who look vaguely familiar, chat in subdued voices.

I touch my mom's shoulder. "Mind if I go out?"

She pats my hand but is still listening to George then realizes what I've asked. "Where are you going?"

"To the Queen of Spades."

"Who with?"

"With myself."

"You're going to a bar by yourself?" She looks at me as though I've just handed her a box of tampons with a snarl of ribbon on top.

"It's not 1953. No one's going to think me a floozie."

The relentless snow falls sullen and quiet. Pull my tuque down, wrap a scarf around my head and face, and steel myself for the twenty-minute walk downtown to the Queen. I miss Aubrey. He'll drown his sorrows for a week or so, then Gina will start to snuggle up, feign concern and support, that's when she'll make her move. He'll resist at first, protest, cry outrage, and then finally succumb. The guilt will tear him apart at first. But he'll get over it, convincing himself that lying to me to spare my feelings is the right thing to do. It was fun while it lasted. Maybe it's all for the best. Just as well I got out at a high point. Before he really got to know me.

Buy a pack of smokes at the Mike's Mart across the street from the Queen. Shake the snow from my head and shoulders, stomp my feet and open the door. Who could possibly be in the Queen at 9 PM on a Tuesday night? Only Reg.

"Hey, Sister Golden Hair, long time no see. What can I do ya for?"

"Black Russian."

"That kind of night, eh?"

He pours two generous Black Russians and plops a maraschino cherry into each glass. It sinks among the ice cubes, bobbing and glowing red like Rudolph's virginity in the shrill lights of the bar. I ask Reg to dim them a little. Congratulate myself for not calling Tim.

"Dead in here tonight."

"Yeah. It'll pick up in an hour or two once the snowmobilers get wore out. Royal Frenzy done real well on the road. You and him still?" He wraps his index and middle finger around each other in a lurid twist.

Shake my head. "Good for them, wish 'em well."

Glug my drink.

"Stephanie's gone."

"What happened?"

"I'm a fuckin' idiot." He runs his hands through his salt and pepper hair and throws them in the air with a sigh.

Remove the plastic from my Du Maurier Extra Light Regulars and offer him one. I hate those long cigarettes Tracy smokes, can never get a decent haul.

"Got caught with my pants down in the walk-in with a new waitress. I know, I know." Reg flips a Zippo for us both. Up close, under the bar lights, the skin on his cheeks looks craggy and dry like a toasted crumpet.

He leans against the bar, smacks his hands firmly on the counter and says, "What's done is done. 'Nother drink?"

Throw back the remains of my Russian, chew my syrupy cherry and plunk the glass on the bar where Reg already has my next one waiting. "Met a guy in Australia."

"Aussie?"

"Nope. Yank. Floridian. Last name Santiago."

"So, where's this *Latin lover* now?"

"Back in Darwin, top of Australia. Plays guitar in this restaurant we worked at."

"Always the guitar players."

"It's a curse."

"So, if he's there, why are you here?" Tell him about grandma. "Gonna be in town long?"

"Couple of months. Gotta stick around and give mom a hand. Maybe make a little money to get back 'down under.'"

"Wanna work the bar? I got no one else. Maybe my sister's kid. It's slow most nights so between the two of us and the kitchen staff, and you know them guys, we should be all right."

Sip my drink and consider his offer. If I have to be here anyway, I may as well have a good excuse to get out of the house and make a little money. How bad could it be? Reach across to shake his hand and look in his eyes. "Deal."

He places another Black Russian before me. Eventually I stagger and hiccup my way down the street considering, occasionally, the merits of falling asleep in a ditch. A cop car drives up beside me, flashes his lights. Fuck. Imagine being dragged home by the police on the night of grandma's funeral, my parents and their friends still talking around the table. The car stops, the lights and engine still on.

"How are you tonight, ma'am?"

I turn to look up at the cop sheepishly. It's Ritchie Ferguson from high school.

"Holy shit! Serena! What are you doin' out here? You're gonna freeze your ass off." He escorts me to the front seat and buckles me in.

"Had a little too much good cheer tonight I'm afraid, Ritchie."

"Staying at your folks'?" I nod. Speak as little as possible. "Still going out with Tim Thompson?"

"No, no, no, not for ages. So, you're a cop just like your dad, like you always wanted."

"Yup. Made it through last year."

Pulls into the driveway of the house. There are a few lights still on, but the extraneous cars have left. "What luck running into you! Or you into me. Thanks a million, Ritchie."

"No problem, that's what I'm here for. Let me walk you to the door."

"No, no, no. Really, you've been too kind already I got it from here." Last thing I need is Dave and Margaret inviting in my new best pal here for some egg salad.

"Hey, since you're in town for a while, if you want, maybe we could go for coffee sometime?"

"Sure, yeah, thanks. That'd be fun. See ya." Is he possibly that blind to the sloppy disaster that stands before him?

Kathy, George, Melissa and Mathew are up bright and early for their drive back to London. It's just mom and dad, Stanley and me. Dad takes us out for Chinese before he drives Stanley to the airport for his flight to Lethbridge. We eat a totally inauthentic lunch of chicken balls, chop suey and egg rolls at the Golden Dragon. My mom says something completely bone-headed to Stanley about how wonderful it must be to have Hazel introducing him to new foods. Instead of letting it go, Stanley gets all snippy snappy, says, *She's from Calgary, Mom, her family's been in Canada as long as ours has. She'd just as soon eat hot dogs as dim sum.*

The phone rings around 2:30 that afternoon. Margaret passes me the receiver with a big smile on her face. It's Aubrey.

"Serena! Oh, lover of mine!" he says. "Your mother's voice is so lyrical. I see where you must get your wiles." His call, his voice begins to rattle some of the mortar between the bricks that I've been stacking one by one. I quickly calculate as he gushes love for me that it must be the middle of the night in Australia. He's totally wasted. But thinking of me. Calling me. The sound of him fills me.

Chris grabs the phone in the middle of our conversation. *This guy's lovesick over you! You should see him. It's pathetic.* A tumult of hoots and jeers clutter the background. Gina's there. I'm here, feeling so ordinary, so stuck in rotten old Mariposa, a lone black-capped chickadee singing my name over and over again to a bunch of parakeets busy learning new things to say.

From the sound of things, they've been partying at the Flash and couldn't stand Aubrey's pining any longer. Though the conversation is brief and pointless, I take comfort in it anyway. Then I hang up and slump on the bathroom floor with the door locked.

February: Four Months Before

RUST NEVER SLEEPS

In grandma's condo, the bed is stripped down to its Searsopedic essence, the bedside table swept clean of evidence. I lie down in the dip where she would have lain. How would it feel to let yourself fall asleep knowing the last time you'd ever wake up was already behind you? Wonder if Jimmy rammed that egg into his mouth on purpose. What if he'd been trying to off himself for years, to free himself from his human cage, and the only way he was capable in the MNC was to choke himself?

Sit up and swing my legs over the bed. Rummage in the pink-lined jewelry box and find among a lot of junky broaches, and strings of beads, the brass dowsing pendulum and the opal necklace I sent from Australia. Wonder if she ever wore it. What if she was wearing it when she died? Hope it helped her astral projection. I stick the pendulum in my pocket and tie the necklace around my neck a little tighter than the Jimmy Birchbark so that it's more like a choker, the wire wrapped opal sitting at the base of my throat. Pin an enamel clown broach on my shirt.

"You want me to toss all this jewelry type stuff?" I shout down the hall.

"Unless you want something. Anything of value is already in the safety deposit box."

The sickly scent of fake flowers rises from the drawer liners as I empty them of giant stretchy granny briefs, bras and girdles, socks and stockings, night gowns, camisoles, slips and polyester elastic waist pants. Figured it'd be better for mom if I did all this personal stuff.

I look to the drawer of the bedside table for an explanation of sorts. A journal entry perhaps. *Janunary 11th. Feeling crazy, can't*

remember anything, fearful I'll be walking naked down the street like
Barnaby, or medicated into oblivion and confined to an old folks home
wearing Depends while some stranger wipes my arsehole. Begin to hatch
plan with stinky friend Jean to off myself with booze and pills. There's
nothing of course. Just a King James Bible, a tasseled flowery old-
lady book mark embossed with some religious verse in golden
script, a TV guide, a book of days and a tube of God knows what
kind of jelly but the label says it stops drooling.

Mom continues to remove dishes from cupboards, wraps
them in paper and stacks in well-labeled plastic totes. "You won't
be needing any of this sort of thing for a while will you, Serena?"

"Probably not. Not here anyway."

"What exactly are your intentions?"

I back out of the kitchen, organize some boxes for my own
sorting. She can't see me. I can still see her. She slows her packing, doesn't stop completely, doesn't look up, waits for an
answer. Guilt swells. I will honour my Dad's request though they
can't expect me to stay here forever. How could they even think
that good for me?

"I'm going back to Australia. Aubrey and I are thinking
about travelling around Southeast Asia, like to Indonesia." Said
with confidence, but do I even believe it?

Later, mom's on her hands and knees, her head and shoulders
stuffed under the sink. She removes herself taking care not to
bump her head and sits on the beige linoleum.

"What did you see when you found grandma?"

"From the moment I opened the front door and called for
her, it felt strange. I could see from the bedroom door, her feet
lying still on the end of the bed. It wasn't like her not to be up
and about with make-up on, a dress and a handful of necklaces,
maybe a broach."

"She did like to accessorize." We both laugh. "How'd you
get to be so conservative?"

"I don't know, I think maybe you're inclined to do the
opposite of your own mother. In a lot of ways, you're more like
her than I am."

"In a crazy sort of way?"

"In a free-spirited sort of way." She points at the linen cupboard. "You should save any of the good blankets and comforters for yourself. You might be glad of them some day."

I do as instructed and set aside a few blankets without a thought as to when and where I might use them. Also snag a black embroidered purse lined with red velvet. When I open it, it's as though its hinge is attached to a perfume diffuser that puffs a bit of her into the air. I close it again and try it once more. Smells like a pinch of *Yardley Lavender* powder and a sprits of *L'air du Temps,* a recognizable scent, but there's something else as well, a sort of spicy fragrance that's unmistakably grandma.

Avoiding the jam-packed closet at all costs, I probe underneath the bed, crawl on the floor and pat my hands around until they collide with a couple of copper dowsing rods as thick in diameter as a pen and as long as my arm. I hold one in each hand lightly like the reins of a horse and walk through the condo with my eyes closed affecting an entranced voice until Mom notices. "I'm getting warmer, I can feel it in me bones, there's water in these here parts."

She leaves the kitchen to investigate, smirks.

"Can I have these?"

"You know your father hates that foolishness."

"I know." Set the dowsing book and rods by the door with the purse.

Mom stands on the threshold between the kitchen and living room looking around wistfully. "She comes to me sometimes when I'm dreaming, you know."

What? "What? You mean like you have dreams about her or that she's like…"

"It's kind of like a presence. Don't say anything to your dad. He'll think I've gone off the deep end."

Can't believe that Margaret just confessed to the possibility of experiencing anything so illogical. Damn Dorothy. I'm the one you're supposed to be visiting.

Roll out boxes of swimsuits, shorts and sleeveless shirts from under the bed dumping them into a bag for the Sally Ann. The second under-bed box is full of photo albums. Grandma Dorothy goes to Bermuda, to Europe, to Brazil, to China. Whole trips summarized by a mauve pinstriped pantsuit and an arm around some unidentified balding man in front of a tour bus. Two sets of cloudy eyes peering out through large-rimmed, flesh-coloured spectacles, two sets of false teeth grinning at the all the adventures awaiting just one pit stop ahead. Maybe I can make some kind of collage piece using them. Cut them into traditional quilt piece shapes and glue them onto a big canvas. I rip a cardboard flap off of a box to sketch it out.

Tim keeps calling me. Keeps hunting me down at the Queen. I told him straight up about Aubrey. Bet he thinks he can wear me down. Fluttering his thick black eyelashes from across the bar. Staring at me with those watery blues.

Back in the kitchen, mom has really thrown herself into her work. She's scrubbing down the counter and the inside of cupboards. Reminds me a bit of Lillian: as long as everything looks proper on the outside the inside doesn't matter. Dorothy's pill schedule is fixed to the fridge with a magnet in the shape of Florida. A poke in the ribs from Aubrey. On the wall, an embroidered sampler reads, *never put off for tomorrow what you can do today*.

"Mom." She looks up from the Comet-soaked scouring pad oozing light green froth, but doesn't stop working. "What was she like when you were a kid?"

She scours on, measuring her response, deciding what's the right thing to tell the child. "She was…" She laughs and shakes her head a little. Brushes the hair out of her eyes with the back of her wrist. "Never a dull moment."

"You turned out pretty normal."

She laughs again. "From my own daughter—thank you. I've got to finish this and get the cleanser off my hands. It's starting to irritate my skin."

She may wear a hole through the oatmeal laminate counter yet. Return to the bedroom closet and file through red and gold blazer, blue velvet dress, knit wear from the Lanark Kitten Mill and floral gowns whose dancing days are long done. The hatboxes on the top shelf hold a variety of hats except for the large red octagon, which contains old letters and more photos. I dive in and start sifting, then notice mom in the doorway observing thoughtfully. She gestures toward the bed.

"She was lying right there. So still. The covers were around her and an empty tumbler on the bedside table. The light was on. TV too. Vomit pooled beside her on the bed, on the floor. Took her pulse. Smelled alcohol. Called your Dad. Cleaned up the vomit. Called 911. The doctors said it was her heart in the end that stopped. Mother was very resourceful. When I was waiting for the ambulance I noticed a cleaned pot in the dish strainer beside the bottle of rye. I think she dissolved all the pills she'd been hoarding over the years on the stove, in the alcohol, and casually drank the concoction throughout the day topping off with the rest of the rye in the evening. Pills for sleep, pills for pain, pills for depression, pills for blood pressure, angina, acid reflux. Her body was old. Guess she was ready to go."

"You got all that from a washed pot?"

"When she finally had to put Barnaby in the nursing home, she went to great lengths describing for me what she would do should she ever become mentally and or physically incapacitated. Years ago, of course, but it fits."

"It's obviously what she wanted."

"Suppose. But is it really what she wanted or was she ill?"

"If she had Alzheimer's, that choice sounds sane to me."

"Dr. Stephenson seemed to think it was early onset. He said it could be readily contained for many years with medication. I don't see why she gave up so easily. Her memory loss could have been linked to her antacid medication for all we know. I've read about people having severe vitamin deficiencies that lead to secondary conditions like memory loss. She just got it into her head that she had Alzheimer's and was going the way of Barnaby. If she'd listened to the doctor, and to us and waited it out, we may have found a solution."

"What if you didn't? What if she had to be institutionalized?"

"Rash thinking followed by rash action. Story of her life."

God. What must she make of my life? And what if she knew the truth? Maybe Dorothy's perception of her life, of her reality, simply differed from my mother's. I would have liked her to meet Aubrey. Would have liked to have said a proper goodbye. Now's probably a bad time to bring up that ticket to Australia.

The sixth time I almost died, I convinced Tracy to join students' council. We organized the biggest dance of the century, an homage to the Age of Aquarius. Once tickets were sold and students from across the county began arriving dressed in full hippie regalia, we parked Brian's red truck across the street at the Hook Line and Sinker bait and tackle shop to watch everyone stream through the school doors. We smoked cigarettes and joints and toasted our fabulousness while downing a twenty-sixer of Bacardi with coke and listening to Neil Young vacillate between electric and acoustic versions of the same song. I found out later after having had my stomach pumped, the dance was a huge success. Tracy said I vomited non-stop on the tarmac in front of the bait and tackle shop and the clerk told her if she didn't get me out of there, he was going to call the cops. I still remember staring up at the bedraggled faces of Dave and Margaret from my hospital bed.

Bedroom packing more or less complete, I turn my attention to the bathroom cabinet under the sink. Pond's cold cream, Noxzema, powders and talc and roll-on blushers left over from her burlesque days on stage, or so it would seem. Bottles, jars, tubes and mousse containers of pink and purple hair rinses with names like frivolous fawn and sumptuous sable await their landfill destiny.

Reg joins me behind the bar.

Tie my white apron over my jeans, say hello to the kitchen guys.

"You wanna start with a Russian?"

"I can't drink and work. At least not this early, I won't be able to make change in a couple of hours."

"Who are you kidding? I seen you put 'em away. It's dead. C'mon."

He pushes a Black Russian at me and lights a smoke.

So, Reg wants a drinking buddy. Twist my rubber arm.

I imagine Aubrey at the Flash tuning his guitar, Gina cracking him a beer. Now, now, don't be like that. Chris and Martina will look out for me. Have a little trust, a little faith in the guy. Besides, how could he want her when he could have me? Proximity? Stop. Stop it. I've got to believe what Aubrey and I have together is true even in the absence of empirical evidence. Tim's right, I have no faith.

Reg takes his drink and sits at one of the booths with his paperwork. Sheets of numbers, a book, pencils, a calculator. I wipe the dust and drips from some of the liquor bottles when in saunters my old high school English teacher.

He looks startled, like he was thinking about something completely different, then his face lights and he smiles.

"Mr. Williams."

"Serena Palmer. Call me Byron."

I pull him a Kilkenny cream ale and get the milky froth just right.

"Never thought I'd see you back in Mariposa."

"Well, what can I say? I did manage to graduate OCAD with a degree in Art, then I went to Australia, then my grandma died so I came home to help my mom out, and now I need to get some coin together to go back."

"And in Australia you?"

"Fell in love. And I was pretty much doing this too. I'm between lives at the moment."

"Between lives. I like that." He sips his beer thoughtfully. "I retired last September. I've been working on a novel the breadth of which has grown to mammoth proportions. I need to trim, to fearlessly edit. But instead…" Takes a big drink of beer. "And you fell in love." Raises his glass to me.

I blush.

"Must be serious."

I am a beet.

"Alas." He looks around the empty bar, makes a show of glancing over his shoulder. "Your love remains in the land of Oz?"

I nod.

"In the immortal words of Mr. Vonnegut, and so it goes."

"How does your wife like being a real estate agent? She enjoying the change in careers?"

"My wife? Oh of course, she was your art teacher before her rebirth into real estate. And now you've seen her ads. Ex-wife. She left me several years ago. Was it four?" He accounts for time in his head, "Yes four years ago. Almost five."

"Sorry."

"No need, no need."

He raises his glass to Reg as an air toast, Reg responds and sucks his ice. I make him a fresh Russian.

"Serena. If I remember correctly, you were an artist?"

"Yes, still am, sort of."

He cocks his balding head, age spots appear in the centre between the greying tufts above his ears.

"I'm not really painting much at the moment."

"Perhaps I can help you with that. You be my muse and I'll find you an artistic venture."

Byron wanders over to the couch and board game area and motions for me to join him in a game of Jenga. I tell him I'm supposed to stay at the bar.

"Then Mohammed must come to the mountain," he says, setting the game down in front of me. "Leave all that wiping. There won't be anyone in here for another hour."

"So Byron, I've been coming here for years. Sporadically, I mean, but I've never seen you."

"Recently fallen off the back of the ol' proverbial wagon, m'dear."

He pours the wooden bricks from the Jenga box out across the bar. One by one we build the tower by layering the bricks and carefully removing them hoping not to be the first to crumble the stack.

"You know, Serena, life's a bit like this children's game. It's a messy pile of disorder we struggle to make sense of and just when we think we've got the world by the tail, the world swishes its butt and everything begins to crash around us. For if we get too close to the sun the universe says nice try silly mortal and melts our wings like Icarus."

Such an English teacher analogy. What's wrong with reaching for the sun anyway? I slowly pull a wooden piece from the tower. It's Byron's turn. The tower still stands. He continues.

"Happiness is transitory. The bricks of life fall down around us. And one by one we build them up. Real happiness is not external and does not come from those people and circumstances that surround you. It's internal. Has always been there. Whether you see it depends on how you look at things. So, in the end, no matter what knocks your world you'll be able to hold that small egg of happiness within."

He extracts the next Jenga piece and those remaining collapse on the bar creating a noise throughout the Queen that belies their insignificance.

"That's some good shit, Byron. You should write it down," I say.

Byron smiles in whiskery creases and finishes his beer. "Words of a drinking man." Passes me his empty glass.

And Aubrey and I phone talk. He asks me what's so wrong with life in Mariposa except that he's not there. Try to explain. He says, *You're always so down on your town, what's the matter with it?* Apparently my MNC descriptions weren't enough, so I tell him things like I was playing Scattergories at the bar with some customers and we had to come up with nouns that start with F. I write Filipino on my sheet and everyone tells me I'm wrong, that it starts with ph. So I say the Philippines starts with ph but if you are from the Philippines you are Filipino and they still wouldn't give me the point.

Then I tell him about going to see *The Rocky Horror Picture Show* in high school. Hardly anyone arrived at the theatre in costume. And instead of throwing rice and toast and carrying a newspaper, as per Rocky Horror custom, people just whipped rotten eggs at the screen. So, the movie theatre called the cops and the News Packet ran a story about the trouble with youth today.

—

Reg's losing his shit. He boozes every night at the Queen and whines about Stephanie. I play the sympathetic listener, but I feel no sympathy. I need him away from me. He's making it too easy for me to listen to the lonely beast inside that tells me to drink, to stuff it all down. I ask him to show me how to do the books and tell him I'll take care of the place for a while so he can leave, go somewhere and pull himself together.

He takes me at my word and two nights later stands behind the bar showing a woman how he likes servers to wear their white aprons, folded in half and crossed around the waist. She's about thirty-five, long black hair tucked behind her ears, deep grooves around her mouth. She wears a plaid shirt overtop of leggings and looks like a barrel-chested, female version of the lead singer of Aerosmith. There's a little leather pouch around her neck.

"Come meet my sister's kid Lisa," Reg says. "You know how you were saying I should get away? I took your advice. Went to the Missinaba Reserve last night and did a sweat. Ran into Lisa here at the community centre. Said she was looking for work until the casino opens late spring. Then I had one of those," he points his finger and snaps at me as I try to fill his gaping vocabulary.

"A flash of clarity? An epiphany?"

"Yeah, that's it. So, I decided right then and there I was taking a break from the business for the winter. I'll be back in spring when things get busier, but for now, you and Lisa can do what needs to be done. I'm goin' surfin' in Costa Rica."

"Wow. How long are you gonna be gone?"

"April. Won't be around booze. Learn how to surf. I'm gonna come back fresh, with a new attitude. That reminds me." From behind the bar, he lifts up a bouquet of pink and yellow gerberas, white baby's breath and fern leaves stuffed into an empty pineapple juice can. "These came for you."

"Card?"

He shakes his head. I can't imagine Aubrey sending these all the way from Australia. Reg claps his hands, and points to Lisa. "Lisa will man the bar tonight and I'll show you all the books."

Lisa salutes. I nod. She smiles back. It's snowing outside again. Can hardly see through the front windows, flakes falling thick like grated chalk. Another month and then some?

Reg pours us each a draught, shuffles through his paperwork. "I seen your friend Tracy the other day. She came in here with that old guy."

"Her dad. Yeah, she's been kicking around town keeping an eye on him since her mom died last year. She's heading to Ottawa soon."

"What for?"

"Some post-grad Human Resources program."

He only half listens, hands me a yellow piece of paper scrawled with blue ink. "Here's the address list for stock order- ing, usually buy my paper products from Bob's Towels."

Then Tim saunters in. Stops by our table for a quick hello, orders a coffee, spreads a newspaper out on the bar and starts reading. Put my head down and make notes. The flowers. Don't want to forget anything Reg is saying but I can't concentrate on anything for long with Tim over there. He smiles at me. I smile back. What am I doing? Close my eyes and think of Aubrey walking beside me all the way around Uluru.

April: Two Months Before

So Long Crapwalker and Good Luck

Reg squeezes my shoulders with a tanned, furry forearm. "TCB," he says smiling, invading my eye space with his pupils.

"What?"

"TCB," he repeats and holds his fist up for a dap. I look blankly, bop his knuckles with mine.

He throws his hands up in mild exasperation. "Taking care of business in a flash. Elvis used to have that on his ring, you know, TCB with a lightning bolt."

"Really?" As if I give a rat's ass. He flits around the bar in his post-tropical glow undoing some of the little changes Lisa and I made in his absence. Whistles while he pulls the high-end scotches to the front. "So, Reg," I wrap the white apron around my hips. "Now that you're back, I think it's time for me to move on."

"That was always the plan. Congratulations." Slips a meaty hand up the back of my neck, touches the nape, waggles a finger at the hairline. "Don't leave without a parting gift. Got some of B.C.'s finest." He kisses his thumb and forefingers and like an haute cuisine chef throws the gesture into the air.

Byron arrives, says, "Spring is in the air, ladies. T.S. Eliot knew nothing of cruelty: early April lifts the clouds of winter despair." He nods toward me. I shove a beer with coaster under his reddening snout. "Had my first Elvis sighting yesterday and you know what that means."

Reg steps in rubbing his thumb against his other fingers, says, "Elvis festival—mucho dinero," and disappears into the kitchen.

Of course, the Elvis thing.

"Where'd ya see him?" Lisa asks.

"Corner of Missinaba and Highway 12."

"Na, that wasn't Elvis. That was Crapwalker. You're all mixed up." She points her chin at Byron and says to me, "How can such a wise man be such a fool?"

"Wise enough to play the fool!" says Byron and then to me, "So, Serena. Your last week." He beckons Lisa to bring over her glass of Diet Coke. Tells me to grab a drink as well. I pluck a Heineken from the beer fridge and pop the cap, unleashing the fruity vapor of hops. The three of us clink drinks and I can't stop myself from grinning.

He pats his leather satchel. "As always, Serena, we are in perfect step with the timing of the universe. I was scouring the Book Nook for information on Lisa's animal medicine when I saw a book and thought of you. Lisa, I'll have you know, there is no such things as *ass medicine*."

She laughs her silent toothy laugh.

From his worn case he produces a small white novel. The drawing on the cover is of a bear in black pen and ink. Orange letters say, *Bear,* by Marian Engel. I reach for it just as Byron yanks it back. "Ah, ah, ah, now that I know you've committed to leaving, I need to inscribe it. But, I didn't know until now what I was going to say." He writes and thinks and taps his nose with the end of his pen. Slides the book across the bar to me. "I think this book was a bit of a Can-Lit joke in its day. Still, I thoroughly enjoyed it. I think you will too. And don't forget about that mural. It's an excellent opportunity. I'll give you one year from today."

I crack the cover of the small paperback, strangely nervous, eager to see what he's written. In black calligraphy: *You never really leave, you know, though you may journey far. Thank you for lighting my evenings with joy and reminding me why I write. Remember, the world is full of people who don't listen to themselves, don't be one of them.* Still holding the book, looking intently at the bear on the cover, I say to Lisa, "Did I ever mention that I've had some pretty intense bear dreams this year?"

"Told ya. Bear medicine. Dreaming's a sign from the ancient ones, trying to help you find your way."

"You think so?"

She nods.

"If they're helping me, guiding me, why am I such a mess?"

"Fucked if I know. Pass me them ketchups. Alls I know is that if your spidey senses are tingly, you better pay attention." She throws the gooey red lids into a sink full of hot water wiping the screw ring tops with a damp cloth. As she deftly pours the sickly sweet, tomato sauce into the bottles from giant black and red cans, the same ones we used at MNC, I think for the first time in a long time about Jimmy B. "My cousin Clara says nothing is decided. Everything is decided."

"What's that supposed to mean?"

"You got bear medicine, Serena. Go in your cave and think about it."

Next night, Lisa barges through the door to the Queen carrying the News Packet. "It's the end of an era. Crapwalker is dead." She unfolds the newspaper and spreads it out on the bar.

From the front page, Crapwalker in his soiled grey parka stares out with beady, unhinged eyes from the red, weather beaten creases that pass for skin. Imagine, virtually ignored by nearly everyone in the town for forty years and now he's splashed across the News Packet with his very own headline. *Gordon Moodie, Dead at 62.*

Reg shakes the paper open, reads the accompanying story aloud.

"Born in Montreal in 1932, Gordon Moodie has been a fixture in Mariposa since the late 1950s when he became a permanent resident. Many believe him homeless, a hobo of sorts. His family tells a different story. He had a typical upbringing by a schoolteacher mother and a mechanic father and attended McGill University studying Economics until his diagnosis of schizophrenia while in his early twenties. His elder sister, Sherry Marsh, explains: *Gord stayed with mom and dad in the city for a while, but he wouldn't take his medication regularly and it got to be too much for mom, they were getting on in years. That's when he came to live with us, but he and my husband never saw eye to eye especially after Gord refused the prescriptions. We decided he was an adult and should be allowed to live his life as he saw fit.*

"He landed in Mariposa shortly thereafter, deciding that he wanted to be where his grandparents had always cottaged, a place where he felt at home. His parents and sister arranged for him to have a permanent room, if and when he desired, at the Pleasant Manor Motor Inn on Highway 12 and to take his meals at the Ranchero Country Griddle truck stop. Waitress Penny Buchanan says of Moodie, *People called him Crapwalker, but he was a goddamn gentleman. Was the heart of our community here at the Ranchero. Him needing us held us together, suppose you could say. He was a reason some days to come to work. We looked after him and he looked after us. If there were rabble rousers looking to cause trouble late at night, you could be sure Gord would be there cursing and grumbling and shaking that wild white hair at them. He did look a fright when he wanted.*

"A candlelight vigil will be held at Wissanotti Beach Park across from the Champlain monument where his lifeless body was found face down on the tarmac last night."

Life as I experience it may be a projection of my own mind but it's the relationships we form that define us. Without relationships, how would ever know we existed? We'd all be invisible blobs, our words asinine shouts into the wind. Though, without other people, we may never have to declare ourselves I.

Crapwalker is the talk of the Queen all night. Too bad he never knew he was a super star. Or maybe he did. When the kitchen closes at eleven, I push through the swinging doors to take beer orders from the guys. They huddle around the prep area discussing the merits of their experimental late night hors d'oeuvres.

"Serena!" The sous-chef, if you could call him that, walks toward me with a plate of something. "You gotta try this. Deep fried pickles. Awesome."

Sour, salty, greasy. Marvelously so. Still smacking oily lips, pickle juice at mouth corners, I push back through the doors into bar world incredulous at what I see. Right there at the bar in front of me grinning like an idiot in a brown knitted sweater and black down vest sits Aubrey. He stands when he sees me and we rush at each other while I pray silently to the forces that be that neither Tim nor Marty will drop in on the Queen tonight. Damn. Indonesia just got that much farther. And, *oh my God if we stay at my parents' they'll make us sleep in separate rooms* and *oh my God he's going to have to meet my parents* and then I distract the monster from eating my monkey brains. Let joy flood my head, float my heart. And I really don't care what I think, because Aubrey's holding me. He came for me. Came to guide me home from this godforsaken underworld.

My arm around his waist, his arm around my shoulder, we walk down by the lake, toward the Spruce motel.

"How did you get a ticket so fast?"

"Martina. Chris' wife. She knows someone in the travel industry through her shuttle business in Darwin. Somebody cancelled at the last minute. Hopped on a couple of planes then onto a coach in Toronto and rode up here to the *Sunshine City*. Isn't that what the yellow wood chips say when you're coming into town?"

He grabs me, hugs me, squeezes me. Lifts my feet off the ground. "Fuck. I love you. I need to be with you. Couldn't stand thinking that Tim guy might get his hands on you."

With steps coordinated, we continue to walk as one. "I was worried about Gina."

"Gina? She couldn't hold a candle to you."

"True, but I bet she put the moves on you."

Under the luster of streetlight, beyond the cold of his cheeks, I swear I see a pinch of red.

"I knew it! There's something you're hiding. Something you haven't told me." I stop walking. Drop hands to my sides.

"Some flirty, drunk girl jumping on your lap while you're hanging out with your friends is not something you tell your girl-friend over the phone when she's like three thousand miles away."

I knew it. I'm not completely psycho. He tries to pull me to him. I stiffen, resist. Paralyzed, a deluge of numbness. Why wouldn't he just tell me?

"Oh c'mon, you *know* Gina. Even if I'd never met you I wouldn't have gone for it. It was ten seconds of nothing. Please don't turn it into something."

I reach for his hand, softly touching our palms together, feeling his warm energy inside.

We keep walking.

"Get this. When I checked into the Spruce, the guy at the desk asked if I wanted the *waterbed suite*. Can you believe it? The waterbed suite! That's so 1982. I half expected James Spader to come out of the bathroom wiping coke off his nose. Don't worry. I said yes. It's all heated up and ready to go, baby."

Off-white paint on the side of the Spruce motel peels and flakes from the stucco. Hasn't changed since I was here last. In one of these hotel rooms, can't remember which, months before I got together with Tim I lost my virginity in a matter of seconds to a trombonist from my high school's band. An endless source of mirth and teasing for Tracy and the rest of my friends. Yup. Good ol' Mariposa. Around every corner, untoward memory lurks.

Aubrey asks me to wait outside a minute. Scurrying sounds leak out from around the hollow green door. The ghost of an old argument with Jason bubbles up in my head. Things will be different this time. I'll try harder. I'll smile and act happy even if I don't feel like it.

Inside, dim lighting. It's really hot from the heater being left on while he was at the Queen. A black bottle of something chills, leans to one side of a plastic ice bin, its neck beading with condensation, water droplets pooling on the plastic wood night table. Aubrey lights candles on the dresser. Sitting on the edge of the bed, on a faux quilt of burgundy and cream coloured triangles, I fall back into a sea of rippling rubber. Forgot about the waterbed. Cork pops, plastic glasses on the verge of overflow. Romance and thoughtfulness, a beautiful man who loves me, it's too much. I need to ruin it somehow.

"Do you think it will always be like this? Even after you know me better?"

"I feel like I already know you."

"You do, it's just, like, what if I get all mopey and depressed sometimes and it irritates the hell out of you, what then?"

"It would take a lot more than moping to change the way I feel about you."

So he says.

Lips on lips. Wine sloshing over cup edges, spilling onto a scratchy nylon bedspread stretched tight across the skin of this massive breast implant of a bed. Kisses greedy and wet at first, then settling into a rhythm of inhale exhale. Nimble guitar-playing fingers unhook, remove. His is the smell of salt, the sweat of man. He breathes his love into me. I shiver. I could shatter. It was so easy for Jason. Renouncing attachment is such a convenient precept.

Aubrey brushes the hair out of my eyes, wraps gently on my skull with knuckles. "Ground control to Major Tom?" I keep on kissing him.

Tear the likely filthy bedspread up from the corners and off the bed resuming on less scratchy sheets. Aubrey covers me with his naked chest, envelops me with arms like wings. "I wish you could know how much I love you," he says.

For now, it's enough and when we wake, it's to exhausted candles, an empty bottle, and sunshine sneaking through the centre crack between hideous drapes and pinky-cream motel room furniture. "I was thinking," says Aubrey, "it's time for us to move into the next phase of our lives together and Mariposa is the perfect launching pad."

Panic. This is getting serious. What do I do, how do I get out of this? Say something funny, break the mood. Jump through the window. Dive into the mirror. It was all fine and dandy in Australia so far from real life. Stop. Stop these thoughts. Get ahold of yourself! Why are you giving Jason all this power? You think he's all apprehensive about jumping into his next relationship? No. Of course not. You gonna drag him around with you the rest of your life like an anchor tattoo? No. I will not.

Another thought flutters: maybe I've been wrong about having to do things on my own. Always believed I was supposed to make my own luck, take care of me, find my own damn self, not depend on anyone especially not a man. I am woman charging through the brush, machete in hand, ready to go it all alone, listening carefully to hear the sound of my own voice. But no one, really, has ever done life on his own; every hero's journey has male and female helpers along the way. Why shouldn't I benefit from a partner's support through the darkest regions of the forest, the privilege of relying on my compliment? Isn't this what women have been fighting for—the opportunity to live, grow, discover, create just the same as men have always done and with the same advantages? Why shouldn't Aubrey have a place in my mythology?

Deep breath. Can I muster the strength to trust? Can I maintain the strength to hold my own in partnership? Courage. Walk into the flames, into the darkness, into the fear. Throw myself on top of Aubrey. Right now, this is right, right now, we are here. Now. And maybe that's all that matters.

Sipping weak coffee that tastes of chlorine from the motel room's mini coffee maker, I wonder if the square packet of creamer will improve it. The back of the packet says edible oil byproduct. And while it smells faintly chemical, the ingredients shocking, I dump it in anyway—can't be any worse for me than all the other crap I've crammed down my gullet. As I drink my oily, chloriney coffee water, Aubrey in the shower, I consider his proposal.

My parents greet us at the front door with hugs and handshakes. Margaret's just had her hair highlighted and coiffed into a neat bob. Perfectly painted lips and neatly penciled eyebrows, natural yet manicured, like an English garden. My dad in green pleated cords and button-down is less well turned out but eager to please nonetheless. He slaps a second hand over Aubrey's during his firm introductory handshake, breaks the ice with some fun facts about fonts. A casualty of working in the print industry. When Dave leaves to fetch Aubrey a beer I mouth *fun with fonts*.

Aubrey points toward my dad's unique, shall we say, birdhouse collection with the large Dr. Suess-style martin condominium—purple, red, white and turquoise—and asks him about it. Dave needs no further cajoling, all too eager to let slip that he's been invited to show them at the folk-art exhibit at the

McMichael next fall. I leave the three of them to it, casually slipping into the kitchen to glug my wine and refill my pinwheel patterned crystal stemware with nobody the wiser.

Aubrey, with a gentility honed in the American south from long summers at his grandparents' where he was served crab cakes by maids in uniforms, has impeccable manners and he leaps to help Margaret before she even knows she needs any. During dinner, shockingly, the conversation turns to the incinerator. Aubrey asks my parents the right questions and they see that he is well informed on the subject. Dave gives him a copy of his pride and joy, a SIN pamphlet. When they inquire about his career plans, Aubrey waxes enthusiastic about his music. I cringe, knowing how they feel about jobs that come without pensions or benefits. But Aubrey is valiant and plays the *music is how I serve my community best* angle, so they can't argue with that. And Dave passes the Caesar salad, winks at me, and asks Aubrey if I'm being difficult. Scarlet inflames my skin like an Australian sunburn. Aubrey smiling, replies, "Well, sir, she is a pain in the ass but I feel pretty lucky just the same."

So, I pack my mouth with white-coated romaine leaves, stuffing down the laughter and betrayal and buying time for a witty retort. When I'm done chewing, the moment has mercifully passed and I'm able to keep my mouth shut by clearing the table, carrying plates into the kitchen. Mom follows me. Says Aubrey is welcome to stay in the guest room. I say we have a room at the Spruce Motel. She stares blankly. We haven't seen each other in nearly three months. Did she expect we'd put on our jammies, give each other a peck on the cheek and sleep in separate rooms? Is this part of her whole pretend game?

Since we're close enough to the city for a day trip, thought I'd bring Aubrey to *Miso Phat,* a Japanese Thai fusion place I'd been to a few times when I lived in Toronto. I have no great experience with sushi, except for the odd dinner with Jason. Aubrey loves it. He pincers his chopsticks around a fat maki roll, dips it in wasabi and pops it in his mouth. A server with a floppy red flower and chopsticks in her black bun sets down a fresh wooden rectangle of rolls. Tuna, salmon, avocado, cucumber, egg—no problem. Roe? I examine the tiny scoop of fish eggs wrapped in nori with black sesame speckled rice. Little pliable sacs like vitamin E capsules with an undeveloped entity inside. Has it already decided what it will become? Is the essence of fishness imprinted on its nascent soul? Does the little speck inside the jelly get any say?

Aubrey reaches across the table with sticks extended. I imagine the embryos rolling across my tongue, slipping into my cheeks, cold, sticky, primordial. "Sorry." I push the tray toward him. He struggles to keep his lips closed, the rice and seaweed in as he chews. From across the table, his eyes water and I vicariously share his wasabi burn.

As we make our way north, up the 400 from Toronto back home toward my grandma's condo, which my parents have generously allowed us to inhabit on the condition we prepare it for sale, I say, "You know, the Komodos await."

Aubrey rolls the passenger window down and then up, cleans the residual water from melted spring snow so he can see where we're driving. "Maybe we should go to New York."

"Kind of expensive," I say.

"True. We'd probably get two weeks there including travel. If we went to Thailand or Indonesia, we'd get two months of bumming around not to mention awesome weather."

"Could we teach English? Would that give us enough to stay longer?"

"Heard there was some good surfing off Vancouver Island. We could camp, keep it cheap, keep it goin' even longer," he says.

"Bet Dave and Margaret will let us use grandma's car to drive cross country. I gotta come back in time to finish Byron's mural, though."

"Maybe I could help you."

And then, just like that, a plan as though already written in the universe presents itself and we seize on it like it's the only thing we ever wanted to do in the first place and we're ready to fly out from Mariposa and into the rest of our lives.

Late June

THE EIGHTH TIME

When I open my eyes, a bald man in a white coat with a silver mustache, a doctor likely, towers over the edge of my bed and scribbles onto a clipboard. I say, or I think I say, "What are you doing and who are you?"

"Who are you?" he says.

And in my dreaminess all I see is the hookah-smoking caterpillar from *Alice in Wonderland* puffing out smoky words: Who are you? Who are you?

Who am I? Who are any of us? My mind smiles laughing heartily, though I'm not certain my body follows suit. I'm worn and weary but manage to say, or I think I say, "I'm energy. We're all just energy."

A tall nurse with a head full of brown curls enters, noticing perhaps, my open eyes. Lifts my slack hand, snaps a clamp on my finger, gauging a pulse, shushing me when I try to speak, so I stare at a long white whisker on her chinny chin chin and try not to choke on the questions in my throat. Questions like how long have I been here—hours, days, weeks? One finger still pressed to her lips, she scribbles something on a clipboard chart from the end of my bed, pats my hand, shakes the tail of my drip sending the liquid shivering, and goes about her requisite barnyard business mentally striking lines through a to do list.

The doctor enters in a waft of authority. Attempt speaking and to my great relief sound more coherent.

"Plenty of time for that, dear," he says, looking everywhere but my face. "Allow your body to wake. You've absorbed enough of that tranquillizer to knock out a bear. That's probably six times what would have felled a slim gal like you. Not to mention whatever else you kids were ingesting. It'll take a while for your brain to catch up."

He says something else, too, but my awareness wanes. It sounded like he introduced himself saying his name was Shaw or something. Squint to see his nameplate because I can't be sure. When I twist, a searing pain shoots from my ass up through every nerve into my brain or maybe it's the other way around. My left butt cheek aches. I may not know exactly where I am or how or when I got here, but that, I know for sure.

"The fluids in these pouches are to keep you properly hydrated, to stabilize your erratic brain activity and to flush the animal tranquillizer out of your system. We've kept a close watch on your vitals. You're already responsive, awake, a good sign. There's a very worried young man waiting by the door. Are you interested in seeing him?"

Who? A man? Oh yeah. I nod.

Tears roll down Aubrey's cheeks. I feel my own face scrunching, eyes dripping as beads of the recent past string themselves together.

"Oh my God, Serena. I am so sorry." He falls on his knees and weeps. "I never meant to hurt you. I was only trying to protect you. I love you so much. I was so scared in the woods. Scared you were gone, dead, that I'd never see you again. I held your body all lifeless and droopy. Could hear your laboured, faint breaths. Put my ear to your heart and heard the weakest little thumping. I was worried, you know, that you were moving on, that you really, literally, had transcended the Bardo."

"What?" My voice cracks from dryness.

He pours me water from the clear plastic pitcher at my bedside, props my head up with a hand at my neck and holds the cup to my lips. "You don't remember."

"Sort of I do. But I'm not sure what's real, like what really went down out there, and what might be some kind of dragon-chasing nonsense from all this shit in my veins."

Aubrey takes a deep breath, exhales. "We ate the heart that Ted brought. Right?" I nod. "Then Ryan and I were jamming, I'm sorry, I was caught up in my own world, guess I sort of lost track of you. You know how I get when I'm playing, especially when I'm fucked up. Ted was sitting with the two of us, tapping and singing and tripping on the Peru juice and the music and then the radio on the ranger truck starts buzzing and a call comes through that there's a second grizzly in the area. They think it's the Missus of the one we, you know. Guy on the radio says the location of the bear is right on the trail by our campsite. Ted goes, *Must have been sighted by that group of campers near the trail-head, down the way from us toward the water.* That's when we notice you're missing. So anyway, Ted's like, *Holy shit! I saw her go in the woods, I thought she was just takin' a leak but it's been a while* and he grabs a gun. Meanwhile, Ryan is totally incapacitated, staring at the fire, banging on his bongos and I see Ted taking off along the trail into the woods and follow him. I didn't know if he had his rifle or the tranq gun or what. So, we're all high and running, running down the trail yelling for you, calling, 'Serena! Serena!' Nothing. Then Ted keels over, leans into some tree and starts barfing. Seriously, heaving his guts out. Turns out Ryan forgot to tell us ayahuasca makes you puke. I say, *Ted! We have to save her!* He goes, *Take the tranq gun, it's pre-loaded with darts, if you see the bear shoot it a couple of times and I'll eventually catch up. Sorry, dude, I'm totally pale.* Thanks, right? So I charge off with this stupid tranq gun and I'm looking all around and calling you when I see it. See this massive bear running through the woods. Kneel down, aim and shoot the gun. I think I miss the bear, it's too far. I follow it, shoot again. I'm jogging behind it in the woods thinking I'm gonna find this hulking bear but all I see is you, crumpled in this tiny heap. I swear to God I thought it was a bear I shot." He rests his cheek on my chest.

It was him. He thought I was a bear. Flash vignettes of last night trickle through. Maybe he was not wrong. "I think I *was* a bear." He looks at me weird. "I think I like shape-shifted, you know, like a shaman." I can almost see the information, the words, rolling through the cogs in his brain turning over and over desperate for a frame of reference. "But you didn't shoot me, you shot a bear! Don't you see?"

"I guess. I dunno, it kind of makes me think of that cheesy Snoop Dogg video from last year where he's screwing some girl and then her dad knocks on the door and he morphs into a Doberman and scampers away."

"Couldn't it be like magic or voodoo spiritual something? That after eating the heart of a bear I embodied its essence, became my animal totem?"

"Fuck. I don't know what I believe. I never would have said I could have shot you."

"You did, though." I roll over as best I can without straining too much and lift the sheet corner to show him my left cheek. "You shot me right in the ass."

"Oh my God. I shot you in the ass. My gay philosophical dad would be so proud."

And then we laugh like crazy because what else is there to do?

Aubrey wipes his eyes clear of laughing tears and blows his nose with tissue from the bathroom. Sits back down and plays with the fluid bags on the IV tree for a while. The doctor arrives, ushering him out in flurry of medical formalities. He pokes and prods me, scrawls things on my chart. Wonders if I feel up to answering some questions. Sits beside me in the peach vinyl armchair and takes a moment to push his wire glasses up on top of his baldhead. Crosses and uncrosses his legs. Navy blue socks slouch out from beneath his green trousers, and arranging his clipboard and pen, he strikes a contemplative pose.

"Now that you've returned to us, allow me to properly introduce myself. I'm Dr. Snow."

Snow, not Shaw.

"I'd like to ask you a few questions to understand how you came to be here. Let's begin at the beginning, shall we? What is your full name?"

"Serena Elizabeth Palmer."

"And do you know where you are?"

"B.C. In or near Prince George, I think."

"Correct. You are in a hospital in Prince George. Now suppose you tell me what you remember about how you came to be here."

What I remember and what Aubrey has just told me hovers fresh behind my eyes. I'm open, still woozy. It spills out raw without censor. "We drank this South American herb, can't remember the name, starts with an A. Then we were hanging out by the campfire listening to Aubrey play guitar, this really slick rhythm, and the bongos were thumping, and I went into the woods, had the strangest sensation that it was where I belonged. You know?" Head nodding, scribbling. "I started running, felt good, felt alive. Started to think that I was like, no, started to think *like* a bear. I could move like a bear, see like a bear, hunger like a bear. When I breathed in, I could distinguish the difference between cedar, pine and spruce, could tell that above me was an owl, below me, an ant. Had this insatiable lust to fill myself with whatever I could stuff in. Started digging in the dirt pulling up roots. I heard voices feathering out into the wind and the rustle of branches, looked down and instead of my hand, I swear, I saw a paw. Furry and clawed and capable. It was like, for the first time, ever, I felt absolutely free. Untethered. Felt this rush of warmth. Love. Power. Like there was nothing at all that could ever defeat me. As though I'd reached, at last, this transposed state of higher being. And I was like…!" A squawk of a laugh escapes my throat, reverberating against the band-aid beige walls. Doctor Snow shifts uncomfortably in his chair. I've said too much. Words tumble back into my ears. My cheeks flush.

"I see." Snow scribbles something. "And have you experienced any of these feelings before?"

Already I feel his self-righteous judgment, his labels coming down around me like a net. "Ummm, no. Not at all."

The scrape of the pen along the paper overrides the silence. Fear like a fever rises in me as I realize what I might have done. "Are you a GP?" I ask. He tries to act natural.

"I'm a psychiatrist. And let me tell you, you're lucky I was on call when they brought you in otherwise you might really have hurt yourself." He stands and organizes his papers, tucks pens in his breast pocket. "I'm going to arrange for you to be transferred out of general care and onto the fourth floor."

"What do you mean? Can't I leave?"

His immediate paternal chuckle implies foolish girl. "Not for a while yet, I'm afraid. We need to keep you safe."

I'm afraid. "Keep me safe? What do you mean? Where are you taking me?"

"Calm yourself. The fourth floor. It's our psychiatric ward. I feel you need more observation. We certainly don't want you hurting yourself."

"I feel I need to get the fuck out of here." I panic. Smell the MNC. Kick the sheets off, rip out my IV, nearly fall to the ground as my legs buckle.

"Nurse Carmichael!" shouts Snow. "There are restraints on the side of the bed."

Nurse Carmichael, the beach ball, dives at me, grabbing my wrists. "Smarten up, Missy," she says, dark eyes glaring, "we're not going through this again. Three strikes and yer out."

I will not play Bruce to her Natalie.

"No. Stop. I will behave." Limbs weak, shaking, I climb into the bed. Snow looks at me with distrust. Holds me in his gaze until he's sure I'll comply.

"Good." He rips off a piece of paper and shoves it at the nurse. "Prepare an additional injection of Thorazine to be administered immediately. And, if effectively tolerated, the dose may be reduced gradually. Prepare patient to be moved to the fourth floor, Kaufman wing."

"Catheter, Doctor?"

"If restraint is required."

"I won't move. Promise. Can I see my boyfriend? Just for a minute. Please? Is he here?"

"I think that's enough excitement for one day."

"Wait, Dr. Snow." I keep my tone submissive. "Please tell me one thing. What's wrong with me?"

"Clearly you are experiencing some kind of psychotic break. Likely a drug-induced psychosis. Could be schizophrenia, bipolar disorder and possibly even some version of clinical lycanthropy. Time will tell. Do as you're told, and you'll get better faster. If indeed getting better is what you want."

The nurse returns and shoots my arm full of yellow liquid. Eyes fall heavy and I float again into a restless dreamtime. How can they think *these drugs* are good for me? My mind's a ball of string some laughing god has dropped from the top stair of the CN Tower giggling as he watches it unfurl. Dead grizzlies dance in pink tutus before devouring me whole. Frankenstein's monster stalks me with his stitched together body while I wander the frigid tundra, hollow with fear. The doctor is dressed like a 1930s German physician with giant steel instruments and electrical wires dangling all around him in the basement of the MNC in a room full of my former clients bleeding and screaming and moaning in their mournful way.

I wake to darkness with a gasp.

"Psst!" A hand on my arm. "Serena, shhhh. It's me."

Aubrey crouches in the corner of my room. Pale green walls surround. No peach chair, no seaside landscape art on the wall opposite the foot of the bed. "Where am I?"

"You're in the hospital. Different room. They moved you last night. Psych ward. They don't like me seeing you up here. Guess some people get all weirded out by visitors. I had to sneak in."

"Why? Why wouldn't it be good for me to see you?"

"I'm starting to think there's something up with this place, especially with that doctor. He's gotta relax, man. He's giving me bad vibes, like I shouldn't trust him."

"Me too!"

"Whatever you told him freaked him right out. You know what he told me? He says he thinks you have drug-induced mania or schizophrenia manifesting itself as clinical lycanthropy. You know what that is? It's when a person thinks they can turn into a fucking werewolf. He thinks, you think, you can turn into a bear. We got to get out of here before he tries to give you elec-tro-shock or lobotomize you or some shit."

"I was talking like an idiot to him. Still half out of it. Barely knew what I was saying." What was I thinking telling all that to someone with such a criminal lack of imagination. Hearing it aloud, I'm not even sure if I believe it. Aubrey leans in from the side of the bed and rests his head on my stomach careful not to put too much weight on my sore spot. "Let me get this straight," I say. "*You've* been scared mental for weeks over bears, *you* shot me in the ass with a tranq gun, and now *I'm* the one on the psych ward?"

"You're not psychotic. I thought you were a bear, you thought you were a bear. Same difference. Who cares? We should all be so lucky. Let's just focus on busting you outta here."

"Can't you try and convince him that I'll be fine, that it was a brief drug-related incident?" If it's not Mariposa trying to put me in a leg-hold trap, it's something else.

"Seriously, I tried. That guy. He's trying to use me to hunt down your parents. Luckily he could only pull up one of your old Toronto addresses from your health card. I don't want to piss him off in case he tightens security."

Imagining Dr. Snow calling Jason at our old place to tell him I'm crazy makes me laugh so hard: dirt in truth is clean. I stroke Aubrey's hair, though the action soon exhausts me. Dave and Margaret would have to fly all the way across the country to Vancouver then drive or fly halfway as far again up here to Prince George. The expense, the worry, just to hover over me with frightened disappointed faces full of generational deference to Dr. Snow. No way.

"He says it's imperative that they understand the severity of your mental illness. Says you need close monitoring. I think he wants their signatures so he can keep you here for *observation*." He runs his rough fingertips along my forearm caressing cautious circles around the IV at the bend.

"He says it's for your own safety and wellness. He's a doctor, I'm sure he means well. It's not his fault he's unenlightened. Bugs me him acting like he knows everything, and we're a couple of stupid kids. Everything you said was out of context. You don't need fixing. Or observation." He squishes in the bed between the guardrail and me. "This weird part of me thinks that maybe he knows you are precious and rare and wants to keep you for himself. That probably sounds crazy. Better watch what I say around here, or I'll end up watching Jerry Springer in the next room with that freak show in the plaid robe who keeps writing lip-stick messages on his door window." He holds my left hand with both of his for a moment then drops it to blurt his scheme.

"We'll go to Miami; if there's anything seriously wrong with you, I'll get my grandpa and his doctor friends to figure it out. If you're ill, you need a real doctor not some fucking small town Quack. Okay? I have a plan. Be ready for me tomorrow night."

Kisses me, slips one leg over the side rail and then the other, landing softly on the floor and skulking away.

A squat nurse I don't recognize peers in at me through Plexiglas, asks me *how we are doing*, replaces the empty bag with a new pouch and administers an injection.

Late June

ESCAPE FROM PRINCE GEORGECATRAZ

It's dim when I wake. Aubrey sits beside my feet on the bed playing his guitar. When he realizes I'm awake, he sets his guitar down and climbs into bed. Momentary bliss, our bodies nestled together, a cloak of security. Then I get a whiff of my stale pajamas and become conscious of my appearance for the first time since arriving. Nothing like getting shot in the ass to lay you bare. A mulleted orderly peers in the door, sees two heads on the pillow, and stops.

"Visiting hours are over." Twists and tilts his wrist. "It's eight o'clock."

"Oh c'mon, man," says Aubrey. "She just woke up. Half an hour. What's your favourite song?"

"Know any Floyd?"

Aubrey smiles at me. "I might know a couple. How about something from the *Dark Side of the Moon*?" He sings *Brain Damage*. The orderly holds his lighter and sways in the doorway.

"All right. You just bought yourself half an hour. Don't fuck it up."

When half an hour is done, Aubrey makes a big show of saying goodbye to him, shaking his hand, cracking a joke.

Later, he yanks my sleeve, whispers from under the bed. "Shhhh. It's gotta be tonight. Break-time is 11:30 until 11:45. They get lazy during breaks. We got fifteen minutes to get past the girl at the front desk. She's a serious Tetris addict and won't even look up from her computer screen. Even if she does, what's she gonna do? We'll be so far gone by the time she tries to cover her own ass."

He unhooks my intravenous lines, peeling the clear surgical tape from my veins and applying gentle pressure with his thumb as he extracts the needles. Dresses me back in street clothes, tugging the shirt over my head, helps pull on one pant leg at a time. A different night orderly passes the half open door and I manage to shield our bodies with a sheet, pretend my eyes are shut, squinting only enough to spy his white-trousered legs, his hands tossing an orange up into the air and catching it as he walks past.

And then we're in the car again only this time driving south. So. The eighth time, I almost died, I didn't almost. I did. And was promptly born anew.

"I'm such a fucking idiot. What was I thinking suggesting Leary's bullshit as a path to enlightenment. I'm supposed to protect you," he says.

"No, don't you see? I did transcend. Though I suppose you could say, all life is a state of Bardo, one monumental act of transformation. There is no finite self. You're born, you live, you die. Born, live, die a hundred times before this body quits. It's not that I've been between lives, the in between is life. If I hadn't tried the Peru juice, I wouldn't have gotten to this place, to my higher consciousness. Does that sound crazy? Oh my God, do I have lycanthropy?"

"No. But, you also wouldn't have wound up in a hospital in Prince George because of your dumb-ass boyfriend."

"No such thing as a free lunch." I write this on the ceiling of the Tempo along with a likeness of my grinning self. Jason used to tell me that a Buddhist had no self. Tracy always said you have to love yourself before you can love someone else. And I'd think, how can you love what doesn't exist? But maybe they are both kind of right. To love yourself, you have to know yourself. Once you know yourself you can renounce yourself. Once yourself dies, you realize, there is no self, only oneness and love and that energy doesn't dissolve or destroy, it simply changes form. Maybe life is bigger than an Escher staircase. Maybe it's more like an ocean and all of us merely water drops.

Through my Thorazine fog, I realize that there may be some grain of truth to Dr. Snow's concerns, that on the crazy continuum, I may etch a mark. I went from the dark spiral of angry desolation and self-destruction last fall into the height of golden energy attraction and awesomeness in Australia and then back again—a continual inch worm of undulating moods and states of mind—up and down like a bride's nightie, as my grandma would say. "Aubrey, what if it's true, what if I really am fucked up?" I can't bring myself to look at him, just stare out at the yellow lines illuminated by the headlights on the road ahead.

"You're not crazy. No crazier than I am. Everyone's crazy. Have I told you about my parents? A little crazy is good, makes people perceptive, sensitive. Maybe even extra sensory if they can tap into it. Besides, even if you are crazy, crazy is not all that you are."

"Yeah. What does crazy even mean?" We're always asking these big questions, but we need never know the answer, can never know the answer. For the answer alone belongs to the infinite, still we demand explanation, feel static until we think we receive it, cannot move forward without, and yet, to ask that simple why is to simultaneously admit our lack of knowing and our desire for control, fueling our fear of the unknown. Maybe we're not asking the wrong question maybe it's that we're asking the question at all, and we ought to just be accepting and loving the not knowing.

So go ahead, Dr. Snow, just try and confine me with your labels. Hold fast to your barbarian heart and the evil that men do when they pretend to know more than they do, when they fear what they can't understand.

Aubrey steers into an all-night gas station for fuel, coffee and water. My body quietly reels, stomach clenching, muscles contracting and relaxing as it struggles to flush hospital drugs. Fall asleep against the window. Wake when it's light. Must have been driving for hours. We pull into a highway rest stop, get out and stretch our legs. Breathe the warm damp air of summer. Prop myself up against a picnic table and pick at the peeling red stain with my fingernail. Watching Aubrey walk toward me from the bathrooms, I begin carving our initials inside a heart on the table-top like so many before me have.

"Why do you think you were so fucked up about the bears?" I ask him.

"Yeah. Been asking myself the same thing. Think I fell pretty hard for you." Wraps his arms around me, kisses my neck. "Like intense. No guarantees in love, huh? Suppose I was insecure, like what if you woke up one day and realized I'm a big dope and you could do better. Probably channeled all that anxiety onto the poor ol' bears. So fuckin' scared of you."

"Me?"

"Not *you*, the leaving myself too wide open. Never fun thinking about your heart getting ripped out and trampled on." Pulls me onto his lap. Traces the carved heart with a fingertip. "You know when you're a kid and you climb up on top of the slide but instead of going down the slide you jump off. And even though you're scared, even though you might get hurt you do it anyway because you don't want to miss out on the thrill of the flight? I don't know in the end which I was more scared of, you, me or the bears."

"Maybe we're one and the same."

Guess Jason was wrong again: it's not attachment to others, but attachment to the idea of others' separateness that causes all the trouble. And all of a sudden, I notice the moon, reflective sunlit surface that it is, lighting the night sky and Aubrey's face and the sharp edges of his nose, the way his freckled skin pulls taught across his cheekbones.

Back inside the Tempo, finish off a couple of granola bars, look out the windows as the landscape changes west to east, north to south. Are all the trees in Miami palms? Will I find a place among them? Suppose I was scared of him too. More though, think maybe I've really been afraid of me, of my own power. Of what might happen when I give myself over fully to loving, to creating.

TRUE NORTH STRONG AND FREE

Summer in Miami is sun-seared greenery spilling from planters, leaves pale and crisp like over-processed hair. It's honking and traffic and boulevards that never end, the smell of sea air and pulp and paper, exhaust. It's white and pink art deco buildings; glass and steel monoliths spiking up from the sand, Latin music that thumps through sidewalks and on into the feet, women in tight dresses and men with slicked back hair. It's air conditioners and Spanish grandparents going to bed early and giving hugs and kisses with old people breath. It's twin beds and separate sleeping quarters, sneaking around a sprawling bungalow in the middle of the night to fuck. It's watching Aubrey in the Miami he knows, the way he loves his grandparents, his friends, the way he takes the stage in clubs each night with confidence.

It's me drawing and painting bears in the garage next to tennis rackets and golf clubs, empty tubs of lawn fertilizer. It's me using pencil, pen and ink to draw representational bears catching salmon in rivers or pausing in long grass. It's me painting huge abstract canvases of bears in flames, bears in the shadows, bears hibernating inside a transparent tent with a giant moon pressing down on the sway back triangle. It's bear country expressed as a physical landscape where fear and shadows and knowing lurk. It's me painting pictures of myself curled inside the body of a bear, of dead bloody bears lying still in rays of pink diamond light, a Swiss Army knife open upon the ground. It's me doubting the improbable feat of shape-shifting and transcendence ever happened. It's me wandering through galleries soaking up colour and visiting the university to ask staff about their art therapy program. It's my parents calling Labour Day weekend to tell me that my grandma's condo has officially been sold, that Stanley and I are each entitled to an inheritance—so long as we come home to sign papers and collect.

In Mariposa, Byron white-washes the mural wall and provides a projector to illuminate my final sketch, never once questioning my intentions. Aubrey manages technicalities of scale, helps me line the work and fill in large patches of colour with paint.

Since the incinerator plan was scrapped, thanks in large part to the efforts of SIN, there's a lot of talk and excitement around our house about trying to keep the momentum of *feel good do good* going strong in the community. Margaret suggests starting a watchdog nature conservancy for all of Mariposa. One phone call leads to another and suddenly there's a fundraising celebration event to coincide with the unveiling of my mural. As if I don't feel like enough of a sphincter, everyone my mom knows driving by and gawking, asking questions as I work, without that kind of attention, that kind of pressure.

Stanley arrives the same day as the official unveiling all morose and quiet. Hazel has dumped him.

"You know," I tell him, "If you weren't such a jerk maybe you'd be able to keep a decent girlfriend."

"You think I'm a jerk?"

He looks wounded. After all the insults we've tossed between us? I cuff his shoulder. "We're all jerks, Stanley."

He sniggers, flicks my ear, stuffs his hands in his pockets. "When are you going to pull the sheet off that ugly mother?"

Twenty-two times now I've been around the sun. It's a warm September Saturday almost exactly a year to the day of Jimmy Birchbark's death by egg. One single revolution and here I am again, right back where I started. And everything so different now somehow.

Lisa waves from across the parking lot. Pats the seat beside her on a bench beneath a maple tree covered in paper cranes from a nearby elementary school's feel-good environmental project. Loops a leather pouch necklace over my head. "Bear medicine," she says. And though I think about it, I just don't have the heart to tell her what really happened. Or what might have happened. To speak of it diminishes it somehow, like it was only meant to exist for a precious blip to help me along my way like a sacred vision maybe.

I squeeze her hand. Remove my opal necklace and place it in her palm.

My dad, with his megaphone, links arms with my mom. Mary Wieder and her new boyfriend, Ritchie the cop, stroll alongside them wearing grey terrycloth ribbons as they campaign together and recruit walkers and sponsors for the next big charity affair promoting mental health awareness, to be known hereafter as Gordon Mooney's Journey, a twenty-kilometer event retracing a portion of his well-traveled stretch of highway. The Raging Grannies sing and can-can with bent legs and tight hamstrings, celebrating the strength of the collective voice of individuals and of the incinerator's demise. Tracy's dad rubs his bowl-full-of-jelly-belly, shells out mini candy canes to children, tells me Tracy has a job interview in Ottawa. Reg sells glasses of beer from a keg, apples and bags of chips for a dollar a piece. Tom and Candice weave through the so-called normals followed by a clutch of clients. Barney is there, mole intact, Maurice, Lenny and Mucker too, their expressionless Buddha-like faces squinting into the sunlight along with everyone else, just as it should be.

As this alternate universe, Mariposa in the raw, oozes up from the cracks in the tarmac all around us, the tailings of my life are exposed acid green and nuclear. Aubrey looks around, tugs my sleeve, says, *What the fuck?*

"Told ya," I say. But I no longer really care, for this is the ground that grew me.

Tim and the band set up black boxes, plug stuff in. He sees me, waves, gives Aubrey a nod. As the moment of truth approaches, the Royal Frenzy honours the occasion with a drum roll.

Aubrey's on a ladder with one corner of the veil and I'm on the scaffolding with the other. On the count of three we let it drop. Directly across the street from the pastel mural of Leacock with his *great believer in luck* quotation is now a giant visual manifestation of my very own *Sunshine Sketches of a Little Town*. In form and feeling it is as though Peter Max with his psychedelic pop art and Norval Morrisseau of the Woodland school shook hands with Jonathan Swift in a sci-fi molecule scrambling pod and splattered the results on the side of a building. The entire street corner is colour-saturated, vivid, intense and full of Serena. For as long as it lasts, for this brief moment in time, all heads will swivel on necks to stare. A clamor swells. People try to guess what the guy beside him thinks before committing to either outrage or applause.

It's Mariposa through a skewed perspective. In the centre of the scene is a giant semi-circular incinerator resembling the sun at the horizon line. Radiating out from the incinerator, elongated pie slices create a layer of background in yellow and orange over an intricately patterned sky in shades of blue. On top of the rays, as if smoke belched out from the incinerator, are cloudy caricatures of McLaughlin and Banbury, Leacock riding past on a book like a magic carpet, tipping his fishing hat to the crowd below. Magenta. Purple. Trippy swirls of yellow, green and white. In the right foreground, the MNC. Jimmy Birchbark's there under a parasol stuffing his face with dual chicken legs like a medieval king beside a bowl of hard-boiled eggs. All the other sketches of people and places from town come together too, in grand scale, right down to Crapwalker in his grey parka holding a lamb in a portrait of stained glass in a church-like rose window of the casino. On the far edge of town, a giant Penalty Box donut shop sign reaches heavenward, stretches far above the humble beings of the city like a colossal probe pressing into the cervix of the sky. It's almost like a perversion of a Jehovah's Witnesses' account of the afterlife straight off the cover of a *Watchtower* magazine where the lion and the lamb lie down together and the lion never hungers for flesh. Kind of a perversion of a perversion.

So maybe I'm not making the world a better place, maybe this is not what Dave and Margaret mean by *service*. And maybe someday I'll enroll in an art therapy program and do some good.

Or not. But right now? What I love is this. Watching all these befuddled smiles ripple through this sea of people gathered here together to celebrate the end of something wicked and the start of something, if not beautiful, at least colourful like a TV room full of clients, like one of grandma's bawdy stories, like a psyche-delic trip, like wildflowers sprouting up in a parking lot of black and grey.

Byron takes care not to spill his pint as he drapes his arm around me. Watches carefully as beer sloshes up and over the sides of his glass, sips the frothy overspill and shakes his head. "Leave it to you, Serena," he says with pride, with fondness. "The sweetness of truth."

And then we laugh and laugh.

"Two minutes to core melt down," Tim screams into the microphone, drowning the murmuring beribboned throng with arm pumping, wrist strumming adolescent metal that incites sur-prise, ear covering and old people feet shuffling. No matter. They encircle the phony incinerator just the same.

McLaughlin holds a bottle of lighter fluid awkwardly in both hands as though butting an automatic weapon up against his fleshy navel. Flaps his striped tie over one shoulder and squeezes for all he's worth demonstrating with the inherent madness of a native Mariposian, that sometimes the very thing that threatens to divide and destroy is the very thing that in the end unites. Throws the empty plastic bottle on top of the model and gestures for Banbury to light a match. Ever the politician, he flashes a grin with hands held high still grasping at votes as his tiny dream burns down.

With the mural as my backdrop, I look out into Mariposa. Hand at my throat, I fondle my necklaces, and through flames, chemical smoke and ash, the crowd stares back at me one face of folly divine.

Aubrey uses my knife to pare a heart-sized apple, wipes the blade on his jeans and passes it to me unsheathed. Steel reflects a ribbon of white sunlight across my eyes. I fold it back into itself, back into the place fear no longer lives. His soft hand with cal-lused fingertips pries open my other palm, sets in a neatly quartered, red skinned apple. Smile. Raise wet, white flesh through lips to tongue. Taste sweet, tart juice. Remember dropping apples with Tracy from hilltop down into culvert, running alongside, watching as the water swept them down and out into Lake Wissanotti as we cheered, patting each other's backs in schoolgirl triumph at the feat. Like Paddle to the Sea, whooshed through the Great Lakes into the warm Gulf Stream at the mercy of high winds, currents and tides, all the way to the Grand Banks of Newfoundland and on into the Atlantic Ocean where he bobbed and floated, a little piece of carved wood set loose to divine his way through the vast primordial flow.

Acknowledgments

This book was written slowly over many years as I worked full-time, raised (and continue to raise) a family, performed (and continue to perform) all manner of domestic labour expected of women, wrote twenty-two short stories, seven of which have been published, pursued a master's degree, and earned a yoga teacher designation. There were many setbacks and times when many doubted my ability to bring this novel to fruition dubbing me a hopeless, hapless, talentless dreamer. Thank you to Chris Needham and Now Or Never Publishing for sharing my creative vision and for publishing my work. To my friends who always believed in me: Janet Myers, Niki Martin, Michelle Hodge, Maureen Uren, Grace Eagan, Janice Kinney and Jay Rothenburg. Your faith means the world to me. To early readers Sally Cooper, Dorris Heffron, and Larry Mathews, thank you for your feedback. For writerly conversations, thank you to Tracey Waddleton and Vaughan Dickson. To my parents, thank you for encouraging my creativity and critical thinking during childhood. And to my partner and biggest cheerleader, Doug Leeper, I wish everyone had the privilege of a relationship as supportive and loving as ours. And last, thank you to my children to whom this work is dedicated: Thank you for teaching me how to open my heart, thank you for teaching me patience, thank you for your brutal honesty, thank you for loving me. Thank you, thank you all for everything. I am filled with love and gratitude. I am filled with loving awareness. Merrily, merrily, merrily, life is but a dream.